Don't Worry about the Kids

Other Books by Jay Neugeboren

Big Man

Listen Ruben Fontanez

Corky's Brother

Parentheses: An Autobiographical Journey

Sam's Legacy

An Orphan's Tale

The Story of STORY magazine
    (*as editor*)

The Stolen Jew

Before My Life Began

Poli: A Mexican Boy in Early Texas

Imagining Robert: My Brother, Madness,
    and Survival—A Memoir

DON'T WORRY ABOUT THE KIDS

STORIES

Jay Neugeboren

University of Massachusetts Press

AMHERST

Copyright © 1997 by
Jay Neugeboren
All rights reserved
Printed in the United States of America
LC 97-14706
ISBN 1-55849-113-9
Designed by Steve Dyer
Set in Fairfield by Keystone Typesetting, Inc.
Printed and bound by Braun-Brumfield, Inc.

Library of Congress Cataloging-in-Publication Data
Neugeboren, Jay.
    Don't worry about the kids : stories / Jay Neugeboren.
        p. cm.
    ISBN 1-55849-113-9 (cloth: alk. paper)
    1. United States—Social life and customs—20th century—
Fiction.   I. Title.
PS3564.E844D66   1997
813'.54—dc21   97-14706
                                CIP

British Library Cataloguing in Publication data are available.

For Catherine

ACKNOWLEDGMENTS

The author gratefully acknowledges the magazines that first published
the stories—all now somewhat revised—contained in this volume:

The Atlantic Monthly: "The St. Dominick's Game"
Boston Review: "The Year Between"
California Quarterly: "Department of Athletics"
Columbia: "Romeo and Julio"
Contact: "Workers to Attention Please"
The Georgia Review: "Don't Worry about the Kids"
The Gettysburg Review: "What Is the Good Life?" and
    "Your Child Has Been Towed"
GQ: "Minor Sixths, Diminished Sevenths"
Inside Sports: "Fixer's Home"
The Literary Review: "Leaving Brooklyn"
New Letters: "Tolstoy in Maine"
Tikkun: "In Memory of Jane Fogarty"
The Transatlantic Review: "Connorsville, Virginia"
Willow Springs: "How I Became an Orphan in 1947"

Several of these stories have also been anthologized: "Don't Worry
about the Kids" in *Prize Stories: The O. Henry Awards 1988;* "Fixer's
Home" in *The Twentieth Century Treasury of Sports;* "Romeo and Julio"
in *Sarajevo, an Anthology for Bosnian Relief;* and "Workers to Attention
Please" in the SOS Anthology, *Louder Than Words.*

Contents

Don't Worry about the Kids

Don't Worry about the Kids

MICHAEL IMAGINED that he could see the fragrances coming at him in waves, that each wave was a different color. He sat in a small Italian restaurant in the Cobble Hill section of Brooklyn, Langiello, the court-appointed investigator, across from him. Langiello was talking about his own marriage and divorce, about how he had begun living with his second wife before he had filed for a separation. It was crazy, he said, what love could do to you when it took hold.

Michael tried to smile, felt his upper lip quiver, stared at his plate. The gnocchi seemed to be carved from balsa wood, floured with potato dust. He thought of radio waves, outside the restaurant, shimmering in the air, passing through the metal roofs of automobiles, the brick walls of apartment houses, the windows of office buildings and storefronts. He inhaled, tried to separate the fragrances, to name them. He saw low smoky-green S-curves for basil, high rolling mountains of barn-red for tomatoes, graceful ripples of ivory for garlic.

"So you can relax, Mike, let me tell you right off that I think the present custody setup is lousy and that I'm going to recommend some changes." Langiello smiled easily. "Okay?"

Michael nodded. He liked Langiello, liked the man's manner: the streetwise directness, the rough-edged tenderness. Langiello reminded him of the Italian guys with whom he'd gone to grade school and high school.

"I read the complaint you filed, and I read all the diary stuff you gave me. You've been through some rough times."

"I suppose."

"We never had kids, me and my first wife, but I feel for guys like you, when their wives use the kids against them. I mean, it's one thing if some broad tries to kick shit out of you herself. It's another if she gets your kids to start kicking too. How can you fight that?"

"I don't know."

"Still hard for you to talk, isn't it?"

Langiello reached across, put his hand on top of Michael's. Michael felt like a child. Why? At the present time Michael had his children with him only one out of every four weeks, and he'd known that in filing for primary custody he would be blamed by them for stirring things up. It would be the same old story—their mother's story: that he didn't really love them, that he only wanted to prove he could get his way. He had been prepared for this. What had surprised him, though, was how tiring it had become to hold back, to *not* answer his children's accusations. *When did you stop loving your children?* The question was there, in his head, and the only thing more absurd than the question, he knew, was that in Langiello's presence he felt what he sometimes felt when he was with his children: the need to answer it.

"Listen. I was nervous too, before I met you the first time—all I remembered from when we were in high school, you being such a hot shot. I mean, two guys like us, two old schoolyard ballplayers from Brooklyn, we'll get along fine."

The waiter appeared, asked if everything was all right. He spoke to Langiello in Italian. He wore a midnight blue tuxedo, fingered the dark lapel. Langiello and the waiter laughed together, and Michael imagined Langiello as a boy of seven or eight coming across the ocean on a ship, huddled inside a blanket.

Michael touched his napkin, thought of white drapes around an open wound, a scalpel in his palm. He saw the skin spread and bleed. He saw subcutaneous tissue, the layer of pale yellow fat below that. He saw muscles, like brown steak, thin tissues of white tendon being peeled away. The waiter was gone. Langiello was buttering a piece of bread. Michael smelled onions, parsley, sweet red peppers. He imagined Coleman, his anesthesiologist, staring into a green monitor, at hills and valleys of fragrances that flowed above and below sea level. Oregano. Grated cheese. Lemon. Michael wanted to reach out and touch the smells, to flatten them to the horizon. He wanted the moment he was living in to become a thin white line, to disappear.

"Tell me what to do," Michael said.

"First thing?"

"First thing."

"Eat."

Langiello skewered a strip of scungili on his fork, talked about how his father had brought him to the restaurant when he was a boy. Michael felt frightened, in need of reassurance. He tried to visualize himself earlier in the day, taking the subway from Brooklyn to Manhattan, entering the hospital, greeting receptionists, nurses, doctors, residents. He saw himself in the operating suite, putting the X-rays on the viewbox, hanging his clothes in the locker, walking into the operating room. Bach's Suite Number One, his favorite, was already playing. His nurse helped him scrub up, tie his gown, put on his slippers. She held a pair of gloves for him, stretched the wrists wide. Langiello talked about the diary he kept while he was going through his own divorce, about how crazy things had been.

Michael closed his eyes, could feel the thin skin of latex coat his hands like a film of talcum. The hip was exposed, draped inside a white rectangle less than a foot square. He prepped the area, watched his fingers, smooth and white like a dead man's, work inside the wound. His fingers retracted muscles, moved to deeper muscle, cut, cauterized. His resident suctioned blood. He told the resident to be careful of the sciatic nerve, to move it aside gently. If you harmed it, the woman would have a dropped foot forever after. Bach became Mahler—the Andante Moderato from the Second Symphony. They were using his tapes today, not Coleman's. His fingers worked on. Mahler became Bach: Preludes and Fugues on harpsichord. Landowska.

He held an electric saw as if it were a pistol, cut through the bone, removed it. With a mallet, he banged a reamer into the middle of the bone, inside the hip, put down his trial prosthesis. He removed the remaining cartilage, drilled holes, cleaned them with a water pik, washed out the femur, the socket. He mixed cement, white and creamy like Elmer's glue.

He chewed his gnocchi now, imagined a piece lodging in his throat, Langiello leaning across, grabbing his jaw, prying his mouth open, reaching in with a hooked finger. He saw himself suturing heavy tendons with violet thread. He smelled potatoes, butter, sausage.

Langiello asked about his brother, about how it felt to have a brother who was crazy. Michael wanted to protest, to explain that Jerry was not crazy—that he was retarded, perhaps, damaged, disabled—but he told Langiello that he had stopped by the day-care center before coming to the restaurant. Jerry was heavily sedated: two thousand units of Thorazine a day, Benadryl for the side effects. Michael was concerned about Jerry's eyesight: the corneas were becoming filmy, glazed. He must remember to call later, to suggest an exam, a change in medication. He imagined the top of Jerry's head, sliced open, lifted up as if on hinges, and he saw himself standing on a stepladder, pouring a mixture of glue and corn meal into Jerry's head.

"You said he's been like that most of his life, that he was never really normal."

"That's right."

"I don't mean to pry. It's just that I like to find out these things—so I can get the big picture, you know what I mean?"

Michael had long ago stopped believing in the diagnostic terms the doctors used: autism, schizophrenia, manic-depression. Who would ever know what had actually happened thirty-nine years ago—genetically, neurologically, in utero?

Michael saw himself closing the wound, binding the skin with a staple gun, laying on the dressing. Langiello asked Michael to describe his marriage and Michael gave Langiello a few sentences, then talked about how hard things were on the children, about how he wished he could get them into counseling. Langiello nodded sympathetically, said that he might be able to make a recommendation, that he didn't think their objectives were far apart.

"Then you *agree* with me?" Michael asked. "You really do think I should have the children with me more?"

"Sure. Only you have to remember that I don't have final say. I do my investigation, I file my report, I make recommendations if I want." Langiello smiled. "But don't worry. We have leverage. My uncle just happens to be the judge, or did I tell you that already?"

Michael felt his heart surge, pump. He tried to show nothing.

"You got some time?" Langiello asked.

"Time?"

"Afterward. You got any appointments, or are you free?"

"I have time. I left the afternoon open. I don't have to be back in the city until four-thirty."

"Good. So how about after lunch, we walk around the neighborhood? I'll show you where I was born—where my old man had his store."

If Jerry were reasonably calm, Michael thought, he would bring him here the next time. Jerry loved Italian food. If they succeeded in getting through the meal without incident, he decided, he would bring the children the time after that. Michael looked down, knew that the spirals on the gnocchi were there so that they would resemble seashells. He ate. He told Langiello that he would love to walk around the neighborhood with him, and while he talked he thought of the ocean, of Brighton Beach, of sand castles. He saw himself on the beach with Jerry, smoothing down a spiral runway that ran from the top of the castle to the bottom. He set a pink ball at the top, watched it circle downward. Jerry clapped. They dug out tunnels that let in the ocean. They built moats. They mixed water and sand, and let the mixture drip onto the castle's turrets.

Jerry's back was red. Their father screamed at Michael, slammed a newspaper against his head, kicked in the castle. Jerry wailed. Their father yelled at Michael for letting his brother burn up while he kept himself protected. He grabbed at Michael's polo shirt but Michael was too quick for him. He ran off. All he ever thought about was himself, his father shouted. His father was kissing Jerry's back in a way that made Michael feel embarrassed. Michael looked down, watched the ocean foam around his ankles.

His father was dead, Jerry was crazy. Michael was forty-four years old, a successful orthopedic surgeon, the divorced father of two boys and a girl. Well. He had worked for seventeen years to create the kind of family he himself had never had, and now that family was gone, had *been* gone for over two years. Why, then, was he still so surprised?

They walked along Court Street, turned left, passed the Baltic Street Day Care Center. A line of patients, Jerry not among them, moved toward a Dodge mini-van. Most of the patients were in their thirties and forties. They wore housecoats and ragged furs, plaid shirts over heavy wool sweaters, brightly colored silk scarves, frayed slippers, men's ties for belts. Such sad flamboyance, Michael thought. The patients shuffled along in pairs, eyes downcast, skin colorless, holding hands like schoolchildren, looking as if they were emerging from a storm-tossed flight, airsick.

Next to the van a young Hispanic couple embraced. The man, about thirty years old, wore a long olive-drab Army coat. While his eyes and shoulders showed fatigue, his mouth and jaw were set in anger. The woman was attractive, young, her glossy black hair pulled back neatly, her eyelids shaded in pale lavender. Michael watched her lips move at the man's ear. *I love you,* she said. *Oh I love you.*

The woman stepped into the van. The man started to walk away, turned.

"Don't worry about the kids," he called back. "You hear me? Don't you worry about the kids."

Then he pivoted, raced across the street at a diagonal. Cars screeched, honked. He was gone.

"That's heavy, isn't it?" Langiello said, touching Michael's arm.

Michael saw that Langiello's eyes were moist. Had he misjudged him? By the end of their lunch, as now, Michael had become quiet again, uneasy. He wanted desperately to make a good impression. He wanted Langiello to know just how much he loved his children—how he *liked* them as much as he loved them—and yet, without his children physically there, he was afraid that anything he said would sound hollow.

Langiello talked about the neighborhood, about what it had been like growing up there. Michael answered questions. Yes, he liked to cook, to clean, to shop, to do the dishes, to do the laundry, to help the children with their homework. Yes, he had worked out a schedule with his partners that allowed him to be at home most days after school. He was on call only one out of every four weekends. He *liked* being a father, being at home with his children. And yes, as he had written in his diary, he did fear for his ex-wife's sanity, for her influence on the children. For months, before and after the divorce, she had threatened to commit suicide by hanging herself from the boys' climbing rope. She had thrown scissors and bricks and kitchen knives at him. She had threatened to harm the children.

She continued to tell the children she had never wanted a divorce, that she had done everything to save the marriage. She told them Michael had left her for another woman, that he had been playing around all through the marriage. She told them that he had beaten her. She told them he was planning to abandon them, to leave New York and take a job at the Mayo Clinic in Minnesota. Langiello nodded sympathetically, said he'd seen a lot of guys in Michael's spot, that he admired Michael.

"Sometimes—" Michael said, encouraged by Langiello's words "—sometimes I feel like the Jackie Robinson of divorce." Michael paused. Langiello smiled, and when he did, Michael felt his own heart ease. "What I mean is, sometimes I feel that I have to take all the crap my kids can throw at me, yet have the courage *not* to fight back."

"Sure," Langiello said. "I know what you mean. Don't I remember Jackie, what it was like for him that first year, everybody calling him nigger, going at him with their spikes?"

Langiello touched Michael's arm, pointed to a set of windows on the second floor of a three-story building, to the apartment in which he had lived for the first twenty-six years of his life. Bruno's Pastry Shop, on the ground floor, had always been there, Langiello said. They entered the shop. Langiello told Mrs. Bruno that Michael was a friend, a famous surgeon. Mrs. Bruno inclined her head, as if in the presence of a priest. Michael closed his eyes, inhaled the fragrances: butter, almond, chocolate, yeast. He saw Jerry, in the bathtub, himself on his knees, beside the tub, rinsing shampoo from Jerry's hair. He was carrying Jerry to the bedroom in an enormous pea-green bath towel. He was sprinkling talcum on Jerry, rubbing baby oil into his scalp, inclining his head to Jerry's head, closing his eyes, inhaling the strange, sweet fragrance.

Michael and Langiello walked along Court Street, passing fish markets, antique stores, restaurants, funeral parlors. Langiello said that his father had been a shoemaker, that when he was a boy he had believed the neighborhood was called Cobble Hill because of men like his father—all the Italian cobblers who worked there. Langiello pointed to the narrow store, now a locksmith shop, that had once been his father's. Langiello said that his great regret in life was that he had never been able to let his father, who died when he was fourteen years old, know how much he had loved him.

"My father died when I was sixteen," Michael said.

Langiello put a hand on Michael's shoulder, and when he did Michael found that he wanted to tell Langiello *everything*. They passed a yellow brick building set back from the road like a small museum: The Anthony Anastasios Memorial Wing of the Longshoreman's Medical Association. In the distance, no more than half a mile away, Michael could see the Gowanus Parkway, the gray turrets and smokestacks of ships beyond. Michael talked about his father, who had been a book-keeper for a small manufacturing company, Wonderwear Hosiery. His mother had worked as a practical nurse, taking care of invalids at home. Whenever she was on a case—this was before Jerry was hospitalized at the age of twelve—he would be in charge of Jerry and of the house: of cooking, cleaning, shopping, laundry. It was one reason, he sometimes thought, taking care of his own children came so naturally for him.

They sat on a bench together in Carroll Gardens, watching old men in black jackets playing *bocce,* schoolchildren playing tag. The sky seemed lower, as if being pushed down by an enormous slab of gray steel. Michael thought of aircraft carriers, their decks stripped and lifted by giant cranes, then welded together until they stretched across the heavens. Had Michael resented having to care for Jerry? Some. Still, the days he had spent alone in their apartment with his brother were among the happiest of his childhood—the only times when the rooms were quiet, when he could be close to Jerry, could tend to him without being scolded—times when Jerry felt free to return Michael's affection.

Langiello asked if Michael had talked with his ex-wife since their last interview. She had called two nights before, Michael said, at three in the morning, exploding at him with obscenities, threats, accusations; and she had called again just a few hours ago, before he left for the hospital, to wish him good luck in his interview with Langiello. She had sounded rational, normal. She had told him that she was still willing to get back together.

"And I'll bet she's been giving the kids the same line," Langiello offered. "Sure. I know all about it. The kids need a punching bag and you're it. They'll know the difference, though, Mike. Kids are resilient. I mean, they'll take her side now—she's the victim, right?—but you'll get your reward some day."

"Maybe."

"You will, Mike. I've seen enough of these cases to know. The open agenda is reconciliation—the hidden agenda is revenge. Hot and cold, cold and hot. The problem is that they had this great family once upon a time, see, and now they don't—and she gives them a story that helps them make sense of what can never really make sense. It's what I was trying to tell you before, about going to court: it's not who's right or wrong that counts, but who comes up with the best story. What you need is a good *story*, Mike."

"Jackie's story?"

"Not a bad idea." Langiello laughed. "I got close to him once, at this clinic for our team at Ebbets Field. I was in a group assigned to him, him showing us how to take a lead, get a jump on the pitcher. Jesus! I forgot about that for ages."

"Where did you go—New Utrecht?"

"Yeah. I played second base, only I wasn't much. Good-field no-hit. You play baseball at Erasmus?"

"No."

"I remember how great you were in basketball—first team all-city, right?"

"Yes."

"For a little guy you were something else, Mike. We had these two big Italian guys that clogged up the middle—surf and turf, we called them—and in practice our coach got this kid from the JV to try to imitate you, the way you'd dribble through any defense we could throw up."

"You were on the team?"

"Sure."

"Why didn't you say so before?"

"Maybe I was hoping you'd remember me." Langiello shrugged. "Ah, I wasn't much. Seventh man, my senior year. They'd send me in for surf or turf if they got into foul trouble."

Michael tried to picture Langiello as an eighteen-year-old, in uniform. He tried to recall the game, but instead he saw Jerry running in circles around the schoolyard, screaming with joy, a basketball held tightly against his stomach.

Langiello laughed. "You faked me out of my jock once, going in for a drive, I didn't know what happened, you were so quick." Langiello leaned forward, hands clasped. "You were all-Ivy at Dartmouth too—I remember following you in the papers, but you never went to the pros. In those days I guess you could make more being a hotshot doctor than an athlete. You read about the contracts these guys get now, out of college? It really pisses me off, you want the truth, twenty-year-old kids making all that dough." Langiello paused, cocked his head to one side.

"Let me ask you something, Mike. How much do you think I earn, the job I got?"

"I don't know. You have a law degree, don't you?"

"I have a law degree. Brooklyn Law School, Class of '68. But take a guess at how much I make. C'mon—"

"I'd rather not."

"Twenty-three thousand."

"That's *all?*"

"That's all. Sure. But I got no complaints. I mean, I like my work, right? Child-abuse cases mostly—I get to be *guardian ad litum* for a lot of kids, get to make a difference in their lives." He stood. "And I get to meet some fascinating people too, right?"

Langiello suggested that he walk Michael to the subway, that Michael had more important things to do than to pass the time of day with a guy like him. Michael clenched his fists, angry with himself because he hadn't seen that each time Langiello had asked him a question he had doubtless been hoping Michael would ask one back, would show interest. They stopped at the Gowanus Canal, leaned on the bridge railing, looked down into water that seemed thick with black clouds. He answered a few of Langiello's questions, then asked him about his work with child-abuse cases.

"Ah—crazy things go on behind doors once people close them," he said. "And the craziest thing of all is how most of the time, the women and the kids, banged up to hell, all they want is for us to get the fathers to live with them again. They'll almost always drop the charges if only the bastard will come back home."

"I'm not surprised," Michael said.

"You know what the hardest thing in the world is, Mike? It's getting a kid *not* to love a parent." They came to the Bergen Street subway station. Langiello said he would be seeing Mike's ex-wife later in the afternoon. Langiello smiled. "But don't worry, okay? You'll get more time with the kids. I promise—"

"Thanks," Michael said. He moved toward Langiello, wanting to touch the man. "I wish I—"

"No need to say anything," Langiello said. "I mean, it's been good to reminisce about the old days, the way things were when we were growing up. Times change, Mike. Times change and who's ever ready?"

They shook hands. Michael watched Langiello walk off, then started down the steps. He felt exhausted suddenly—drained—and he couldn't understand why. All he wanted to do was to lie down, to dream of lush green lawns and pale blue skies. Three teenagers, two in black leather jackets, stood below, where the staircase turned.

At the landing he made a right turn, then saw bright lights flare inside his head, welding sparks spraying crazily. A hand was jammed over his mouth so that his teeth cut into his lips, drew blood. He was being dragged backward by both arms. He resisted, saw a knife blade flash. He relaxed, let himself be led to an alcove. He stood on a soft mass of wet newspapers. Above him were rusting girders, sagging wires, a clogged grating coated with swirls of brown slime.

"Don't fight back. We ain't your enemies, okay? We don't want to hurt you unless we have to."

Michael nodded. They were taller than he was. The man in front of him was well built, wore a black T-shirt, the sleeves cut off.

"You a friend of Langiello's?"

"Not exactly."

"What's it worth to you if we take care of him?"

"I don't understand."

"Don't give me crap. We know what Langiello does, the hold he got on you. You want us to do a job on him, it'll cost you five thousand bucks, cash, unmarked bills. Five thousand ain't much for a rich guy like you, the clothes you got on."

"Hey Lobo—ask him if he owns oil wells."

"Shut up, jerk." Lobo pulled on Michael's tie. His eyes were dull, without cleverness. Michael thought of sludge at the bottom of the Gowanus Canal. Why did he call himself Lobo, Spanish for wolf, when he was not Spanish? "What do you do for a living?"

"I'm a doctor."

"Oh yeah? What kind?"

"A surgeon. An orthopedic surgeon."

"Langiello makes bundles off guys like you."

"You're wasting your time," Michael said coldly. "I have nothing against Mr. Langiello."

"But he got plenty against you, I bet. He always does. Who'd you beat up, your wife or your kids? You rape your seven-year-old daughter, mister, or are you one of them new kinds of pervert who gets off on old people?"

"I haven't touched anybody. You've made a mistake."

"Don't crap with us." Lobo sliced buttons from Michael's jacket, one at a time. "What's he got on you? C'mon. How much you gotta pay him so he don't have his uncle send you up the river?"

Michael moved forward.

"If you'll excuse me, I—"

He saw the gun pointed at his chest.

"We're on your side, mister," Lobo said. "Believe me, okay? We just want to talk with you for your own good, understand? You want the truth, there's lots of guys on your side. Lots of guys would chip in for a contract on Langiello. His uncle's the judge, see—"

"I know that."

"Only there's no profit in us killing the judge. You will one judge, there's another judge in his seat the next day. But Judge DiGregorio, he only got one investigator who's his nephew. You get rid of the nephew, you're home free. You think it over, who you can trust, us or Langiello. Like they say, our rates are competitive."

"My story is different," Michael said. "I'm not involved in child abuse. I was divorced. I have three children. My ex-wife and I are in court because of a custody dispute. I don't think Mr. Langiello means me any harm. Really. I—"

"Let him go," Lobo said.

The two men released Michael's arm. He heard a switchblade click shut, but not before it had slashed his jacket, upward, on the right side, from the waist to the armpit.

Langiello smiled and shook Michael's hand, asked if Michael had had breakfast yet. He tapped a manila envelope, said that his report was ready for the judge. He was sorry he'd made Michael come out so early, but he had to be in court by ten o'clock for a child-abuse hearing. Michael ordered coffee, talked about how cold it was outside—a freakish hailstorm turned to slashing rain, crazy for the first week of spring— and of how, coming along the street from the subway station, he had seen daffodils and crocuses sheathed inside ice, looking as if they were made of stained glass.

Michael was surprised at how good he felt, how relieved he was to know that the report was complete, that the ordeal, for him and the children, would soon be over. And he was pleased too, he knew, simply to be in Langiello's presence again, to feel that he had an ally, somebody who understood that, despite all his worldly successes, he was still just an old Brooklyn schoolyard ballplayer heading for his middle years.

Michael sipped coffee, talked about his children, his brother. He said that when the trial was over he intended to have his children spend more time with Jerry. He wondered: should he mention having met Lobo and his two henchmen the week before? He didn't want even to *appear* to be testing Langiello, to be doubting him.

"Listen," Langiello said. "I always like to do this with clients—not all investigators do—but before I file my report I like to sit down with them and tell them what's going to be in it. I like to be up front."

"Of course."

"Your case has been a real tough one for me, Mike, and I guess the main thing I want to say to you—and I hope this is a help, given how much pain you've been in—"

"Pain?"

"The stuff you told me last time about how it hurts you to take crap from your kids all the time, to be their nigger—how your kids are always taking their mother's side."

"I don't understand."

"Your kids love you, Mike," Langiello said. "Absolutely." He paused, leaned forward, his eyes suddenly bright. "But they don't *like* you. Do you understand what I'm saying?"

Michael tried to laugh. "I know they love me," he said. "I never doubt that. As for liking me—well, they're in a real bind, as I explained. If they even let themselves *think* they like me—that I'm not the monster who made everything go bad—it makes them feel they're rejecting their mother. The more they punish me emotionally, the more brownie points they earn with her. That's why I—"

"Mike," Langiello said sharply. "You're not *listening* to what I'm saying. That's one of the things the kids said too—that you never really listen to them, that you always have to be right, that you think you're perfect."

"That's ridiculous." In his mind, Michael was on the court at Madison Square Garden, looking toward the bench, seeing the coach tell him to slow down, to take his time in setting up the next play. "Look," he offered, forcing a laugh, hoping to appeal to their common past. "I missed a foul shot in a game against Jefferson that almost cost us the championship my senior year, didn't I?"

Langiello stared at Michael without expression. Michael thought of Lobo's dull brown eyes. He thought of daffodils thawing, wilting. He thought of reaching inside his chest, of sawing ribs, retracting muscles, of stroking his own heart gently, of calming it.

"I mean, there are dozens of times I admit to them that I was wrong about something, that I made a mistake," Michael continued.

"They love you, Mike, but they don't like you. Can you *hear* what I'm saying? I'm telling you the truth. I'm trying to help you."

"I don't understand," Michael said. "Last week you said you were going to give me more time with them, that—"

"I hadn't met your kids yet. I hadn't met your wife either." Langiello paused, as if daring Michael to reply. "They're good kids, Mike, and she's a terrific mother. And what I think is that they've shown a lot of courage in putting their lives back together since the divorce."

"Courage?"

"The kids want to live with their mother, Mike. Can you hear me?"

"But they *have* to say that. If they don't, they're scared she'll stop loving them—don't you see *that*?"

"No, Mike. I really don't. I don't think you give your kids enough credit. They said that too—that you never believe them."

"Oh come on," Michael said. "I've never said such things to them. What's going on is your garden-variety emotional blackmail and you know it. I mean, ask yourself this question: Would the kids ever be able to tell her they want to live with *me*?" Michael stopped, realized his voice was rising. "When they're afraid to reject me or criticize me, then I'll worry. Then—"

"You're not listening to me, Mike." Langiello sat back. Michael saw himself passing off, circling under the basket, getting his wind back. He wondered if Langiello had an arrangement with Lobo, had *sent* Lobo. He wanted to be ready for Langiello's moves, to be alert to all possibilities.

"I don't understand," Michael said again. He looked down. Play defense, he told himself. Stall. He decided to try letting Langiello think he was bewildered, wounded. Perhaps if he didn't threaten him, if he gave him his ounce of flesh . . .

"Let me put it this way," Langiello said. "I met your kids and I met your wife. She's a wonderful woman, Mike—soft-spoken and somewhat shy, I'll admit, but warm and loving and gentle and—"

"Sure. When she doesn't have a knife in her hand."

"You're interrupting me again." Langiello smiled. "You can't resist, can you?"

Michael said nothing. He tried to let his mind go blank. He tried to let it fill up with air, but as it did he saw gray swirls of smoke, he smelled coffee and bacon, he saw fragrances drifting through his head as if through canals, as if they were dyes that had been injected into his spinal column and were journeying toward his brain.

"I listened to everyone," Langiello went on, "and what I kept asking myself was this: What was it that could have caused a woman like this to act the way she did? I mean, I admit her behavior's been bizarre—but what I wanted to know was what made her *get* that way?"

Michael let his shoulders sag. There was no way he was going to win, he realized, and what surprised him was neither Langiello nor his own foolishness in having trusted Langiello, but something else: that he was *still* willing to trust Langiello, if in a totally unexpected way. He almost smiled, but he didn't want to give himself away, he didn't want Langiello to know that what he was tempted to do suddenly was to throw aside all his old rules—his crazy devotion to *fairness*. For the first time in his life he was tempted, he realized, to make a deal, to offer a bribe, and the discovery delighted him.

He tried to play the scene out in his head, before it happened. What if Langiello were to double-cross him after being paid off? What if Langiello took the money and submitted his report without changing it? Michael could, he saw, lose both ways: he could lose the children *and* lose in his own eyes—for having betrayed a set of values that . . . that what? Michael looked up.

"And what did you decide?" he asked. "What was your answer?"

"You're a tyrant, Mike," Langiello said. "It's as simple as that. You were always the big shot—the powerhouse. She showed me notes you left for her when she was putting you through medical school, when she didn't do things exactly the way you wanted—"

"But that was *before* our problems—almost twenty years ago."

"There's no doubt in my mind that she struck out at you through the kids and did a lot of crazy things—I mean, who doesn't when a marriage breaks up?—but it's also clear to me, and this is the essence of my report, that you drove her to it."

"Sure," Michael said, and he smiled for the first time. "The devil made me do it, right?"

"They talked about that too—her and the kids—the way you get sarcastic whenever you can't face up to taking the blame. I *learned* from them, Mike. It wasn't difficult to figure out why they were willing to talk about the marriage and you weren't."

"But the marriage is over," Michael said. "It's been over for two years. I didn't think it was *important* to talk about it. I thought that what was important was putting all the old battles to rest so we could get on with our lives." Michael stopped, aware that the words were coming out automatically, that he himself hardly believed in them. "All right. If you want to talk about the marriage, let's talk. What do you want to know?"

"Too late." Langiello tapped the envelope. "I've already put more time into your case than I usually do."

Michael hesitated, shook his head sideways, spoke: "You're not giving me a fair shake."

"Could be." Langiello gestured, palms up. "You and your lawyer are always free to ask for another investigator."

"No." Michael saw himself wandering around an empty court, looking up at the game clock, at championship banners, at ducts and wiring and fans of bright lights. Was the game over already? He supposed he could do it—that he could compromise his values in order to save his kids, to win for all of them—that he could humble himself if he had to, even if he *and* Langiello knew he was only putting on an act. "I just want to put all this behind me, but I suppose that as long as she can stay involved with me, one way or the other, she's gratified."

"But the two of you *are* still involved, Mike. You're still mother and father to these kids. She showed me letters—the way you tried to persuade her to come back into the marriage when you found out she was having affairs. But what else could she do? The men she loved didn't run her down the way you did, Mike. They were kind and gentle. They—"

"They were married and they had kids, damn it!" Michael felt his heart blaze. He stood. "I really don't have to listen to this. I don't have to sit here and—"

Langiello was smiling. Michael stopped in midsentence. Had he, by accident, given the man what he was looking for?

"You're angry, Mike. You're a very angry guy, aren't you?"

Michael sat. He looked into Langiello's eyes and he imagined himself making small incisions in the corneas. When the corneas were deprived of oxygen they drew blood vessels from surrounding territory. Michael imagined Langiello's eyes laced with spider webs of pale red threads. He imagined himself lifting the corneas—peeling them off—freezing them so they would be ready for the lathe. He shivered. Refractive surgery—flattening the corneas to correct nearsightedness—was the one new surgical procedure that, in his imagination, could give him chills. He saw diamond blades cut into his own eyes, into the eyes of his children, into Jerry's eyes.

"I'm upset," Michael said. He tried to be ready for what was coming. He tried to prepare himself for asking Langiello how much money he wanted, and how and when he wanted it. "I mean, you're telling me I may lose my children."

"That's right."

Michael smelled sausage, onions. He felt nauseated. "I love my children," Michael said. "I mean, how can I *not* be upset?"

"But when you don't get your way you also get a little crazy."

"No."

"Your kids say different. They say you're like your brother sometimes."

"But my kids hardly know my brother."

"I wondered about that too—why you didn't want me to meet your brother last time, us going right past his place. Your wife says that after visiting him you throw fits sometimes, you hurl things around the house."

"It's not so."

"The kids say it is. Your wife says that you used to wake her in the middle of the night to go on crazy tirades."

"It's not so." Michael looked down, head in hands, hoping Langiello would think he was fighting back tears.

"Are you ashamed of him?"

"Of who?"

"Of your brother."

"No." Michael looked up. "Did she say that *too*?"

"You should see your face, Mike. You should go look in a mirror. I have to say I agree with her, that there's something off-center there when you get angry. And you did have a breakdown once."

"It's not so."

"But you told me you had once put yourself under psychiatric care."

"I was in analysis for six years. When Jerry was—"

Michael considered saying more—considered talking about the analysis: why he entered it, how difficult and rewarding the work had been. He smiled. "Can I ask you a question—a few questions?"

"Shoot," Langiello said.

"I take it you're going to recommend that my ex-wife get primary custody of the children and I assume nothing I say now will change your mind. But tell me, Mr. Langiello—is a good parent one who *lies* to her children about the other parent? Is a good parent one who threatens to put her children in a foster home when they don't do what she wants? Does a good parent deny counseling for her children? Does she threaten to kill them and maim them? Does she encourage her children to lie for her, to spy on their father, to steal things for her, to join in her war against him?"

"Who knows?" Langiello said. "Wouldn't you tell lies to protect your kid?" Michael said nothing. "I mean, who knows what a good parent is, Mike? Who really knows?"

At the corner, Michael went into a telephone booth, called the hospital. He spoke to a nurse who said that because of the weather the vans had not gone to Brooklyn. Would Michael be coming out to Staten Island? Michael said he had office hours midafternoon, but he promised he would visit Jerry later in the week. The nurse said that Jerry had been telling everybody in the ward he was going to a fancy restaurant with his brother; he had spent most of the morning preparing—washing, shaving, deciding which clothes to wear. She had never seen him dressed so handsomely.

"I'll be there," Michael said. "Tell him it may take me a while—I'll go by ferry—but I'll be there."

Michael called his office and arranged for one of his partners to cover for him, then took the subway to Manhattan, exited at South Ferry. When he arrived on the Staten Island side he would take a taxi to the hospital.

The rain had stopped. Michael stayed at the back of the ferry, on deck. Despite what had happened with Langiello, he was looking forward to seeing Jerry. A group of schoolchildren were on tour, and a middle-aged ferry-boat captain was telling them that cows had once walked across the Bay, near where the Brooklyn Battery Tunnel was, from Brooklyn to Manhattan; if the cows did not get back before the tide came in, they would often drown. Michael watched Manhattan grow smaller. Gulls followed the boat, the captain said, not for garbage, as most people thought, but because the warm water churned up by the boat's propellers brought fish to the surface.

When the schoolchildren went inside, Michael stayed on deck, looking not toward Brooklyn, but toward the Statue of Liberty, Ellis Island, New Jersey. The water seemed pockmarked, a murky brown spotted with filmy stars of blue and black and green. The ship rolled gently through row after row of whitecaps. Michael thought of dirty dishwater. He thought of Jerry on a stepladder, remembered teaching Jerry how to wash dishes, how to use the sponge and soap and steel wool. He saw raw spinach rising to the surface of cloudy water. Was he inventing the picture, or had Jerry once tried to wash spinach leaves as if they were dishes? He recalled his father coming home and praising Jerry, ranting at him.

Michael walked to the port side. Brooklyn was gone, bathed in gray fog, and Michael sensed some light—the sun, behind the mist, slowly transforming the air to the color of unwashed ivory. Despite the fact that the air was now warm and moist, almost feathery in its tangible balm, Michael found that he was trembling, his teeth clicking. He should go inside, buy a cup of coffee, rest. He should forget Langiello. He should tell himself again and again that the hard thing would be to believe in his heart what he understood in his mind: that there was, literally, nothing he could do about what had happened and nothing he could have done. All he really wanted was to get to the other side of the Bay, to see Jerry, to spend time with him.

Were Jerry to ask him about the children and were he to begin to tell Jerry the story of what had happened, he knew that Jerry would walk away, turn in circles. He wished that it wasn't so important to him that others understand what, in fact, had truly happened. He wished he could be certain that he cared more for his children than he did about losing them, about losing his fight *for* them.

Michael held to the iron railing, reminded himself to stop on the other side, to buy something to bring for Jerry—a magazine, a pipe, a box of chocolates. He smiled. Jerry would doubtless turn at once and hand the gift to another patient. Michael would tease Jerry about always giving things away and Jerry would laugh, would say something about their childhood that only he and Michael would understand. What do you think this is anyway, he would ask. Your birthday?

The craziest thing of all, Michael sometimes thought, was that the two of them actually liked being together, enjoyed spending time with each other even though they both knew that their conversations made no ordinary sense.

Jerry loved to ask Michael questions about surgery, to walk around his ward reciting the procedures to everyone he met. Jerry had an uncanny memory that made Michael believe he was not brain-damaged so much as brain-scrambled—all the pieces there, but in the wrong places. Michael considered: he could pretend that he needed Jerry to help him in surgery, that there was this guy he knew they had to operate on, so that the man would never walk again.

Michael could imagine taking Jerry to the Italian restaurant, Jerry's eyes bright with pleasure as he explained the procedure, repeated Michael's words back to him: first you make an incision in the knee and put the fiber-optic light in. Then you look into the TV camera and you fill the knee with saline fluid. Then you make a cut of about five millimeters. Then you make an incision on the other side and you watch in the camera while you work with your scalpel and clamps and trocar and Army-Navy retractors. If there's too much bleeding, you buzz the veins.

Michael smiled. Jerry loved the idea of buzzing veins and arteries—cauterizing them with lasers—loved to use the word *buzz* as often as possible. The anterior or posterior cruciate ligaments would be the ones they'd cut, Michael explained, so that forever after the knees would—without warning, but regularly—give way. Or perhaps they could, Jerry offered, go into the neck and slice the carotid artery, or one of the vertebral arteries, so that, as if the guy had had a stroke, his brain would never again be able to tell his body what to do.

The ferry slowed, turned, began backing into its spot in the harbor, foam boiling up above green scum. Michael went inside, moved quickly, pushing his way through the crowd so that he would be first off.

Workers to
Attention Please

HE WAS A SMALL MAN standing on a large box. One percent of the population owned forty-five percent of the nation's wealth, he cried. I held my father's hand and we moved forward through the falling snow. Did we know about the six hundred families? The six hundred families controlled everything that controlled us: railroads, coal, gas, electrical power, movies, newspapers, radio, banks.

Below us subway trains thundered through warm tunnels. In the Soviet Union, the man proclaimed, a new world was dawning, where men and women were not wage slaves—where men and women worked side by side and owned the means of production! The man's hands moved through the snow as if he were already dismembered—as if pieces of him were flying here and there like clumsy pigeons.

I have seen the future, my father said, and it is bloody. Come, darling. We moved closer, to the outer edge of the circle of listeners.

Evening to you, Mr. Krinsky, Officer Kelly said.

Good evening, Mike, my father said, and he tipped his hat.

My father lifted me onto his shoulders. I could see the sign for S. Klein on the Square blinking faintly through the snow.

The man turned to the side and I saw half his face, his eye glowing blue like the pilot light on our gas stove at home. The workers of America had to be educated to the fact that their true enemy lived in Washington! I thought of trains rumbling high above us in the heavens, knocking loose huge pieces of snow from the sky as if they were chunks of ceiling plaster. The man looked directly at me and spoke about children of nine and ten years old who worked in subhuman conditions at subhuman pay—in coal mines and paper mills, in factories and sweatshops right here in New York City.

My father set me down and kissed me. Watch this, he said.

Even though he walked through snow, below the level of the man's box, my father was taller than the man. My father was taller than everyone, including Officer Kelly. My father was so large he could carry small pianos on his back. Six days a week he worked for the Santini Brothers Moving and Storage Company. On the Sabbath he rested. When I visited him, after school and on holidays, to watch him load trucks and move furniture in and out of storage, the Italians bragged that my father was the strongest man in New York.

Sir, my father said.

The man stopped talking.

Your Mr. Stalin is a gangster worse than Mussolini. Your Mr. Stalin cleans out Hitler's ass with the undergarments of poor Jews like you and me.

The man gaped. My father smiled. Officer Kelly moved forward, slapping his billy club against his black-gloved hand. I moved with him. We had seen my father like this before. The man reached to one side and grabbed a pole that held the American flag. He lifted the flag high above his head, but the flag did not stop the terror in his eyes. My father took the pole from the man's hand, and set it upright. Then my father drove his fist into the middle of the man's face so that blood spurted and spread, like a rose flowering in snow.

My father turned, lifted me in his arms. Come, son.

The man screamed for help, but people moved away quickly. The man shouted for Officer Kelly to arrest my father, to do something. He had a right to give speeches! He had a right not to be abused by capitalist thugs.

Yes, my father said. Because this is a free country. But since you don't like it here I want to help you. Since it is better in Russia, I want to help you to get there. I want to help you fly.

My father set me down and lifted the man bodily, one hand between the man's legs, the other around the man's chest. The man thrashed in the air like a small boy trying to swim.

That's enough for now, don't you think, Mr. Krinsky?

My father threw the man forward as if tossing a log into a fire. The man's head cracked against a lamppost. The man rolled over and lay on his back.

An old woman slapped at my father with a large paper bag. The bag split open and the leaflets tumbled into the air. On the top of each page were the words WORKERS TO ATTENTION PLEASE. My father tipped his hat and smiled at the woman.

Is he your son? my father asked.

The woman cursed my father. She said that someday men like him would be lined up in front of firing squads.

I already been, my father said. So what I am trying to do now is to knock some sense into people's heads when I am given the chance. This is a wonderful country we live in, with abundant opportunities. This country has been very good to people like you and me. Here we can pray without being arrested. Here if you work hard, people pay you enough so you can feed your family.

The woman dropped to her knees and packed snow onto the small man's face.

I couldn't sleep because of how loud my mother was yelling at my father for what he had done. No, she wasn't proud of him. No, she did not believe that might made right. I got out of bed and opened the door, to see. The angrier my mother became, the happier my father seemed.

I love you, he declared. I love you when you yell at me.

My father grabbed my mother and pulled her to him, so that she sat on his lap. He lifted her hair from the back of her neck and kissed her there.

She shivered, then pounded against his chest. You're a child, she said. You're such a child.

I'm sorry I hit the man. But he was saying very stupid things.

Will you promise you won't do it again?

I promise.

She rested her head against his chest.

I worry about you, she said. All day I worry.

Don't.

I closed the door. My brother was snoring. I lifted the board from the side of his bed and kissed his cheek. He woke up and bellowed like a cow, then rolled over and fell onto the floor. My mother rushed into the room. I moved back. My brother was as tall and strong as my father, except that he did not understand how to read or to work. Sometimes my father brought him to the warehouse, to try to teach him to use his size and strength, but my mother always ended by bringing my brother home early. Then she put my brother in his bed and sat in my room and cursed my father for making her love him.

Get the rope, my mother said. Quickly.

I brought the rope and while my mother talked to my brother, my father tied up his hands and legs.

In Russia and in Germany they would have killed him, my father said. In many nations of the globe he would already be dead. Here they let him live.

When my brother snapped his teeth sideways, so he could chew the skin from his own shoulder, my father took out his handkerchief and began to bind my brother's mouth.

Then blood spurted from my brother's mouth in a quick stream, like red tobacco juice. My brother stopped howling. Between his teeth, he held onto two of my father's fingers.

My father closed his eyes but he didn't scream.

I told you, my mother said. Someday. I warned you.

Do something, my father said. Please.

Because you don't want to hurt him?

Please.

I stared at my brother's teeth, and listened to a sound that came from them, like wind trying to move through water.

My mother left the room and returned with a hammer.

She looked at my father and again he said please. She banged my brother on the head, between his eyes. My brother's eyes closed. My father's eyes opened.

I'll get the police, my mother said. God willing, maybe this time he's dead.

My father tried, but he could not open my brother's jaw. My mother told me to leave the room, but I held on to my father's arm, and when my mother pulled she could not break me loose.

The St. Dominick's Game

THOUGH I MISSED MY FATHER most at school football games, when the other boys' fathers were there, I never told Mother. I didn't feel I had the right. My father died over eight years ago, and I was too young then to remember him much, so I figured the best thing was not to bother Mother about what I was feeling. It wasn't even as if I ever knew him well enough to miss him, I'd tell myself. It was more that at things such as football games, I was aware of his absence.

Mother didn't attend any of our football games and I could understand that. Ever since Father died, any kind of violence upsets her terribly. There are some days when she can't bear to look at raw meat or raw fish. Maybe if I'd been there when he died I'd feel the same. Mother has never told me what it was like, but it seems they were both sitting up in bed and reading that night, when he suddenly grabbed her arm and then blood started spilling from his mouth. She screamed and locked the door and wouldn't let me into the room until others had arrived, so I never got to see my father again until the funeral. He lived through the frozen hills of Korea, I heard her say to her sister, but he died in our bed in New Jersey. Go figure.

I used to try to picture what the scene was like, and I always imagined that his eyes must have been as wide and round as they could be— as if somebody had just surprised him—and then I'd find myself picturing Mother scrambling back and forth across the bed and the floor, trying to wipe things up, and the look I'd see in her eyes would be awful—so frantic and helpless and dazed that I'd just clench my fists and get more and more angry. Sometimes, trying to feel what she must have felt, I used to wonder if it was possible to love another person too much.

What I couldn't understand, though, was the way she acted when I told her I was trying out for the Fowler football team. Mother had been teaching French at the Fowler School since before Father died, and sometimes she worried that I was too quiet or too much of a loner, and I thought she'd be glad to hear that I wanted to participate in a team sport. But the first thing she did when I gave her my news was to threaten to get Dr. Hunter, our headmaster, to remove me from the squad. If she didn't receive satisfaction from him, she declared, she would go straight to Mr. Marcus, our coach.

I liked Mr. Marcus and I didn't want him to think I was a sissy, so what I did the next morning, despite her threat, was to talk with Dr. Hunter myself, before she could get to him. I told him about going out for the team and about how Mother was against it and about how I didn't want to disobey her, but that I was continuing to play anyway, and he sat in his big leather chair for a while, just thinking. I looked right at him, trying hard not to stare at his left arm, even though it fascinated me. It was shorter than his right one, and sort of hung from his shoulder, swinging gently to and fro whenever he walked, as if it were made of foam rubber. Most of us at school figured that, given his age, he'd maimed it in World War II, but nobody ever asked him, or knew for sure.

"You know," he said, "that your mother has not had the easiest life."

"I know," I said.

"Still, you can't be expected to sacrifice your boyhood because of the misfortunes she has endured, can you?"

I shrugged and said I didn't know. He nodded then and asked me a few more questions, all of which made me feel very uncomfortable, and then, after making some remarks about how contact sports built character, he said he would speak to her for me. The next evening he stopped by our house. Mother was upstairs grading papers, and when I told her who was there, she didn't seem to know what to do first. Finally, after starting down the stairs and coming back up two separate times, she sent me to entertain Dr. Hunter while she changed clothes.

My mother is a very attractive woman, with reddish-brown hair and very beautiful eyes. People tell me that I inherited her eyes. They're blue, but not pale blue—slate-blue, I would call them. She's tall and she makes a lot of her own clothing. When she's upstairs working at her sewing machine, which her mother used when my mother was a girl, and looking out the window, she always hums to herself in an easy way that lets me know she's feeling very peaceful. She's thirty-eight years old now, but people are never certain of her age. Sometimes she looks as if she's in her twenties, and other times, especially when she wears her hair up, she can look as if she's in her forties. It may sound strange, but one of the reasons I was sorriest she objected to my playing football was that I'd always hoped I'd see her at a football game. She has the kind of face and coloring that's perfect for a football game—what I would call an autumn kind of face.

When she came down the stairs that evening, she looked absolutely gorgeous. It wasn't what she was wearing—it was more the proud way she carried herself and the high color in her cheeks. Dr. Hunter must have noticed also, because he seemed a bit awkward when he stood up and shook her hand and said hello.

I went upstairs and tried to do my homework, but I couldn't. I put on the radio so they wouldn't think I was eavesdropping, and then I took out the sheets of plays that Mr. Marcus had passed out and I studied my assignments. At about ten-thirty, when I closed my door to go to bed, Dr. Hunter was still downstairs.

The next morning at breakfast Mother said that she'd decided it was all right for me to be on the football team. She warned me not to get hurt, and I said I'd be careful, and then she changed the subject. I tried not to smile too much, but I felt really good, and at practice that afternoon I nearly killed myself trying to impress Mr. Marcus. I dove for fumbles like a maniac, I was a tiger on defense, I wore myself out on wind sprints, and somehow I managed to intercept two passes. That was the day Mr. Marcus began using me as an example. At first I liked the idea. I wasn't an especially good athlete and I knew it. So did Mr. Marcus. But he kept pointing me out to the other guys and telling them that if they would only try as hard as I did, they *might* have a good team.

Mr. Marcus wasn't very tall—maybe five-foot-seven—but there was something powerful about him and, like the other guys, I used to be scared sometimes that he would get so angry at us that he would pick us up, one by one, and smash our heads against each other. He yelled and screamed and never stopped moving. "My Aunt Tillie could do better—"

he'd shout. Then, when the guys laughed, he'd counter with, "What are you laughing at?—Get in there and drive. What do you guys think this is—a church social? Put your shoulder in there and drive. Come on, girls—let's hustle. *Hustle!* Watch Eddie—there's guts for you! Watch that little guy give it his heart—" He could keep up patter like this for the entire two-hour practice, and at first I was thrilled with the way he praised me so much. After a while, however, I saw how it made the other guys resent me. Still, even though I didn't want them to, I kept giving it everything I had. I couldn't do anything else. I'd be as calm as could be during the day, or when I was standing on the sidelines watching—but the minute I was on the field and there were players opposite me, something inside me went click and I turned into a virtual madman. I didn't care what happened to me! It wasn't because I was angry or bitter or anything like that. In fact, whenever a fight broke out during a scrimmage or a game, I'd move back a step or two, instinctively, and stay away.

When I got home for supper, at about six-fifteen, I'd be totally beat. I'd stay in a hot tub for a long time, soaking my bruises, but when I came down for supper, Mother never asked me about practice or about Mr. Marcus or about any of my scratches or black-and-blue marks. As the weeks went by, it made me feel more and more depressed to sit with her each night and talk about the weather or her classes or my home-work or our vacation plans, when all the time I was wanting to share the practices with her, and how great I was feeling just to be on a team with other guys. Finally one night, after a day on which a few of the guys had really had it with the way Mr. Marcus kept praising me and damning them, and they'd gotten me during a pile-up and given me some hard knuckles to the nose and eyes, I asked her straight out if, when he was young, my father had liked football.

She seemed surprised that I should ask, but when she answered, she didn't seem at all nervous. "I don't know," she said. "I suppose he did, but he never talked to me about it. Handball was your father's sport."

"Handball?" I asked.

She laughed then. "He grew up in a city, remember? Not out here with birds and trees. That came later—with me."

"Was he good?" I asked.

She wiped her lips, and when she sighed I could see that she was making a decision, to tell me something about him. "I suppose so," she said. "He was good at most things he tried. He was a very competitive man. He took me down to Brighton Beach once—this was when we were courting—and I stood behind the fence and watched him banging this little black ball against a brick wall on one of the hottest days of the year. He wore leather gloves." She brushed her hair back from her forehead and breathed heavily, almost as if she were feeling the heat of that summer day all over again. "I couldn't believe it, if you want the truth. And, as I recall things, it made him happy that I kept suggesting to him that it was too hot to play. I think he liked the idea of resisting my suggestions." She leaned forward then, her chin on her hands, looking very young. "Oh, Eddie," she said. "Your father was very special, did you know that? There was nobody quite like him. My parents couldn't understand for the life of them how a *cultivated* young woman like their daughter could be attracted to such a rough-and-tumble young man from the streets of Brooklyn, but there it was, wasn't it?" She smiled, as if dreaming, and I told myself I'd been right about why she always had such a hard time talking about him before—that it was because they'd loved each other too much, that for her it was always as if he'd died only a few weeks ago. "I mean, there was something about the way the sweat dripped along his chest and the ferocious look he got in his eyes when-ever he slammed the ball, and then—the instant the game was over—that easy smile of his. Oh, he had a smile, Eddie! Bright and white in that dark surly face. And not just for me, I can assure you. Not just—"

She stopped and her smile became a straight line. "Not just what—?" I asked.

She looked away, and then stood and went to the sink. "Nothing," she said, and she changed the subject so abruptly—asking me about our Spanish class's magazine drive—that I knew there was nothing I could do to make her tell me more.

Although our school went up to the twelfth grade, we fielded a team that represented only the seventh through ninth grades. The Fowler School wasn't very large—four hundred students, including girls—and the other schools that were in our league were about the same size, so we played six-man football. We wore full uniforms and the rules were basically the same as in eleven-man football, except that no direct hand-offs were allowed and you had to go fifteen yards for a first down. The second week of practice Mr. Marcus made me a defensive end; I liked the position, especially when a blitz was on: this meant that instead of "boxing," and protecting my end against a run, I just crashed through the line and tried to knock over everybody I could until I got to the ballcarrier. Except for Charlie Gildea, who was the best player on our team, I seemed to be the only player who tried hard during practices. At games, when everyone's parents and girlfriends were there, the other guys would exert themselves, but it didn't matter much. "Games are won from Monday to Friday," Mr. Marcus would say, and he was right.

At the end of every practice session we would "run the gauntlet." We'd line up in a straight line, about three yards apart from each other, and Mr. Marcus would give the first man a football and he'd have to run through the entire team, one man at a time. When he finished he'd become the last man and the second man would get the football. The guys hated him for it. By the time you came to the fifth or sixth man you were usually dead, but Mr. Marcus wouldn't let you stop to get your wind back, either, so most of the guys would just fake the rest of the run, falling to the ground before they were tackled. What I'd do, though, would be to tuck the ball into my stomach, both hands around it, put my head down, and charge ahead, ramming as hard as I could into each guy I came to. I suppose it hurt me more than it did the others, but it made me feel so good! Mr. Marcus would tease me because I never tried to fake anybody out or even to sidestep. "Here comes Marcus Allen," he'd say. "Come on, girls, are you going to let this little runt bowl you over? Or is he too fast for you? Move toward the runner—*toward* him!" His voice kept me going, I think. "Way to drive, Eddie," he'd say, as I got up after each guy had rolled me to the ground. "Way to hang in there—"

Mr. Marcus wasn't very big, but we all knew he'd played halfback at a teacher's college in Pennsylvania, and once, on a hot day at the beginning of the season, he came to practice in short pants and I'd never seen such powerful legs. They weren't hairy, either. Just broad, smooth, and muscular. When he was teaching during the day, though, all his power seemed gone. He taught social studies and he could never control a class. I didn't have him for a teacher yet because he taught ninth and tenth grade and I was only in the eighth, but the guys on the team from the ninth grade would talk in the locker room about crazy things that went on in his classrooms. They said that some of the students actually smoked or made out right in front of him.

What seemed especially strange to me, though, wasn't anything Mr. Marcus said or did, but this look he had on his face when he walked through the halls. It was as if he were lost. The way my classes were arranged, I used to pass him in the halls three or four times a day and sometimes I'd say hello to him. He always said hello back to me, but I had the definite feeling that when I was out of my uniform, he didn't know who I was. He seemed to be thinking about something else, I thought, and when I was home remembering what his face had looked like as we passed each other, I'd start thinking that I'd been wrong: it wasn't as if he were lost, really—it was more as if he had lost something.

He was never lost at practice, though. His eyes were all fire then. Especially when he began to get us ready for the big game against St. Dominick's on Parents Day.

St. Dominick's was an orphanage about twenty miles away, run by Jesuits, and we were playing them for the first time. Mr. Marcus told us that he'd seen them play the year before and that we would have to play more than perfectly if we expected to win. By this time we'd played six games, winning four of them, and I wasn't starting but I was getting in, usually near the end—at garbage time—when either victory or defeat seemed certain. I didn't expect to get into the St. Dominick's game, however, because even though I was hitting harder and playing better than ever before, so were the other guys. Dr. Hunter showed up at two of our practices that week, and once, when we were running through our kickoff return drill, I saw him pat Mr. Marcus on the shoulder in a friendly way. Until then I'd had the feeling Dr. Hunter didn't like him. It was nothing he ever said, but what he didn't say. He'd stopped by our house twice after that first time, and both times I'd tried to entertain him while Mother got ready to come downstairs, by telling him about our team. But whenever I said something nice about Mr. Marcus, and waited for him to say something back, he either changed the subject or agreed with me. He never added anything.

"You certainly are a quiet lad," he said to me one night, when, as usual, I'd run out of things to say. I shrugged. Nobody else I knew ever used a word like "lad," I thought to myself, looking down at the rug. But then he added something that made me look up fast. "Not at all like your father was, are you?"

"I don't know," I said. "I—I don't really remember him much . . ."

"Of course," he replied, but before I could get up the courage to ask him for more information, Mother had come down.

I went upstairs to my room, so they could talk. After the first time he came by, I'd begun to think of the fact that he might eventually marry Mother. The thing was, though, that every time I began to imagine what it would be like to have a man like Dr. Hunter for a father, I'd wind up by thinking of what it would be like to have Mr. Marcus as one. I knew this was foolish, especially since Mr. Marcus was seven or eight years younger than Mother, but I thought about it anyway and I wondered a lot about what he did after he went home from practice. I kept thinking what a waste it was that a man like him wasn't married, and how sad it would be if he somehow went the rest of his life without a son or daughter of his own.

I tried hard, a few times that week, to get Mother to talk about my father again, but she wasn't very interested. She did bring down a box of photos for me to look at one night—and after going through the first few, of them before they were married, going to Coney Island and Jones Beach and to her parents' home in Connecticut together, she got up and told me to come to her if I had any questions. All the photos were marked on the back, she said. Then she went upstairs.

I looked at the photos for as long as I could, but without Mother next to me, to give me stories about what wasn't in the photos, I got depressed. I closed my eyes tight a few times, and tried to force myself to remember things I'd done with my father, but it was hard, and the only clear pictures that came into my head were ones of him laughing and giving me a ring for my thumb that he'd made out of a folded dollar bill—and another of him tossing me into the air and of how scared I was until I fell back down and he caught me and rubbed his rough beard against my cheek. I went upstairs and gave my mother each of these memories—asking her if he'd ever told her how to make a ring out of a dollar bill, and if he used to toss me in the air a lot or just once in a while, and if his beard had been very thick—but even though she answered my questions, she didn't add things to her answers, and she made me feel I was intruding on a part of her life I didn't have any right to.

The day before the St. Dominick's game, Dr. Hunter made a speech in our assembly about how we should be as friendly as possible toward the boys from the other school. They were less fortunate than we were, and he hoped we would all learn something from watching them and meeting them. The speech made me squirm. Words weren't going to do any tackling for us, I said to myself. But there was something else that was making me uneasy, and that was the way Mother was acting. When I turned to look at her in the back of the assembly hall, her cheeks were flushed, and this annoyed me. A lot of things annoyed me about her during this period, I know—the way she walked down the halls, the way she stopped to look in mirrors so much at home, the way she smiled at Dr. Hunter and the other teachers, the kind of clothing she wore—and the best way I can explain is to say that during this period, for the first time in my life, I was unhappy that Mother was pretty.

I certainly felt this way when we went to Parents Day together. Very few of the mothers came up to her to ask her questions about their children, but a lot of the fathers did, and the way she smiled, and the way they tried to impress her or make her laugh, bothered me. I kept wanting to go over to her and order her to stop—or to grab her and take her far away—and at the same time I kept wishing she would just pay a little more attention to me, and that she'd ask me about the game and about what our chances were and if I thought I'd get to play.

We were going through our passing drills when the St. Dominick's team arrived. They came in a pale yellow school bus, and they already had their uniforms and cleats on when they stepped down from the bus onto the field. Mr. Marcus went over to their coach, who wore a priest's black shirt and white collar, and shook hands with him, and while they talked we kept going through our drills, trying to act indifferent to their arrival. Their uniforms were black and gold, and I think we were all surprised at how new and clean they were.

I noticed, too, how serious they were about everything they did, even their jumping jacks. The other thing I noticed, of course, was the blacks on their team. Almost half their squad was black and there were also a few Puerto Rican–looking players. Although we had seven or eight at our school, and a few of the other teams in our league had one or two black players, I felt certain we were terrified by the sheer *percentage* of blacks on their team. One of the players standing near me confirmed my suspicion by saying that he wished we had "a few of those" on our team. "Can they run!" he exclaimed. I turned to him, wanting to contradict him, but I didn't say anything because I had to admit that my reaction had been pretty much the same. I assumed that black athletes were faster than whites, and that a team full of blacks would be almost impossible to beat.

By the time the whistle blew for the kickoff, our spirits were high, though, and the guys were all patting each other on the rear end and everybody was giving everybody else encouragement. On the sidelines the students and parents were watching and clapping for us, and the girls stood together and did cheers most of the guys pretended to be annoyed by. I looked for my mother, but she wasn't there. We huddled around Mr. Marcus. "They look fast," he said, "but they're not very big. If you hit hard on the opening play, the game is ours. Is that clear? Hit hard and keep hitting. Drive, drive, drive! Let the man opposite you know you're the boss, okay? I think we can win this game. What do you think—?" We yelled back that we would kill them, smash them, obliterate them, and then Mr. Marcus put his hand into the middle of the circle and we thrust our own hands in, pyramiding them until he shouted, *"Let's go!"* and then we all let out a big roar and the starting team ran out onto the field.

We kicked off and St. Dominick's ran the ball back to the twenty-five-yard line, but on the first play from scrimmage, Charlie Gildea red-dogged into their backfield and smashed this little black kid. The ball skittered out of his arms and John Weldon, our left end, fell on it. I threw my helmet into the air and raced down the sideline with the others to get closer to the play. Mr. Marcus tried not to seem excited, but I could tell he was just as thrilled as we were. Charlie Gildea went around right end on the first play after that and gained three yards. Mr. Marcus yelled at our guys to hit hard and I believe they were hitting as hard as they could, but on the next play I watched the way the St. Dominick's team dug in on defense. They dumped Guy Leonard to the ground for no gain. As I expected, Charlie Gildea went back to pass on the next play. I didn't watch him, though. I watched the line. The three St. Dominick's linemen charged through our men as if they weren't there. Charlie sidestepped one of them but the other two smashed him for a ten-yard loss.

Going back to pass again, on fourth down, Charlie was pulled down on the forty-two-yard line. It was their ball, first and fifteen to go, and it took them exactly four running plays to cover the fifty-eight yards they needed for a touchdown. The crowd was quiet. The St. Dominick's coach was yelling at his boys, and none of them were even smiling. Mr. Marcus was angry. "X-15!" he called. "And stop looking at the ground— look into their eyes. I want them to know they're in a ball game! Pick out a man on the kickoff and lay him flat!" X-15 was a reverse play, and it worked. The St. Dominick's team charged too quickly, and before they knew it, Charlie Gildea was in the clear, along the far sideline. Their safety man pulled him down on their own thirty-yard line, and we went wild. The thrill was short-lived. After the first play, when Guy Leonard gained four, our guys seemed to die again. As soon as the ball was snapped, the first thing you noticed was that our linemen seemed to move back a step, in unison. I could tell that Mr. Marcus noticed also because he started calling our guys girls, and right in front of the parents.

A few of us were still shouting encouragement to the guys on the field, but it didn't make much difference. After we gave up the ball, St. Dominick's began chewing up yardage again. "What's the matter?" Mister Marcus yelled. "Didn't you ever see a straightarm before? Christ!" He smacked his head with the palm of his hand and looked to either side of him. "Eddie," he called. "Where's Eddie?"

I ran to him, my heart pounding. "Go in for Shattuck. Show these girls something, okay? You show 'em, Eddie."

I dashed onto the field, pulling my helmet on and snapping the chin strap. "You're out, Shattuck," I said in the huddle. St. Dominick's was on our thirty-yard line. The other guys stared at me and none of them said anything, but I knew they were probably thinking that Mr. Marcus had put me in for spite. I didn't care. The first quarter wasn't even over and I was getting a chance to play. I lined up at right end, and when the ball was snapped, something went click inside my head. I took a step back, so as not to be taken in, and then I saw men moving toward me with the ballcarrier behind them. I charged forward, hand-fighting past the first man. The second man hit me with a cross-body block and laid me flat, however, and all I could do as the ballcarrier went by was to reach out with my hand, snatching for his ankle. I missed, and looking up I saw that he was laughing as he chugged by, his white teeth gleaming inside his brown face. Charlie Gildea came up from the secondary and made the tackle. He helped me up. "Good try," he said.

"I'll get him next time," I said. I heard my name and I looked sideways. Mr. Marcus was having fits. "Eddie! *Eddie!*" he was wailing. "How many times do I have to tell you? When you see men coming at you like that, don't try to fight them all—roll up the play and leave the tackle for somebody else. Is that clear? Roll it up!" I nodded and set myself for the next play. They ran the other end and made a first down. On the following play, though, they came my way again, and I did what Mr. Marcus wanted. Instead of trying to fight my way to the ballcarrier, I faked at the first blocker and then threw myself into him, low and sideways. It worked. He toppled over me and the other blocker tripped over him and the ballcarrier was slowed down long enough for Guy Leonard to bring him down for no gain.

The first half ended with the score 28 to 0, in favor of St. Dominick's. Between halves I lay under this big apple tree in back of the school, alongside the players, sucking on oranges. The St. Dominick's team stayed on the field, under the goalposts. Nobody said much. Mr. Marcus paced up and down, and it seemed to me he had a million things he wanted to tell us and felt frustrated because he'd get to say only a few of them. In the distance I could see some of the fathers playing catch with a football. Beyond the football field I thought I spotted my mother, near where they were serving coffee and hot chocolate. I wanted her to look at me—to watch me sitting with the other guys and to be proud of me. I wanted her to know what it meant to me to have gotten into the game so early, and I wished too that I could just hear her voice—even if she was only laughing at some stupid joke one of the fathers was telling her—but, at such a distance, I couldn't be sure it was her.

"Do you know what the trouble is?" Mr. Marcus asked, his hands on his hips. "Do you?"

John Weldon shrugged. "They're too fast," he said. Some of the players covered their mouths and giggled.

"I see," Mr. Marcus said, nodding up and down. "I see. They're too fast. They're too fast. What else?"

Somebody to his left mumbled something. Mr. Marcus whirled toward him, then seemed to catch hold of himself, and when he spoke he did so firmly. "Would you mind repeating that for the other boys, Phil?"

Phil Siegel looked at the ground. "They got all those jigs on their team," he said. Everybody laughed.

"Do you know what the trouble is?" Mr. Marcus said again, ignoring Phil. "Do you know what the trouble is?—You're not hungry ballplayers." He sighed, as if he knew how useless his words were. "Damn it, pay attention!" he snapped, and he grabbed John Weldon by his shoulder pad, yanked him from the ground, and then shoved him back down.

"In your little fingers you guys don't have—you don't have . . . Oh, what's the difference—" He looked around and his eyes flicked from one side to the other. He took a deep breath, concentrating hard, and then he spoke again. "Do you want to know what else? Do you? I'm glad you're getting beaten. How's that? This is probably the last time any of those boys will ever beat you at anything. When you're coming back here someday, watching your pansy children run around the field against the latest group of orphans or deprived kids, the boys you're playing against will be, will be . . ." He threw up his hands. "—God knows where! And while you and you and you," he said, pointing, "will be reminiscing about that time those jigs slaughtered you, none of them will even remember what the Fowler School was." He stopped. He seemed very tired suddenly, and I wished more than anything that I could help him. "Okay," he said, blinking. "This is the way it's going to be. I'm giving every one of you a chance to play, because I want every one of you, for once in your lives, to know what it is to get hit and to get hurt. Is that clear?" Nobody said anything. I was angry, and I wondered for a second if this was really what Mr. Marcus intended—if he'd only wanted to get us angry enough to go out and play hard-nosed football during the second half.

"That was a most interesting speech, Mr. Marcus." Some of the boys started to stand up. "Sit, boys. Please. Sit—" Dr. Hunter said. "You've been playing hard and you need the rest." He smiled, and when he did I looked at Mr. Marcus and the anger in his eyes made me imagine for a split second what my father's eyes might have looked like when he was moving in for a ball on the handball court, moving in to kill it. "I just wanted to wish you luck for the second half, boys. I know you'll do your best."

Mr. Marcus muttered something under his breath.

"What was that?" Dr. Hunter asked.

"Nothing I haven't said in other words," Mr. Marcus answered.

"Fine, fine—well, I'll leave you to your discussion."

Dr. Hunter left. Mr. Marcus waited a few seconds, then started off toward the playing field. "Follow me, girls," he said. "Don't be scared, now—"

The guys really hated him then, and during the second half they showed it. By the fourth quarter, when almost all the parents had stopped watching, they'd called their girlfriends over and were standing with them, wisecracking and showing off. One or two of them even took drags on cigarettes and necked with their girlfriends. It hardly affected Mr. Marcus. He just kept yelling at us and mocking us and he was true to his word about putting everybody into the game. For their part, the St. Dominick's team kept coming. At the time I would have given anything, I think, to have been one of them. And I kept hoping, all through the second half, that before the end of the game one of them would speak to me—would say something about how hard I was play-ing, about how I was hanging in there—would make some gesture toward me. None of them did.

When the game was over, Charlie Gildea and I were the only players who stayed on the field and shook hands with them. I shook hands with as many of them as I could, even though they hardly seemed interested. They huddled at the far end of the field, gave us a 2-4-6-8 cheer, then walked to their bus and left. The final score was 54 to 0.

After I got dressed in my regular clothes, my gray flannel slacks and blue Fowler blazer, I went back to the field to look for my mother. Most of the parents were gone by now, and I couldn't find Mother anywhere. I walked over to the school building, and went inside, but it was de-serted and her homeroom was locked. I came back outside—the sky was starting to turn orange from the sun—and, scared suddenly of being left alone, I found myself wondering for a second if she'd gone off with some other guy's father, if maybe one of them was divorced or a widower and if they were already sitting together in some plush lounge, having cocktails. I kicked at the ground and then got angry with her for not having told me where she'd gone, and for making me think such stupid thoughts and see such stupid pictures in my head. Didn't it ever occur to you that I might think things like that if you went off and left me alone? I wanted to shout at her. Didn't it? *Didn't* it . . . ?

Mr. Marcus saw me walking across the field, and he called to me and asked if I wanted a ride home with him. He had an old 1966 green Dodge Dart, and when I sat next to him we didn't say anything to each other. He smoked one cigarette after another, and since I'd never seen him smoke at school or practice, I was surprised. I gave him directions to our house, and when we got there I was relieved to see Mother's car in the driveway, and lights on in the kitchen. I asked Mr. Marcus if he wanted to come inside. I told him Mother could make us some coffee or hot chocolate.

"Some other time, Eddie. Okay?" He put his hand on my head and he stared at me for what seemed like ages, his mouth slightly open and a cigarette stuck to his lower lip. His eyes didn't shift or blink at all. Then he seemed to wake up. He looked at his hand as if he were puzzled to find it resting on my head. "Christ!" he said, ruffling my hair. "You're a sweet kid, Eddie. Now get inside, take a nice hot shower, and stay warm."

"Thanks for the ride home, sir," I said, when I was out of the car.

"Sure," he said. He backed the car out of the driveway and I started toward the house. Then he honked and I turned toward him. He looked out of the window and waved to me. "You played a good game, Eddie," he called.

On Monday I looked for him at school but he wasn't there. He didn't show up all week, and in assembly on Friday morning, Dr. Hunter announced that owing to illness in his immediate family, Mr. Marcus had been forced to leave the school for the remainder of the term. He said he hoped Mr. Marcus would be returning for the spring semester. When the spring semester began, Mr. Marcus didn't return. No announcements were made, and I was probably the only student in the school who even remembered what Dr. Hunter had said. I was feeling pretty upset, and when, on the evening after the first day of classes for the new term, Mother told me that Dr. Hunter was calling for her and that she'd have to leave me alone in the house for the evening, something inside me went click.

I stalked off, but while she was dressing, I walked straight into her room and asked her if she was going to marry Dr. Hunter.

"You should knock before you come in, Eddie. I might have been undressed." She looked into her mirror and fastened an earring.

"*Are* you?" I asked again. "I'm serious. I have a right to know!"

She kept working at her earring, as if I hadn't said a thing, but when I saw her mouth open slightly, I didn't give her a chance and I spoke before I even thought about what I was going to say. "How—how could you ever marry a man with a gimpy arm?" I demanded. "How could you—?"

She turned toward me and looked at me sternly for a second or two. Then her face broke into a big smile. "Oh, Eddie," she laughed. "Of course I'm not getting married." She stood and came to me and hugged me. Her perfume was strong, and I struggled to get loose. "You know you're the only man in my life."

"I'm not," I said, freeing myself. "I'm your son. You should get a husband while you're still young and pretty."

She backed off and looked at me for a long time after I said that, and I kept having these alternate feelings—that I shouldn't have said it and that I should have. I think she wanted to kiss me and hug me again, but for some reason she seemed afraid to do it now. She simply closed her eyes, nodded once, and then opened them. She turned back to her mirror. "Will you finish the dishes while I'm gone?" she asked.

"Sure," I said. And then: "How come Mr. Marcus didn't come back this term?"

"You're full of questions, aren't you?"

"Can I ask Dr. Hunter why Mr. Marcus didn't come back?"

She sighed, then smiled again, but in a much easier way than she had a few minutes before. "I don't think that would get us anywhere, do you?"

"No," I admitted.

"Well, then?"

"I guess I ask too many questions."

When Dr. Hunter called for her, I didn't go out to say hello to him. After they left, though, still feeling worried about what I'd said to Mother, I kept walking around our house, going from room to room, upstairs and downstairs. It seemed terribly large to me, and I wondered if Mother was afraid when she stayed in it by herself sometimes. I tried hard to remember what things had been like when Father was there, but I couldn't. I went into Mother's room and took out her box of photos again and looked at the pictures of him, but that didn't help either. Not even when I found a picture of him with his arms around some other guys in sweatshirts, and a football on the ground in front of them.

But looking at the pictures of him, and seeing the way he smiled, reminded me of Mother being alone with Dr. Hunter, and when I saw that picture in my head, for the first time I asked myself if she could actually *enjoy* going out with him. Then I closed the box of photos and went downstairs to watch television.

I must have fallen asleep on the living room couch, because the next thing I knew, Mother was sitting next to me, stroking my forehead with her fingertips. The television set was still on.

"Hi, Eddie," she said. She bent over and kissed me. She held me for a long time, pressing her lips against my forehead in a very gentle way. Then she sat up.

"Did you have a good time tonight?" I asked.

She seemed surprised that I should ask her, but when she answered me I saw that I'd said the right thing. "Thrilling," she whispered. "I talked about irregular French verbs, and he told me about his eating club at Princeton."

"His *what?*" I asked.

"Never mind," she said, laughing. "At any rate, there was one interesting thing that occurred tonight. I couldn't stop thinking about our conversation, and about how much, when you get angry, you remind me of your father. You made good sense, you know . . ." I looked away from her then. She stood up, turned off the television, and sat down across from me, letting her shoes drop to the rug. "All right," she said. "Let me ask you something, Eddie. What would you think of our leaving the Fowler School and moving somewhere else? Maybe back to New York City, where—"

"Do you really mean it?" I exclaimed. My face must have registered how happy I was at the idea, and when she smiled and said that she did mean it, I tried to check myself, to hold back my enthusiasm. "Well, don't do it because of me," I said.

"You?" she laughed. "If we do it—and I'm not promising anything yet—we'll do it for the two of us." She leaned forward, and bit her lower lip before she spoke again. "I think we could both benefit by giving ourselves the chance to meet new people, don't you?"

"I suppose," I said, trying not to appear too excited. I didn't fool her, of course, and soon I stopped pretending and we were both talking about what it would be like to live in a place like Manhattan and of all the things we might do there together, and all the interesting people we might meet.

When she spoke about selling our house, though, I began to feel sad, and when she began talking about my going away to college someday and beginning a life of my own, what I wanted to do was to cry out that I would *never* leave her. *Never!* I didn't say anything, though. Because I guess I knew she was right about my leaving her someday, and what I was hoping was that by the time I did she would be married again. But I knew that she might not be. I guess she knew it too, even though you never would have guessed it from the sweet way she kept smiling at me.

Romeo and Julio

JULIO LAY ON HIS SIDE, as if, Tony thought, he had been folded into position like a paper swan. An aide gave Julio an injection, then wrapped him in a straitjacket. Patients swarmed around, chattering like birds, shuffling in carpet slippers, bare feet, broken shoes. They asked Tony for money, for golf lessons, for candy bars, for skate keys.

Tony imagined that Julio's skin was made of glass, that he could see through to the skeleton below. Julio was a large prehistoric bird—more deadly and beautiful than an eagle, his bones held together be gleaming black railroad spikes. Julio was flying home, his wings spread to the width of the highway, his eyes bright as emeralds.

Tony went over his lines, so that, afterward, when he brought Lynne home to Brookline from the dress rehearsal of *Romeo and Juliet*, he would be ready. *O, Wilt thou leave me so unsatisfied?* he would ask. He saw Lynne lean against her door, smile, take her cue. *What satisfaction canst thou have tonight?* she would reply.

He wondered: if he were to tell her he had spent the afternoon visiting his brother Julio in a mental hospital, would that make her like him more? He did not want to be liked *because* he had a brother who was mentally ill. Still, it pleased him to imagine Lynne asking questions, gazing at him with admiration while he talked about how close he and Julio were.

You really love him, don't you? she would say, and he would shrug, modestly. *Sure—Romeo and Julio, that's us,* he would reply. Then he would apologize quickly for the bad joke, so that, sensing his embarrassment, she might like him even more.

He had met Lynne at the Cambridge Public Theatre, where, three months before, they were chosen, along with ten other high school seniors, to serve as apprentices. After rehearsals they would go with the other apprentices to a nearby luncheonette, and often they would stay and talk long after the others had gone. He loved being with her—loved her directness, her sometimes strange sense of humor. She seemed always to say just what she was thinking, without worrying about how it would play to others. And he loved, too, the way her hazel eyes flickered, as if filled with fine gold shavings.

Tony dressed, looked past the closet mirror, to the window. Below, in the courtyard of their apartment building, Julio had become a small mud-colored lizard. Julio scurried under hedges, leapt to the wall, began climbing. Julio appeared at the window, crawled onto the sill, dropped to the floor, skittered behind the bed.

After the rehearsal, they rode the train back to Lynne's home. The train rose from a tunnel into the night-lights of the city, then crossed over Longfellow Bridge. Tony saw Julio slipping down from one of the bridge's old stone towers, riding the roof of the train like a cowboy, hanging by his ankles, peering upside down into the subway car, grinning brightly.

The instant they were inside Lynne's apartment building, Tony's chest constricted, as if, he felt, the muscles around his heart were drying out, so that the blood had to force its way through. When, on the second floor landing, Lynne turned away to put her key in the lock, Tony touched her arm. She faced him at once, smiling so warmly that he sensed she did want him to kiss her, and yet, his heart pounding, he told himself to wait, to follow through with his original plan.

"O, Wilt thou leave me so unsatisfied?" he asked.

"Why not?"

"Why *not*?"

She laughed and he found himself too surprised to know what to do next.

"The question's from the play," he said. "I was saving it. I was hoping you'd remember—that maybe you would recite Juliet's reply back to me . . ." He felt dizzy. "I'm sorry," he added.

"Oh Tony—don't be sorry—"

Her eyes seemed nearly transparent, as if made of the thinnest gold leaf. He shrugged. "I just . . ."

"You just what?"

I was just thinking about my brother, he wanted to say. I just love look-ing at you. I just can't believe a girl as pretty as you would like me as much as I like you. I just don't know what I'm doing and I don't want to put on an act and make a stupid joke from my brother's name and yet . . .

"Nothing," he said.

She smiled and brushed her hair back. He wished he were her hand. He wished she could know, without words, how much he loved being near her. But he was frightened that if he began telling her about Julio he wouldn't know where to stop and that the moment he'd been hoping for would pass and never come again.

He felt faint. He imagined a twister of frigid air swirling up the staircase, tunneling around him, wrapping him in white. He blinked, looked down, saw nothing but her mouth, her lips.

"Would you like to come in for a few minutes?" she asked. "I have to get up early tomorrow to help my mother bake. Before ten o'clock mass. Then we're going to my aunt's house."

"I'll be visiting my brother Julio tomorrow," Tony stated. "He lives in a mental hospital. He's been there for almost three years. He's my only brother and he's a year younger than I am. We were always very affec-tionate with each other."

Lynne cocked her head to one side, and he saw a look of such intense compassion on her face that it made him stiffen.

"That must be hard for you," she said.

What Tony wanted more than anything in the world was simply to hold her and to have her hold him, yet when her fingers touched his cheek, gently, he was too ashamed of himself, and too furious with her, to risk being repulsed again. What right did she have to know about Julio's life, and why—what he would never be able to take back, he knew, and what she would surely despise him for—had he been so weak as to mention it?

"I'll see you on Monday," he said, stepping back. He moved toward the staircase.

"Call me in the morning," she said. "All right? I'll be home until at least nine-thirty. Please?"

Tony slept. When he woke, near dawn, thirty years had passed. He reached over to stroke Julio's hair, the way he often did, but Julio was not there. Tony sat up. He saw himself taking Lynne by the hand, leading her to this point in his life. They were driving north of Boston, past low rolling hills and endless green fields of gravestones. Tony's wife was beside him, his two children in the back seat. Tony was a well-known film director, his wife a beautiful movie star who had given up her career to raise a family with him, but who, every few years, appeared in a film he made.

They drove on, Lynne invisible, yet strapped to the rear of the car, forced to watch and to listen. Why was he so angry with her? he wondered. Even if she found out the way his imagination worked sometimes—how it could contain the craziest, most violent and most beautiful scenes at the same time—why would this scare her away? Did love and friendship *have* to be opposites, the way sanity and insanity were?

When they drove past an enormous complex of tall prisonlike buildings, he explained to his children, as he did each time, that this was where their Uncle Julio had lived once upon a time. They cruised along curving tree-lined roads, stopped in front of an elegant colonial home. The front door opened and Julio appeared, smiling radiantly. He walked down the steps. Tony emerged from the car and he and his brother embraced. Julio asked him why it had taken him so long to get there.

"Long?" Tony said. "But it's only been thirty years—"

Tony put on a bathrobe, left his room. The apartment was wonderfully still. In a few hours his parents would be eating breakfast, going through the *Sunday Globe,* talking about their visit, later in the day, to Julio. It was just past five-thirty. Tony opened the refrigerator. He could eat breakfast, dress, go out and get the paper, take a walk, come home, shower, shave. Time would pass more easily if he kept busy. He didn't want to telephone Lynne's home before nine.

Leaving Brooklyn

I STOOD IN THE DOORWAY of a luncheonette and watched the children playing in the schoolyard. I glanced sideways, aware of eyes. The owner's head was in the window beside me—a middle-aged Puerto Rican man with deep pouches under his eyes, he was stir-frying onions and peppers on a grill, and the fragrance made me salivate. I imagined some of my students sitting in the booths behind me, inside the warm store, chattering and necking and feeling one another up, and I smiled at the man. He shrugged, and in the slight lifting of his shoulders and the world-weary expression in his eyes, I felt he was sharing something with me—an acknowledgment of the difficulties and trials life had brought to him. He returned my smile.

"Hey Miz Mishkin!"

"*Mira! Mira!* Miz Mishkin! Miz Mishkin!"

Across the street the children were lined up in a long row, on the other side of the wire fence, their fingers locked in its diamonds, their voices screeching in high-pitched tones of delight. They were glad to see me! I felt blood rush to my head, felt my heart catch, but I did not deny their greetings—I'd come for this moment, after all, hadn't I?—I raised my head, smiled, waved to them, and then walked quickly down the street and away from the school, hoping none of the teachers had spotted me.

"Hey Miz Mishkin!" a boy called. "You look real swift!"

I heard cat-calls and whistles, elaborate mock-groans and laughter. I didn't turn around. I'd never see these children again, I knew. Michael and I were moving—his company was transferring him to their new electronics plant in Seattle this time—and I would go with him. They had waited until I was out of the hospital, though. They were very considerate. They had sent me flowers. Flowers instead of a child. But we do have Jennifer, Michael said, touching my hand. And you won't have to go through these months of pain and worry ever again.

That's too bad, I'd said, and Michael had looked at me in the way that made me know I had reached him, had made him worry. There were, I told myself, even in that cold and bright room, still pleasures in life.

We have each other.

Do we?

"Hey Miz Mishkin—he got love real bad for you. He think you just like a real movie star!"

I longed to cross the street and go through the schoolyard gates—to have them follow me into the building, singing and dancing and holding hands in a long line behind me. Still, the instant I turned the corner their voices were gone, severed by the buildings now between us. I slowed down and touched my fingertips to my right cheek, expecting to be burned. My cheek was barely warm. Willa Cather, I recalled, had felt that the years during which she'd taught Latin in a Pittsburgh high school were among the happiest of her life.

I heard singing and tambourines, from a store-front church. Three fat Puerto Rican men sat at a card table in the middle of the sidewalk. One of them wore green wool gloves from which the fingers had been cut off. I saw infants in baby carriages, heard women call to one another from open windows, watched children playing in the small plots of dirt around trees. I thought of how wonderfully comforted I'd always felt in the morning, these past three years, walking from the subway station to my school, and I thought I now knew the reason why: I could not possibly believe, or hope, that anybody living here—the families of the black and Puerto Rican and West Indian children I worked with—could ever know what my past had been like. They came, literally, from different worlds. But on Long Island, the people looked as if they were from *my* world—as if they should have been able to understand what my childhood had been like. It was the illusion that angered me, I decided—and the absence of illusion that comforted me. Walking these streets, I realized—the streets Michael had walked when he was growing up—I usually felt good about myself in a way I rarely did elsewhere; here in Brooklyn I did not fear, at least not as much as I did at other times, that the sweetness others had found in me when I was a girl had been, with the years, altogether lost.

From the train window, I saw a man without legs sitting inside an old tire. Beside him was a black cap filled with silver coins. I was in the Atlantic Avenue station of the Long Island Railroad. I heard the hissing of the train, the scraping of metal, the soft chugging as we began to leave. Soon I would be home. I would pick up Jennifer from her nursery school. Michael would be home after us. Steam rose from under the train, clouding my view. My father and mother were dead. I had no brothers or sisters, no uncles or aunts who were still alive. In my family nobody who knew me as a child knew my child. I closed my eyes and tried to imagine the fragrance of warm wet wool.

Every Thursday night, for all the years I was in high school, when my homework was done, I'd set up our ironing board in the living room, by the entrance to the kitchen, and I'd iron Father's shirts—he put on a fresh one for work each morning—while Mother watched TV. I set the board up slightly behind her so that she would have to turn her head backwards and away from the TV screen if she wanted to talk to me. Father would be in the basement, puttering—or in the garage, working on the car. I loved to iron his shirts, and I loved to watch Mother's hands, busy mending or knitting or sewing . . . And when, at the end of an evening, she would take the shirts from the doorknob, where I'd hung them on hangers, she'd always smile and say to me (the turn of phrase was Father's, and she liked to tease him about it, and explain to me that his father, who'd been a farmer in Illinois, near Staunton, had said the same thing to her when he was alive) *I'm really glad of your help, Ruth.* She'd look at each of the shirts, lifting the hanger into the air above her and letting the shirt bottom twirl slightly, and if there were any creases left, which there rarely were, she'd point them out to me, and when she did I never felt, as I did at other times, that I'd somehow failed.

For me, the feel of the damp bundles of rolled shirts, the lovely odors of steaming cloth when I'd press the hot iron down, the miracle of watching wrinkles made flat, of wetness made dry, the feel of the pink rubber bulb on the old jam jar, for sprinkling—these were sufficient. More than sufficient. My mind would float free while I worked—freer than at any other time in the house—and the rhythm of moving my hand back and forth in even strokes, while I held something solid and heavy and gleaming, was magically calming.

My father's workshop was in our cellar, surrounded by endless shelves, floor to ceiling, of Mother's preserves: tomatoes and pickles and relishes and watermelon rinds and fruits. I always resented those shelves and jars. They blocked the light from the narrow ground-level cellar windows, and darkened the room and closed Father in. I helped Mother with the canning, of course, but what was there that I could ever do to help Father with? I mowed the lawn and trimmed the hedges and weeded the vegetables, but Mother did those things also and Father never thought to ask me to help him with the car or the furnace or the TV—he never thought to ask me to help him build anything or repair anything.

Mother would sometimes try to console me by telling me how disappointed he's been never to have had a son, and she must have informed me a thousand times, though never in his hearing, of how vicious and angry he'd become—inconsolably so—when I was two years old and he contracted a case of the mumps. But the mumps didn't really explain everything, because—a strange obstinate part of him I never had access to—he had not even allowed for the possibility that his first child might be a girl. When I was born, I'd had no name. For years—even into college—whenever I had to write an essay for English class about myself, I'd begin, "I was born Robert Arthur Sutler . . ."

Or was that the story Mother wanted me to believe? I never asked Father about it. Once or twice when I came down to the cellar to visit him—it was the coolest part of our house in summer—his defenses down momentarily, he would smile lovingly at me. But an instant later he'd realize he was no longer alone, and he'd snap at me or ignore me. Didn't I have anything else I wanted to do?

I like to watch you work, I'd offer, but my words seemed to mean nothing to him.

How different when I'd go off with him in his car! At Christmas and Easter every year I'd get one day each school vacation to be with him, and I longed for those days, savored the memories afterward. When he was off and alone in his car, his samples and catalogs of Masonite products in the back seat, he was free too, wasn't he? I'd sit next to him and go through the catalogs, asking him about the different kinds of woods and grains and finishes and panelling, telling him which ones I liked best, which ones I'd like in which rooms of our house—and in my own house when I would be married someday—and he'd talk with me and tease me and laugh with me.

When I was nine he made me a dollhouse with a roof and walls that lifted off—first the roof, then the walls—from Masonite samples he brought home. The dollhouse was a replica of our own house, and he panelled the small rooms according to my wishes. It will be nice to tell Jennifer about my days with Father sometime, won't it? She knows him only through photos. She loves the dollhouse as much as I did, and she can play with it for hours on end. It's the quality in her that Michael encourages most, a quality he claims comes as much from me as from him.

On the long weekends when Father was building our house, while we lived in a small apartment near Greenwood's first shopping center, I'd have to amuse myself for twelve or thirteen hours at a stretch sometimes, without playmates. Mother would help Father—nailing and painting and measuring and bringing him things and holding things for him—and she and I would try to make our picnic lunch an elaborate affair, but he always ate as quickly as he could so that he could get back to work, and most of my day—I'd bring a little satchel of things: dolls and books and a jumprope and crayons and chalk—would be spent playing with woodcurls, scraps of Masonite, pieces of copper tubing, bent nails, asphalt shingles, and tar paper. I hated those days. I knew, of course, that Mother and Father needed to be left alone, that they were anxious to get out of the apartment at last, that they were irritated by costs they hadn't foreseen, and afraid of errors that would delay us, but my knowledge didn't keep me from feeling lonely, abandoned, and resentful. Later on, they would refer to those days when they'd worked so hard together as if they were wonderful ones—and they would remind me of what a good child I'd been, of how everybody had been in awe of me for my ability to amuse myself so endlessly. And for a time, in my own memory, I even came to believe that I agreed with them.

Despite father's irritation with me, I'd often stay in the cellar with him and watch him work. He would make me doll furniture from scraps and samples—a new piece every year especially for my birthday. From the time I was nine until I left home for college, and when he was away at work I would sometimes steal down to the cellar and touch his tools, look in all his jars and boxes, and read through the hardware catalogs. I would lift the tiny bureaus and chests of drawers he was constructing and I'd hold them in the palm of my hand, amazed—remembering his surliness—at the delicacy of his work, his patience for detail. The miniature clamps, securing the wood while the glue dried, always fascinated me most.

After he died, Mother sold his tools, and I was furious with her for it, though—same old me—I said nothing to her at the time. And later on, when we'd moved into our house on Long Island and Mother was watching Michael drill holes on the back deck one day, for installing a barbecue, and she said something to me about wishing she'd saved Father's tools so that Michael could have had them—that Father had loved his tools so much and cared for them so well, and had always bought the best quality even if it meant doing without until he had the money—I'd rushed into the house, too overwhelmed by anger and loss to cope with the situation.

I wished that Michael could have known him. I wished that Michael could have talked to him and worked with him, making things for our house, for his grandchildren. From the time I met Michael—eight months after Father died—I'd always believed that, with his sweet ways—with his directness—he would have been able to draw Father out, to share things with him, to get around Father's irritability.

When Father entered the offices of his clients, I would see just how much others admired him, and it surprised me each time to have secretaries and businessmen tell me how he bragged on me—about my good grades in school, about my achievements—my 4H ribbons and medals, my Girl Scout awards, my swimming trophies, my parts in plays. It used to amaze me to discover that other people were eager to be near my father—that they wanted to please him, and until I saw the way they looked at him when he came into their offices, I'd never really thought of him, I realized, as being especially handsome.

But he was, and when I was about fourteen I first began to have an elaborate fantasy in which I would put myself in the place of some beautiful and shy secretary with whom he was having an affair that lasted for many years and was very painful, beautiful, and tragic. I imagined them taking long drives in the countryside together. I imagined myself writing her diary. I imagined them having elegant dinners at roadside inns. I imagined her early death from a gruesome form of cancer, and the quiet reassurance he would give to her—the peace he gave her soul before she departed this world. I imagined him at her deathbed, holding her hand—and I would dote on the gentle knowing smiles they exchanged, the firm and loving pressure of their hands upon one another. I knew the secrets she took with her to the grave. I heard harps and violins. I saw them kiss and dissolve into the heavens. I saw Jesus folding them gently under his cape.

During that period, whenever actors and actresses kissed in movies, I would lean forward and peer as intently as I could—to see if they really meant it. It was something I *had* to know. I was the prettiest girl in our school, everyone said, and the smartest. I could sing and dance, I could memorize long speeches and poems without difficulty—I accepted the verdict: I would go to Hollywood one day and make our town famous. But what I wondered about endlessly—the thing I feared would ultimately prohibit a film career for me—was how I would ever be able to kiss men I wasn't truly in love with. If I were married, I asked myself, and had children, what would my husband and children think and feel when the whole world would be seeing me on enormous screens, my lips pressed against those of other men? And how would I ever be able to kiss a man I wasn't truly in love with and make people believe that I was? How did actors and actresses manage it? Did the directors step in and put their hands on the cheeks and lips and chins of the actors and actresses to get them in the right positions for the camera?

Sometimes, when Mother and Father were both gone to work, I'd take movie magazines down to the cellar with me and I'd sit on the braided brown and orange rug in front of Father's workbench, and press my lips against photos of actors. I discovered that my fingers—the knuckles of my index and middle fingers pressed against my lips—felt like a boy's lips. I'd close my eyes and dream, trying to let my mind drift off into ecstasy. I'd lick my fingers lightly, and part my lips. I'd open my eyes to stare at photos. I'd glance down and be aware of my nailpolish, at nose level, but I wouldn't smile. When I returned from seeing movies I'd replay the love scenes in my head in front of mirrors, fogging them as I leaned forward, eyes almost closed, for the climactic moment.

At kissing parties, and later, on dates, when I would actually be kissing boys, I would always be trying to imagine what—if someone were filming us—I would, as an actress, have been feeling. How many hours and how many times did actors and actresses have to practice to get it right? Did they get aroused in front of cameras and cameramen and other actors? And did the men—the girls laughed about it in our school locker room—wear jockstraps to the movie sets the way the girls said boys did to dances, to keep themselves from showing? I was intensely aware of how often movie stars became divorced, and when I discovered stars who didn't, and who, according to the magazines, led good Christian lives, and had loving marriages, I'd bring the articles to Mother. The real Christian home, Mother stated, but with a severity that chilled me, was the nearest approach to heaven this side of the grave.

My mother was the local Avon lady and in truth, I'd liked the idea—what could have been funny or wrong about it to a girl born and raised in a small Indiana town?—for it enabled me to know the insides of the houses of all her friends. I liked going with her on her rounds, and sitting on couches next to her, and being proud of how much she knew about the products in her sample case. Nor did I ever question the gentle and discreet way she would, when she delivered completed orders, give the women gifts of Bible pamphlets, for which she'd paid herself. And though I came to realize later on that most of her clients probably did not share her views, all of them seemed to admire her for what she did. Whenever I'm out doing my work, she'd joke, I always try to do a little of His work too.

I used to wonder what Michael could want with stories from my childhood, with such ordinary memories—there seemed so little that was strange about them, so little in them that could be called real secrets. But the truth, I came to see, was that I liked to think of myself as having had the impossible: a childhood without terror. I lived the way everybody lived in my home town. In my dollhouse the rooms contained only those dramas that were derived from the most ordinary and normal of books and TV shows—from Ozzie and Harriet and Sue Barton and Loretta Young and *Anne of Green Gables* and Jane Wyman and *Father Knows Best*. In my dollhouse the mother cooked and shopped and drank coffee with the neighbors and tried out new Avon products. The father came home from work and fixed the car and mowed the lawn. The children rode on yellow schoolbuses and played house and had slumber parties. Everybody admired everyone else's new clothes and new cars and new washing machines and green lawns. In my mother's house there were many mansions, I used to tell Michael, and they were all decorated by Montgomery Ward.

Michael tried often to answer the question I was always asking. Where did I come from? I came from me, he told me. He tried to teach me to value the fact that however banal I may have found my childhood, it was mine, and nobody else's. And to him, of course, born and raised in Brooklyn, my life was, in fact, exotic—a real American girlhood, one in which mother and daughter cooked together for the church bake sale, and in which the daughter was never permitted to see the father nude. Incredible yes, I'd say to him—but extraordinary, no. How I wondered about the little bundles the boys in school carried between their legs! When I was eleven and a half, I went to the local library, took an anatomy book off the shelf, brought it with me to the girls' room, and locked the toilet door. But the only drawing of a man's parts was a cut-away medical diagram, in profile, showing all the major internal organs and arteries and veins, and it made no sense to me.

Often I'd go off my myself, biking, and stop in quiet places and take out my notebooks and my books of poems and the plays I was memorizing parts from and storing up—as I'd stored up the verses Mother taught me when I was younger—and those were the times I felt most beautifully cool and desirable and at peace. Those were the times when I did believe that I had a soul that made me special. It was as if, I'd imagine then, I were seeing myself from the point of view of the mysterious man, who, happening by, would see me there, would understand me, and would desire me.

I see myself sitting on the grass, my old Schwinn bike next to me. My knees are up, my hands locked around them. I'm home from college for the first time—Father is still alive, I haven't met Michael yet—and my hair is tied back in a pink ribbon, my plaid shirt is open at the chest, my cut-off dungarees are tight around my hips, and what I'm realizing, with a miraculous suddenness, is that it isn't so much that I'm waiting there to be discovered by some older man—as I'd imagined before—or that what I want in life is to be able to please some older man the way I felt my mother had never pleased my father. What I'm feeling in that moment is not so much that I want to *have* a man like my father— which thought had begun, during the previous year or two, to disturb me—but that I want to *be* a man like him. And curiously, the connection, instead of frightening me, soothes me.

By then I'd seen photos and statues and paintings, and I knew what the mysterious little bundles looked like, and so I was able to incorporate them into my fantasies. I'd let boys do forbidden things to me now and then—heavy petting—and I'd touched them where they wanted me to touch them and held them there—wanting to please them, and hoping to become excited the way books and other girls said you were supposed to be excited. Sometimes I would feel something like what other girls told me they felt—but neither my fantasies nor my experiences ever seemed to be enough to arouse me as I felt I should be aroused. I was forever outside myself while things were happening, it seemed, wondering if I were feeling and doing the right thing.

When we first met and were falling in love, Michael loved to have me tell him about this part of my life. We could talk for hour after hour about all the years before we'd known one another—about what we'd felt and what we'd wished for and what we'd done and why it was that we now thought we'd felt and hoped and acted in the ways we had. Inevitably, we'd wind up talking mostly, and with great pleasure, about how good we were for each other, about how lucky we were to have found each other: the man inside me, the woman inside him. Having been only children was part of it, we'd tell each other—I the sister/brother he'd always desired and never had; he the brother/sister I'd never had—the sibling we'd each desired, not only for the giving and receiving of love, but, without even having known it then, to help us survive—to give our mothers other objects for their love, and to have been able, thereby, to have eased our invisible burdens.

Whenever we talked about these things, Michael would please me most by claiming that he'd never met anybody as direct as I was, anybody as natural, anybody who was in direct touch with her true self in the way I was. It was as if I came to him—with his wary city ways—from a foreign land. It was why he loved me.

I remembered that and used it against him later on, during a fight once—telling him that studies by Army psychologists and psychiatrists showed that men who chose foreign women for wives, as he had obviously chosen me, wanted, quite simply, that their wives be foreign to them. They tended to desire to live with women from whom they would, in a fundamental way, always be separate, because they perceived that separation—symbolized by the obstacle of language—as their protection.

When I listened to the children who came to me at school—to their stories and problems and feelings—I'd remember that scene and I'd suddenly hear Michael's voice inside my head and I'd find myself thinking of the accusations he'd come, more and more with the years, to charge me with: that I was the one who'd put distance between us, that I was the one who'd been afraid to face real feelings and fears, that I was the one who used my work and my training—my knowledge of how and why our feelings work the way they do, of how our emotional history, our early years especially, can be caught up in any and every act and gesture of our later life—to cut myself off from my own feelings and self—from the sweet young girl he had once loved—and from him.

I'd go on listening to the child who was with me, and I'd be able to respond usefully; yet all the while I'd also be hearing my conversations with Michael and I'd be analyzing the effects his words had on me and I'd be figuring out that what I was doing, most simply, was substituting his judgmental voice for my mother's. I'd remember Michael telling me about my supposed directness, my ability to feel things and to act on these feelings spontaneously—without filters and without dissembling—and I'd think that it was because of this supposed talent—because of his words confirming this talent in me—that I'd first decided to study psychology and to go into counseling. And then—inevitably—I'd wonder why it was that the more I understood and the more I actually used the gifts Michael told me I had, and that I believed I had, to help other people, to have the kind of influence on their lives that I'd had on Michael's—the more I seemed to lose those gifts for my own life.

Then, as now, I became frightened of those parts of my childhood that I feared I would never have access to—those parts I couldn't recall, or that I felt Mother kept from me somehow—and that was when Michael's voice would leave me and pictures of you would enter my head, Mother. I would see you, dressed in your Sears Best, as if you were a statue in bronze—arms extended, eyes radiant—an Avon kit in one hand and a Bible tract in the other. And I'd see you as you were after your stroke, in the nursing home—your senses gone, unable to feed yourself or void yourself, unable to recognize me. I'd see the aides try to take your covers off and lift your nightgown, so they could bathe you, and I'd see you come alive suddenly and battle them with an astonishing fury. They were in awe of you—of the modesty that seemed to have survived all else. They gave me a demonstration several times, and watching your anger—your fists gripping the sheet to keep it pulled to your chin, your head whipping back and forth against the pillow, I remember feeling, to my surprise, that I was proud of you. I remember feeling that I wanted you to win. I remember wondering, from the doorway, as I've wondered since, whether or not I would ever find, before my life ended, that I'd been fortunate enough to have inherited a measure of your passion.

The train was slowing down. I saw pretty houses, in pastels, and flat frost-filtered emerald lawns. I was almost home. It was no secret then, was it? I was more like her than I often liked to admit. The force that through her grim life drove her, drove me too, I supposed. I recalled trying to tell her once how much I loved *My Ántonia*. Though she never showed that the books and stories were about anything more than young girls growing up on farms in the Midwest, yet she was the one who first introduced me to Willa Cather. She was the one who gave me *My Ántonia,* which was her favorite book too. I wrote out the sentence I loved, in my notebook, brought it to her, repeated it to myself again and again: *Some memories are realities, and are better than anything that can ever happen to one again.*

I was crushed, though, when I tried to talk to her of the wonders I'd discovered in it, when I closed my eyes and recited the line. She said nothing back, and so I found myself talking more and more, on and on, about all the parts of the book I'd loved, and asking her which parts she'd loved, but my words all seemed to pass her by.

"Yes," was all she said, when I was done. "Life was very hard in those days. I'm glad you can see that now."

How I Became an
Orphan in 1947

I WAS FIVE YEARS OLD. We were driving to the country and I sat in the back seat with my mother. My father sat in the front seat with Dave. Dave had a title, in Yiddish—and it meant the-man-who-drives-you-to-the-country. That was who he was: the-man-who-drives-you-to-the-country. He had a fine old black DeSoto, with running boards and a kick seat in the rear that I could rest my feet on. It had once been a taxi. Every summer Dave came and loaded our trunks onto the roof of his DeSoto and drove us to the country, where we stayed with my mother and her family in a large cottage that had a communal kitchen. My mother had four sisters, and they all had husbands and children, and all the husbands stayed away during the week, in the city, working, and drove up by bus and train for the weekends. None of them owned their own cars. That year we never arrived at the cottage. We had a flat tire and while Dave fixed it, my mother leaned against the side of the car and smoked a cigarette. When Dave passed her, she let her hand touch his neck. Dave patted her ass. My father went crazy, screaming that my mother was a cockteasing ballbusting slut. My mother laughed. Dave told my father to calm down—what good was life if you couldn't flirt with a good-looking dame once in a while? My father attacked, and Dave slammed him across the cheek with the tire iron. My father keeled over and bled on the grass. My mother screamed at my father for acting like an idiot. Dave finished changing the tire, cursing all the while, and then he and my mother dragged my father into the car, and Dave said he would drive us to a hospital. My father lay with his head on the kick seat, dripping blood onto my sneakers. My mother sat in the front seat, staring ahead as if we didn't exist, telling Dave he had ruined everything, that they had had a good thing going and he had pissed it away. Dave called her the same names my father called her and she laughed and blew smoke in his face. My father didn't wake up. My mother told me that if ever I told her sisters what I had seen and heard she would kill me. I sat back and stared out the window. Then I looked down. It was the only time I was ever to see my father, in the presence of my mother, with a peaceful expression on his face. The more blood leaked from him, the more peaceful he became. I asked if we could stop for a malted milk. I loved vanilla malteds and would always ask the counterman to put in an extra spoonful of malt for me. My mother told me if I was so damned thirsty I should drink my father's blood. Dave took the curves of the country road with great speed and my mother yelled at him that he had missed the turn-off for the hospital. What good is a hospital for a dead man? Dave asked. He called my mother a dirty cunt who should strap a mattress to her back. She slapped him. He grabbed her wrists and punched her in the nose and I leapt forward, across my father's body, and dug my fingers into his eyes. My mother wailed. My father's head fell off the chair onto the floor and his body twitched. Dave beat at my hands. While we bounced down a hill, my mother opened the car door. There was a splendid red barn on the side of the hill, with a handsome stone foundation, and at the bottom of the hill—across the road—a young girl in pigtails was painting a picture of it, the canvas on an easel, and a man who might have been her father standing next to her, giving her instructions. They looked very happy. Dave was too strong for me and pulled my right hand out of his eye. There was blood and skin under my fingernails. I shoved my freed finger into his ear. My mother threatened to jump. Dave told her to be his guest, but before she could make up her mind, the car turned onto two wheels. Crazy Jewish women! Dave shouted. They'll kill us all. But he was wrong. She only killed two of them. Dave swerved to avoid the young girl who was painting the picture of the red barn, and in so doing he rammed into a large maple tree, and the steering wheel broke and spiked his head the way a shaved branch pierces a marshmallow. My mother flew through the side door and landed on the grass and fell asleep, her skirt up across her back. Her blue underpants were flecked with blood. I had seen the tree and the girl and her father and the easel speeding toward us, and had lain down on top of my father. The exhaust system twisted up through the floor between my father's legs, but it didn't reach me. I went to sleep. When I awoke I was in a hospital, sitting in a chair, reciting the alphabet for two young nurses. They hugged me and kissed me and the younger nurse wept. I recited the two, three, four and five times tables for them and when I told them I was not yet in kindergarten they called me their little Albert Einstein. I said that Albert Einstein lived in New Jersey and that my father kept a photo of him on his desk, where he worked doing income taxes for people. They told me I would play the violin some day and sail the seas on sailing boats, like Professor Einstein. I let them hold me close, so that I could smell their talcummed breasts and starched uniforms. They took me into the room where my mother lay with tubes growing into her and her face bandaged from where they had removed slivers of glass and metal. I sat by her bedside and ate strawberry ice cream. I was unblemished. I was, the nurses declared, a miracle. An elderly doctor, tall and hunched over, his moustache the color of dry spring grass, patted me on the shoulder and told me I was the man of the family now. I nodded. Could I see my father? He didn't think so. My father was asleep. Was Dave asleep too? Yes, Dave was asleep also. Would my mother wake up? Yes, she would. But my father and Dave were sleeping the sleep of the angels. The doctor took me into his office. He had a voice like warm chocolate. He said that he had telephoned his wife and that I would come to his house for dinner. They closed their eyes and hands before the meal and prayed that Christ would bless their home and food and guest. Their dining table was made of cherry wood that the doctor had milled and joined himself. He gave me a tour of his workshop. He made artificial legs and hands for young children, and showed me his sketches for movable parts of bodies. Prosthesis, he said. It was a new word to me and it made me happy to spell it inside my head. P-r-o-s-t-h-e-s-i-s. I slept in a guest room that had a porcelain washbasin on a corner stand, and I repeated the word until I slept. His wife called me her poor little boy and I told her that it was not so. We had more money than Dave, but he had a car. He had to drive us to the country to earn his living but we got to stay in the country all summer long and he had to return to the city and sweat. I told her that I did not like Dave because whenever he kissed my mother it made her laugh. The doctor's wife's mouth went sour, but I didn't care. She wasn't my mother. Her mouth was a slit in soft gray stone. Her clothes smelled of camphor.

She wouldn't let me kiss her. The next day my mother woke up. I was there. She told me to get out of her room. She didn't ever want to see me again. She told me to get out of her life. She blamed me for killing Dave and ruining her face. What man would ever look twice at her again, except to gape at her wounds? The only job she could get now would be in the freak show at Coney Island in the winter. I told my mother I would never stop loving her, but I was lying so that the doctor would be kind to me. He was. He and his wife fed me and played cards with me—Peace and Patience—and he took me in his car on his rounds and asked me if I wanted to be a doctor some day. He told me I had very intelligent eyes. Jews made good city doctors, he said. I said I wanted to live in the country and have children who would have a mother they could love and be loved by. He blushed. I never saw my mother again. I never saw her sisters or their husbands or my cousins again. The doctor said my mother had to go away for a while, where they would cure her by the use of electricity and water from hoses. The doctor and his wife drove me down to New York City and put me in the Home and on the way I asked them if I could be their child. They replied that they would keep me in their prayers and hope that the Lord Jesus Christ would one day enter my heart. If He did, there would be hope for me. But not with them, for they were too old and I was too young. They had made their peace with the Lord, accepting His judgment that they would pass from one eternity to the next without having a child. We were all God's children. I said it wasn't so. Some of us were nobody's children. I never saw them again. I found out where my mother lived by looking it up in the office at the Home, when the secretary was gone. And once on a day off, when I was twelve years old, I walked by the house she lived in, on Howard Avenue in the East New York section of Brooklyn, but I decided not to visit her because I didn't want to ruin the hatred in my heart, for that hatred was the brightest and purest thing I owned. I held onto that flame of rage, sensing that it would allow me to survive and thrive wherever I might be in the course of this life. I did not want to have to see that my mother was just an ordinary, boring, and lonely woman—a plain aging woman with scars on her face who had once upon a time given away her only son. I thought of the splintered black steering wheel going through Dave's eye, where my finger had been, and of how I had seen the inside of my father's nose from where his cheek was split open. When I left the Home at the age of eighteen I found my way to the spot of the accident and saw the red barn, which was freshly painted, as it had been on the day my life changed. I walked through the nearby town, hoping that one of the young women I would pass would be the girl I had not killed—that we would recognize each other and the moment we had shared—and that she might fall in love with me and marry me.

Minor Sixths, Diminished Sevenths

HE WAS THERE and he was not there. His brother Eddie was playing lead guitar, Jimmy backing him on piano, Kinnard on bass, Captain Sammy Barber carrying the four-four time on the snare drum, round and round so that Jimmy felt the wire brushes caress the inner curve of his skull. He drifted toward sleep, floated inside the music, low, then rose through to the surface for air, kept rising, looked below and imagined himself heading downstream, feet first, arms rigid at his side.

There's a somebody I'm longing to see—I hope that he—turns out to be— someone who'll watch over me. . . .

The stream widened, curved gently between lush green banks. An old Philco radio, copper wires unfurling from the rear of its wooden case, sat in the center of a meadow. The song he and Eddie had recorded so many years ago drifted lazily across the grass and wildflowers. Cool, brother. So cool.

Jimmy's hands moved across the keys, the blocked chords—minor sixths, diminished sevenths—giving Eddie the solid ground he needed. Without that ground, Eddie was lost; with that ground beneath him, Eddie found purchase on this world, could set the music inside him free, could take off in sweet riffs like nobody else. Play it, brother. Play it sweet and blue. Eddie's left hand was high on the guitar's throat, his fingers glancing against the frets in a dazzling explosion of harmonics: pure crystal bells. Jimmy watched his own hands navigate the keys— steadily moving north in parallel chords, his left hand doubling the melody in the bass—and he wondered, as ever, how it was they knew where to go. He was not aware of giving them direction.

There and not there. Of course: Eddie was in Brooklyn with his wife and his two boys; Jimmy was in Paris, leaving the nightclub. Le Jardin Noir. Jimmy turned back, said good night to the doorman. *Eh bien, M'sieur Jimmy. Bonne nuit.*

Now came Jimmy's favorite time—the long walk home, alone, after a night of making music. I've got it all now, brother. Music. Home. Family. I've got it all and that ain't bad.

Jimmy looked up, imagined green and gold clouds of dry ice spinning through the neon script above the nightclub door. The letters circled gracefully and Jimmy cooled himself by riding inside the glass tubes the way he swam inside his music. Let's ride, brother. Let's ride this song . . .

I'm a little lamb who's lost in the wood—I know I could—always be good—to one who'll watch over me. . . .

He was there and he was not there.

He imagined himself brain-dead, his hands locked in position at the wrists, his fingers marching like tired soldiers across yellowed piano keys. He looked down at black sleeves, white cuffs, mother-of-pearl cuff links. He paid attention to his wrists, his knuckles, his fingers, kept the sound full by adding a sixth note in the left hand, a third below the melody.

Jimmy shook hands with the other musicians. They set down their cases, lit cigarettes, mumbled farewells. *Bonne nuit. . . . Sois sage, Jimmy. . . . A demain. . . .*

Arriving in Paris, emerging from a taxi, Eddie would be impressed by Jimmy's rap, by how well he spoke the language. Elegance. You always had elegance, man. My big brother got elegance and ain't that hot shit! Jimmy would laugh, would introduce him all around. They would go back inside, despite the hour, turn on the lights, open their cases, play a set together, then another, then jam until dawn. Jimmy and Eddie would show them. Music alone would live. Sure.

Jimmy heard the melody, the round he and Eddie and the others had sung on their tour: in Mississippi, Georgia, Alabama, South Carolina, Virginia. White and black, rich and poor, young and old—holding hands, the music swelling. New York City, too. Sure. Pete Seeger and Odetta at the microphone, Jimmy and Eddie behind them.

All things shall perish from under the sky. . . . Music alone shall live. . . . Music alone shall live. . . .

They had believed that things might change, that they might yet redeem their native land. *We must love one another or die.* Seventeen thousand people singing in parts, the minor thirds breaking Jimmy's heart. He wept without shame. *We shall overcome.* Madison Square Garden, April the seventeenth, nineteen hundred and sixty-six. Martin King and Bobby Kennedy were still alive. Medgar Evers was in the ground. Twenty-four years. Twenty-four years gone by under the sky.

Deep in my heart, Jimmy thought. Oh, yes. Deep in my heart I need someone who'll watch over me too. That's why I'm here, in my new life. That's why I have Monique and Henri—my wife and my son. Don't you see?

Jimmy moved forward, separate from the others now, and he imagined he was walking through the streets of Paris with Eddie, talking about music, women, baseball—about the Hollywood Bar, at 133rd Street and Seventh Avenue, the cutting contests Jimmy had been in with other pianists, in the back room, each man showing his stuff, challenging the others to do better, modulating to a key like B or E, doubling the tempo with a strong left hand to make things more *interesting* for the next man up. Oh, yes. You could get by with all kinds of slop in a rhythm section, but there was no cheating when you played solo. You were the main man then. Jimmy had loved those sessions, had used them to educate himself in styles not his own: stride, boogie, swing, bebop.

It would be wonderful to wander this city late at night with his brother, without fear. What *couldn't* they talk about?

I worry about you, though. I worry about you all the time.

Eddie laughed. Well. I worry about you too, man.

When he arrived home, he would telephone, would find out how Eddie was doing. He would ask about Eddie's wife and sons. The boys—Pete and Mike, twins—would be 15 years old by now. Jimmy had never met them. Nor had Eddie ever met Monique and Henri.

Eddie still played with some of the same old gang: Kinnard, Barber, Carr. If Eddie were short on cash, Jimmy would send money, but only if Eddie asked him to. The important thing was not to condescend. The important thing, always, was to act as if they were equals—as if it were so—to let Eddie know that Jimmy would come to him in the same way should things turn sour in his own life, should he be needy.

But you never are.

Monique's tone, calm and knowing, was one Jimmy did not like. What did she know, after all, about what he and Eddie had been through together, about how and why they'd made their choices? She had not been in Mississippi in the summer of 1964. She had not been with them in New York when the noose began to pull tight on the Movement. She had not been with Eddie when the FBI put shotguns to his head and hauled him out of his flat on 139th Street. She had not been with Eddie through the trial, through his four years in prison. She had not been with Jimmy through those years when, though he knew letting Eddie take the rap was the only smart thing to do, he'd burned to change places with his brother. She had never known what it was like to wake up scared and powerless every morning of your life—to wake up with a bucketful of rage and nothing to do with it except swallow.

Earlier in the evening, between sets, a young American woman had approached him, had asked about Eddie, about the albums they'd made together in the Sixties, about their work in the civil-rights move-ment, about Eddie's four years in jail, about the years since they had seen each other. Of course. That was why his head was so full—why he was thinking too much of what he usually preferred not to think of: how well he had or had not watched over his brother once upon a time.

Bien entendu, mon vieux. Ne t'inquiète pas trop. Ton frère t'aime, malgré tout . . .

He spoke to himself in French. Detached in this way, his words and thoughts seemed more precise. Jimmy savored clarity. In his music, there was no mud: no false notes, no shortcuts, no old man's tricks.

Because, he asserted, I have been there and it is so. If you blindfold a group of knowledgeable musicians and have a series of black and white pianists play, the musicians cannot determine if the music emanates from black fingers or white.

Jimmy thought of the blind pianists he'd known: George Shearing, Ray Charles, Watertown Willie. Let the blind judge the blind, Jimmy thought. Let skeptics choose any of the others: Nichols or Tatum or Evans, Lewis or McKenna or Peterson or Tristano or Price or Jimmy Wilson himself. Mister Jimmy Wilson.

Nous vous présentons, Mister Jimmy Wilson . . .

Jimmy saw himself step into the lights and the applause, incline his head. When he finished the first number, he spoke to the audience, his voice rolling at them like warm water over loose gravel. If they were blindfolded, these elegant French, would they guess the nationality, much less the color, of the man addressing them? Jimmy's accent was impeccable. When asked if he'd fought with the French in the war, if he'd been raised in one of the colonies, if he'd attended French schools as a child, he smiled. He loved to speak French, to turn his mouth around the liquid sounds. The French! The arrogant French, never showing their feelings or their souls, never giving away anything. He loved the idea that he could sometimes speak French better than they. Here, he could tell Eddie, was a new cutting contest.

And you're winning, right?

Right, Jimmy said.

Well, my brother always did love to win.

Won't you tell him please to put on some speed—follow my lead—oh, how I need—someone to watch over me. . . .

Was he inside the music or was the music inside him?

The young woman had asked a question about ragtime, about its origins, about African polyrhythms. Was she flirting, showing off? She let him know she was on her junior year abroad, studying at the university in Aix-en-Provence. She was blonde, pretty, a long, thick braid down her back. Her face was boyish, handsome, her lips full, her teeth clean and straight, like those of all the young Americans. She had done her homework, he thought. He gave her that. But she was not, she admitted, a musician. Nor, he wanted to add, are you black or in exile.

Her very forthrightness angered him—the freedom she had to approach him with such openness in her eyes, such unabashed enthusiasm? Her eyes were a pale, marbled green, he recalled: like the eyes of his cat. He'd had the urge, he realized now, to strike her—to somehow blast the innocence from those eyes, to put the red mark of his hand on her smooth, fair-skinned cheeks. Instead, without looking directly at her, he'd given her a speech he'd made many times before: Racists of all colors will try to tell you differently, he stated, but I have seen it happen and it is so. Melanin and the blues are not linked eternally in some perverse biological bondage. Rhythm, harmony, and melody are the property of all men, individual talent the property of some, genius the property of few. The particular music that I play—that derives from our heritage as Africans and as slaves—the gift we have made ours and given to the world, is not particular because a minuscule portion of recombinant DNA has within it both the cause of pigmentation and of jazz but because of history, culture, and individual talent. With enough time and practice, I can appreciate and reproduce Mozart, Bach, and Chopin as naturally as you, had you my gifts, could produce Waller, Monk, and Ellington. . . .

Thank you, she said, her eyes downcast. She held an album under her arm but did not ask him to autograph it.

Oh, you're a bad man, Jimmy Wilson, ain't you now? Takes a bad man to beat on a young white bitch that way.

You would have done the same.

Wouldn't have had the words. Only, tell me, brother—when'd you give that speech before? Ain't one I ever heard.

In my mind, Jimmy said. Many times. I gave her the abridged version.

Yeah. So I wouldn't think you *really* cruel, right?

Jimmy strode across the Pont Marie, toward the Île Saint Louis. He was alone, between the worlds he loved—his working life and his home—living within his favored hour, knowing his wife and son would be safely in their beds, lost and found in their separate dreams, when he arrived.

God bless the child. God bless the child that's got his own. . . .

Jimmy was in Paris and Jimmy was in Brooklyn and in both places the music was the same, although it was night here and morning there. Against probability, Jimmy had *made* the life that gave him his freedom. Monique sometimes accused Jimmy of being distant, of cutting himself off from his past too utterly. But Monique did not walk with him between midnight and dawn. Monique was not inside him when he played, riding the currents that flowed from his brain to his fingers.

When he spoke French, he translated still—he searched for the correct word, for equivalents. His skill with language was acquired, and he worked to master the deep, rolling consonants, the mannered cadences. But when he made music, there was no translation, no shadow needing shape, no darkness needing light. He worked hard, studied hard, drove himself toward perfection. Of course. But when he was ready, he was ready. When his practicing and rehearsals were done and he sat down to perform the music he loved, then all hesitation was gone—then he did not need to search for phrasings or notes, words or feelings. Everything was there, without translation, and he was neither inside nor outside. But how could anyone else understand what he felt, unless they were there too, with him?

He walked next to the Jardin des Plantes, along Rue Cuvier. To his right was the Université Pierre et Marie Curie. He glanced at signs plastered to the walls, urging this or that cause. He did not concern himself with French politics. It all seemed like so much squabbling. Even the Communists and anarchists seemed to him, in this beautiful and civilized city, to be working to advance privilege.

He imagined Eddie coming toward him, the young American woman walking beside Eddie, her hands deep in the pockets of her raincoat. He felt his heart bump down slightly and he did not deny what he felt: that he wanted to be there, in one of those pockets, safe within the hollow of the young woman's warm hand. He saw himself greeting Eddie, kissing his brother on both cheeks. The girl was gone, Eddie was smiling.

It had been too long. Many thousands gone, he thought, and no auction block upon which he could stand with Eddie so that they could, at least, experience the wild pain of being severed from each other forever, of being sold, of being *had*.

He turned the corner, saw French workers hosing down the side-walks, sweeping the cobblestones with a small motorized sweeper. "*COMMENT NE PAS VOTER IDIOT.*" He smiled at the poster—his favorite—mocked himself for the foolishness of his imagination. It was easy to be sentimental about Eddie, easier still to chastise himself for being so. For the price of a single airline ticket he could eliminate such fancies. With a persistence he found irritating, Monique kept urging him to do so—to buy the ticket, to invite Eddie to visit. She wanted to know his brother, she said, and she believed it was time Jimmy allowed himself that pleasure too.

He could talk with Eddie about Henri's condition—about the operation the doctor was recommending: an experimental implant that would connect an amplifier directly to the auditory nerve. Jimmy could tell him about the first time, three years before, he'd accompanied Monique and Henri to the doctor and had looked through to where the light shone, to where the swirling gas of tissue and blood strained against the film of skin. He had been frightened the ear would explode.

Jimmy had been angrier with the boy than he'd intended to be. The boy's wailing had kept him awake for two days and nights, not for the first time, and nothing Jimmy did or said had helped. When he tried to hold his son, to rock him gently against his shoulder, the boy pushed Jimmy away, screamed that he wanted his mother. *Maman . . . Maman . . .*

Punctured, Jimmy declared. The eardrum is punctured. The boy punctured it because that is the kind of boy he is.

The doctor told Jimmy to look into Henri's good ear. Jimmy touched Henri's hair, held the doctor's otoscope, put his eye to the lens. To his surprise, the light revealed a still world that was as calm as any Jimmy had ever seen, all pearl-gray and silent.

The drawing was of a smiling black man at a piano, his fingers larger than the piano keys, his face the color of Baker's chocolate. In the upper-left-hand corner, in purple, Henri had crayoned *"Mon Beau Daddy."* Henri loved to draw, to write his name in script: *Henri Evers Wilson.* Jimmy recalled sharpening crayons in his bedroom, brushing the shavings into a cigar box, saving them, imagining—believing!—that he was creating real gold and silver. He recalled coming home from school—he was in second grade, Eddie not yet in kindergarten—to discover that Eddie had taken the box, spilled the powder. Jimmy had found his brother hiding on the fire escape and had dragged him in through the window, had beat him mercilessly, pounding his open hand against his brother's face again and again.

Jimmy poured himself a glass of Courvoisier, turned off the small light on the piano stand, sat in the corner easy chair of his living room. Who would have dreamed, even a decade ago, that he would be able to walk across the city of Paris six nights a week and arrive at a handsome and well-appointed home in which he was loved and honored? He had, as a boy growing up in Brooklyn, taught himself to believe that he would live his life through without ever having a family of his own.

He sat in the darkness, let the sweet liquor warm his chest. The only thing he loved as much as music, he knew, was a moment like this, when the absence of sound could give him the peace and comfort he loved so dearly.

He took his glass with him to his study, lifted the telephone receiver, dialed the operator, gave her Eddie's telephone number. She told him that he could now dial directly if he wished. She gave him the necessary code numbers. *Merci bien, madame.* Jimmy hung up, lifted the receiver, dialed again. This time a recorded voice came on, telling him that the number he had reached had been disconnected and was no longer in service.

Same as last year, brother. You getting old, forgetting things like that. You *lost,* man.

Surely one of us is.

Maybe. Only difference is, I can always find you if I want.

Do you—do you want to?

Maybe. If I find you, though, what I get?

When her hand touched his shoulder, Jimmy turned on her as if she were an assailant. Come to bed, Monique said. Her eyes showed no alarm. His own hand, he saw, was still on the telephone. He imagined that she knew exactly what he'd been doing and why.

Only after she left him did he realize that Henri had woken up again, in pain. Jimmy walked to the boy's bedroom. Henri was shrieking, one hand covering his right ear. Jimmy stayed in the doorway and watched Monique tend to him. She talked to the boy in French, but so rapidly that Jimmy could not understand what it was she was saying. He was better at speaking French than he was at understanding it. The reason this was so, he knew, was that when he spoke, he could prepare his words in advance.

Monique reached to the boy's night table, took out a small brown bottle, measured liquid into an eyedropper. Henri turned onto his side but did not stop crying. Monique put the drops into the boy's ear. Then Henri clung to her, wept. He looked past his mother's shoulder, to Jimmy. Jimmy did not move. Henri held more tightly to his mother and spoke quickly, gasping as he did. Monique kissed the boy, spoke to him softly. Jimmy wanted to ask them both to speak more slowly, so he could understand what exactly it was they were saying, but he was afraid that if he did they might mock him for his ignorance. What they didn't know, he decided, would not hurt them. By remaining silent, he could be more certain they would not, in the future, join together to use his lack of knowledge against him.

Fixer's Home

TROUBLE IS, I still keep thinking too much about what was. You ever pick a dime off the top of a backboard? You do that, you got it made, man. In the pros, there's guys can do it now— Dr. J, he's the best—but back then, only a few could get up there, most of them 6-10 or over. In the schoolyard—I wasn't even out of high school yet, still had all these scouts and coaches buggin' me—I did it the first time. They boosted Big Ed up on someone's shoulders to put it there, then all the guys cheered me on. Took me three shots, but I made it. I was king then. I mean, you make it big time—high school, college, pro, I don't care where, it never compares with being king of your own schoolyard. You can take all the fame and shove it.

I walk through the gates and the guys sitting along the fence, younger guys, they looking at me the way I look at Big Ed when I was their age, and they say, "Hi, Mack!" or "Hey, Mack, babe—you want nexts with me?" and I see this look in their eyes like they'd give their right arm to be me—man, that was all I needed then. I was home free. Big Ed, he was the one who got me into the fixes, first time. He once got a ladder before we played Duke, in the old Garden on 50th Street, he put a dime up and in the stands, thousands of them, they went out of their boxes when I aced up and snatched the mother. But it still didn't compare with being king of your own schoolyard.

I figured that out a long time ago. You get out there when you're young, on a sunny day, and you listen to the older guys gas with each other about who's got what shots and what moves and who can fake who out of whose jock, and you just ache to have them talk to you. Hell, you get brought up in a white boy's schoolyard, hear them argue for years about every ballplayer ever was, you can't help let it get to you. You play out there, you're real loose. When I sail up there and snatch that dime that first time—man, that was the high spot. If I died right then, I die happy. I think about that lots.

Still go down to the schoolyard on weekends, my age, find we got some other dumb old men like to drag their asses around the court. Mostly we sit along the fence, between games, watching the new kids play. No white boys here anymore. A few years back, they said this was a neighborhood in transition. I liked that. Only what I say now to the guys, I tell them I call it a neighborhood that already transished, and they all laugh, tell me I got a way with words. The white boys, they all gone to live on Long Island and New Jersey, they all doctors and lawyers and teachers. The kids I play with now, I was playing high school and college, most of them weren't born.

Oh yeah, one of them says to me once, he hears us talking about how things were back then. How much you make then?

I too embarrassed to tell him, the pennies I sold out for. So I just look at him hard, say he better mind his own business. Back then, though, anybody mention the fixes, it was like somebody's mother got cancer, things got so quiet. All these white guys always kissing my ass cause I had such a great jump shot, cause I come from their neighborhood, none of them ever man enough to come up to me and ask me to my face why I did it. Or how I felt after. Except this one time, some little kid named Izzie, about 12 years old, he picked me for nexts like he always did. He says to me if you're so good, what college you play for?

So I say back I don't play for no college.

How come? he asks me.

Cause I was in the fixes, I say.

Everything goes quiet then, and I look around and ask the guys on the court how come they stop playing. They start right back in. Nobody like to mess with me in those days. Oh yeah. I'm the big man, real mean. You mean to be mean, Mack, the guys used to say. But his kid Izzie, he asks me what I do if I don't play ball and I tell him I work at the Minit-Wash, washing down cars, you know? That's how come I got such clean hands. Yeah, me, I got the cleanest hands of any fixer around. After that, nobody ever asks me about the fixes.

In the papers, though, these reporters, they get all preachy about us guys who shave points, want to know why we did it. Most of the players, they go to court with me, they get the same Holy Joe voices and tell the Judge they're real sorry they let everybody down and fixed games, but when it comes my turn, I'm the only guy who don't say he's sorry. The only thing I'm sorry about, I say, is when they turn the money off.

All these guys always wanting to know why I did it. I tell this one reporter, Gross, from the old *New York Post,* they give me a pain. I did it for money, what they think? The college paid me, I did what they wanted. Gamblers paid, I work for them. Bookies paid more than gamblers, I signed up with them. Nobody giving me an education cause they like my looks . . .

Sometimes, sitting out there on a nice warm day, my ass on concrete, my back up against the wire fence, drinking a cold Coke and letting the sweat dry under my T-shirt, I can't figure how all that happened 30 years ago. Where you been since then, I want to ask. Where you *been?* Sometimes when I chug through a bunch of bodies and feel my feet lift off the ground without weights in them, feel myself move like somebody I used to know real well—sometimes when that ball moves off my fingertips and hits that metal backboard in just the right spot and goes through that net *swish* like you know what, it all seems gone, like nothing bad ever happened.

But it ain't so, and when I get down to the schoolyard this last time, and I'm warming up between games, pumping in some jumpers from around the circle, listening to the guys tease me about my pot belly and my bald dome, I hear them saying there's this new set of fixes. Oh yeah? I ask. Who they say done it?

Some Catholic kids, one of the guys says, and I got to laugh, them getting only guys from a Catholic school this time. My day, this real powerhouse, he got the Catholic boys off free. Oh yeah, everybody in the schoolyard knew that. Those Catholic players, they shaving points and rigging games along with the rest of us, but when the D. A. Hogan, he gets his lists ready and calls us all in, all you got in that room with Hogan were Jews and blacks. You don't take my word for it, you go look at the names some time. Me, I got their names down in my head like the lineup from the '51 Dodgers, like all those other fixers were brothers who lost the same stuff I did. Oh yeah, Herb Cohen and Fats Roth and Irwin Dambrot and Connie Schaff and Eddie Roman and Leroy Smith and Floyd Layne and Sherm White and Ed Warner, they all still there in my head, floating around our own schoolyard. White and Warner, they the best—I had to go some to keep up with them.

They got some boys from the Midwest, too, and some Catholic kids. Cardinal Spellman, he lived in the powerhouse, corner of Madison and 50th, next to St. Patrick's, and every time I go by, I still spit. Divine intervention, that's what Big Ed calls it when we talk, but I don't laugh. Still, I got to smile now, to see the way things change. That Cardinal gone now and he can't help these Catholic boys even if he wanted to.

They gas on about the new fixes, how this one player, he's a real altar boy, and how the big man this time, he was only doing it for a hobby, cause his main job was running the $5 million Lufthansa gig. Oh yeah, I think, there's still guys dumber than me. Now that this guy puts the finger on guys in the mob, we don't take bets on him getting social security.

The kids on the court, they all in high school, when they sit down between games and hear us talking about the fixes, they don't even blink. They talk to each other about how many tape decks they got and which truck they got it off of and they don't pay these new fixes no mind.

I close my eyes and think about the names of the new boys, and I lean back against the fence, try to see what they look like. I got no photos, though. I listen to how they set this new fix up and I hear the guys talk about how great Connie Hawkins and Roger Brown and Doug Moe would of been, they'd got their chance in the NBA when they were in their prime, and I even hear one of the guys tell me how I was robbed, I got blacklisted. I open my eyes a minute, tell him what I said back then, about what kind of list they got for the white boys. He laughs and when he does I got to close my eyes real quick. All that stuff about clean hands and blacklists and why I did it—who you fooling, Mack? I got this pain down low in my gut, and I'm trying to knock their words out of the way so I can see things clear, try to feel what these new boys must be feeling now.

Oh yeah, that pain tell you something, Mack. You never even been inside that new Madison Square Garden they got, it gonna hurt so much. You never even gone to see Hawkins play, when he got in the pros. Sure. Who you fooling? They take away the only thing you love, and how you ever gonna tell anybody that? How you gonna live the rest of your life, you can't do the only thing you good at, the only thing you been taught to do?

These questions come shooting in my head and I try to knock them out of the way, too, and when I do, I get this real strange picture there instead. There's this long hallway and I'm walking down the middle and I got to stop every few feet to shake hands with these guys I used to know, and they're all sitting in wheelchairs. There's Roy Campanella and Maurice Stokes and Ernie Davis and Junius Kellogg and Brian Piccolo and Big Daddy Lipscomb and Tom Stith and Darryl Stingley and even this guy named Pete Gray, who played baseball with one arm, and Monty Stratton, who played with a wooden leg, and at the end of the tunnel, there's old Jackie Robinson, the greatest player who ever lived, you ask me, and he's got his son sitting next to him. I bend over to shake their hands and I can't figure out why they're in wheelchairs if they're both dead so many years now—Jackie Jr. strung out good on drugs, then clean just in time to get wiped off the highway in a sports car—and Jackie, all white-haired and fuzzy and smiling real broad, dead when he was about the age I'm at now. He reaches up to me with his hand and wishes me good luck with that soft, high-pitched voice, and I tell him I'm real sorry his son died first, before he did.

I open my eyes and see that one of the guys been trying to get me to move and now he's razzing me about my fat ass and how I don't play no different asleep or awake. This kid named Jim, about my height, 6-6, only he weighs about 80 pounds less, he points to my belly and laughs. Why he got to worry? The ball comes to him first thing, down low, he gives me a head fake and he's slamming the ball through and his men slapping his hands and he's grinning real big. One of my guys says to show him how the old fixers used to do it. Jim, he asks me how come the other guy calls me a fixer—cause of the way I let him get around me? I tell him to shut his ass and give his mouth a chance, and he laughs some more.

Oh yeah, I think. They take away my life cause I shave a few points, but that ain't nothing to what athletes been doing since, sniffing and shooting up, and buggering each other and all the rest, only these days they get to write books about it after. Under the basket, back up against the fence, the guys still talking about how these new fixes got rigged, remembering the time, back in our day, when two teams played each other, both teams supposed to go down at the same time for different gamblers, and all I want to do is go over and tell them to shut their big mouths, too. The ball comes into my man and he gives me a head fake. This time, I don't go for it, then he tries to go under me with his dipsy-doodle crap, I get my leg out quick and let him have it where he lives. Then I got the ball from him, he's all bent over, and I roll over this other kid who ain't nearly as big and I'm going up real high, as high as an old man can go, and drop that ball in without touching the rim. Two points for our side.

The other two guys on my team, they try to rank me out about taking it easy cause I old enough to be my man Jim's grandfather, but I don't say anything. The only thing I wait for is the feel of that ball in my hands, dumb me.

Department of Athletics

FROM NOW ON he slept on the couch, she said. She slipped in his puke, she washed out his clothes, she dragged him home from Sheehan's, she tried to believe him each time he promised to change, but she'd been a fool long enough.

My mother was on the phone, complaining to her sister Margaret about my father, who'd come home the night before, twenty-eight sheets to the wind. Nothing new there, only this time—she was already sleeping—he'd sworn he loved her more than Jane Russell, had come up to the bed, unzipped his fly, and pissed on her.

My mother heard me close the front door. She put her hand over the mouthpiece, asked if I'd gotten a job yet.

Not yet, I said.

You know what a good job for an Irish boy is? she asked.

I shrugged.

Listening to somebody else's radio!

She laughed and blew me a kiss. You know what they say, Jimmy—a good joke's like money, right? It can't buy happiness, but it sure helps when you're miserable . . .

I'd heard it all before. I went to my room, set down my books, looked at my homework assignments, at letters from colleges. I'd been named third team All-City in basketball, and the scouts were after my ass: Notre Dame, Manhattan, Fordham, St. John's, St. Francis, St. Joseph's, St. Peter's, St. Wherever. Priests, brothers, sisters, nuns, political hacks—they were all hassling me to go here or there, but I wasn't buying what they were selling. The truth, which I couldn't tell my coach or my guidance counselor or any of the deadbeats who were sucking after me, was that I wanted to go to a place that didn't specialize in Catholic girls.

Catholic girls held out on me, not because they wanted to, but because they always got scared that the Zorro who took confession at Holy Cross Church, where we all went, would know us both, would find a way to get the word back to their parents. It was better with Jewish girls, because instead of closing down on me, or cracking gum and making believe they didn't know what was going on while they hurried to finish me off, they could never get enough. What drove me wild most of all was that they talked about it while they were doing it, asking me if I liked the way they kissed, if I liked the way they did me, if I liked the way they spread their legs.

Some nights, coming home to my place and dreaming about leaving, the only thing in the world I wanted was to spend the rest of my life in dark hallways and carpeted living rooms, hot Jewish pussy coming all over me. When I shot foul shots, no matter how loud and crazy the crowd got, that was what I thought of—their sweat and juices dripping on me, their tongues licking me everywhere, me dozing off afterward and then waking with one of them kissing my eyes or nibbling at my stomach—and it relaxed me, let me shut out all other noise, let me concentrate on what I had to do.

I kept my mackinaw on, left our apartment, my mother yelling after me that there were phone calls to answer, that I should be careful not to ruin my future.

The temple of my body, I said. Sure. Light a candle, Mom.

That's my boy, I heard her say. That's my boy Jimmy. His sense of humor'll save him yet, even if it can't peel potatoes.

I went down to the corner and walked past the Florist Shop three times before Mr. Baldwin waved me in. Did I want to make a delivery for him? It wouldn't take long, he said.

He wrote out directions, and gave me the order—yellow and red flowers in a wicker basket, a black ribbon on the handle, a condolence card taped next to it. He wrapped green paper around the flowers to protect them.

I took the IRT from Church Avenue in Brooklyn to Columbus Circle in Manhattan. It was rush hour and I stood all the way, holding the basket. Between 14th Street and Penn Station the train got stuck for twenty minutes. Under my mackinaw, sweater, shirt, and undershirt, I was slick with perspiration. My palms were pale green, damp from the dye.

At 59th Street, I switched to the IND. I shoved in, grabbed a seat, set the flowers between my feet. Then the longest run of all, rocketing underground from 59th Street to 125th Street. At 181st Street I got out, walked to the funeral home on 183rd Street and gave them the flowers. The man didn't say thank you. The hell with him. The hell with everybody, I thought. If I didn't get into college where I wanted, maybe I'd fool them all and just not go. Maybe I'd do the very thing they were telling me my gifts as an athlete were supposed to keep me from. Maybe I'd become a cop. Another Irish cop, my mother would say. Just what the world needs, right? And he's your son, Mom, I'd reply. Only he'll be gone from home. He'll be a cop out, right?

Coming home, the trains were nearly empty, so I slept. I liked sleeping and dreaming in subways because I woke up at every stop and then when the train started out again from the station and I fell back to sleep, I could have a new dream. I liked having so many separate dreams in such a short time. It was like going to the movies without paying.

By the time I was back in my neighborhood, it was dark, and all the stores, except for eating places, were closed. Mr. Baldwin's store was locked, but I saw him going in and out through the curtain at the back, where he lived with his mother, so I pounded on the door until he opened up for me. He gave me three dollars, plus carfare.

The delivery took me four hours, I said. I want more.

I'm sorry, he said. I don't even make a profit on this kind of order, my having to pay you. It's a courtesy merely.

I shoved my foot in the doorway so he couldn't close me out, then grabbed him by the arm and pressed hard. You cheated me, I said. You told me less than an hour each way when you knew it would take longer. You lied. I want more.

Don't talk to me in that tone of voice, young man, he said. I'll tell your mother. I'm warning you.

Pay up, I said, or I'll tell *your* mother, you cheap creep. I lifted him into the air so that his forehead touched a light bulb. I imagined smashing him against the bulb so that it wound up inside his head, with the chain hanging out of his ear, and his mother tugging on it, to see his face.

His mother came through the curtain then, to where we were. Is everything all right, Arthur? she asked.

I set Mr. Baldwin down and he opened the cash register and took out another two dollars.

Hoodlum, he said.

You watch the way you speak to me, chiseler, or I'll get the police after you.

It confused him, for me to tell him I'd be the one to call the cops.

I used to love Mary Astor best of all, his mother said to me, her hand on my sleeve. Some people said I resembled her. My, but she was a looker. She was wonderful in *The Prisoner of Zenda,* which was before she cut her hair. She spelled her name differently from the flower, of course, but did you ever think of it, of how many people are named for flowers? Rose and Lilly and Daisy and Iris and Buttercup and Hyacinth and Dahlia. When I was in the second grade, my best friend was a girl named Hyacinth . . .

It's been nice seeing you again, Mrs. Baldwin, I said. My mother sends regards. Take good care of your son for me, okay?

Of course, she said, and smiled. What a sweet young man, Arthur. It's lovely to see them grow up and turn out so well.

I walked to where the party was, in an apartment house on Linden Boulevard that doctors, lawyers, dentists, and successful businessmen lived in. The building had a large courtyard, with separate entrances to each of its four wings. When I knocked on the door a second time, the peep-hole opened. Jane Silverman unlocked the door, pulled me into the front living room, closed the door behind us. Three other couples were already going at it. The lights were out. Toni Arden was singing "Come Back to Sorrento."

I thought you'd never get here, Jane said.

She led me to her couch and even before we lay down she was in my pants with her hand and in my mouth with her tongue.

I smell bad from sweat, I whispered. I'm sorry. I had to make a delivery and it was rush hour.

She licked my chest. Do you like me? she asked.

No, but I trust you.

She laughed and told me I was crazy. God, but I was the craziest guy she'd ever met. I had three fingers in her and she moved round and round as if she were spinning in circles on a bar stool. She'd saved the news for me, that she'd received the letters after school a few hours before: she'd been accepted into both Vassar and Mount Holyoke Colleges. Doris had acceptances from Radcliffe, Tufts, *and* Cornell, but didn't know where to go.

I do too. I'm going down, Doris said.

Freddy Cohen got into Brandeis.

Jew U, Freddy said.

If the Jew fits, wear him, I said.

You're nuts, Doris said. Your boyfriend's really nuts, Jane.

He sure is, Jane said, and she began kissing me everywhere. I closed my eyes, to make things darker—so it would seem more like a dream—and let her do what she wanted. When she unbuckled my belt, I grabbed her hair in my fists and pulled the way she liked, just hard enough so she could pull back and keep doing what she loved most. Then she held me close, her cheek against my stomach and I knew she wanted to talk for a while, so I opened my eyes and listened to her tell me about everything she was feeling—about how much she hated living at home, about all the things she might do with her life after college, about how much she'd miss me, about how she had this awful feeling that except for a few rare moments, like the one we were living in now, together, she was never going to be happy. Will you visit me? she asked. Will you come visit me? Please. Say you will. Please . . .

I'll come, I said. Sure. A Mick in time, right?

God, I'm so crazy about you, Jimmy, she said. You're the best. You're wonderful. I hope you get everything in life you want. I really do.

I let my fists open then so I could rub her head and feel the shape of her skull with my fingers. I did that for a long time. Jesus, Jimmy, she said later. Oh sweet Jesus. She was crying and she didn't wipe away the tears. It's like the ocean coming right through me. Oh sweet Jesus, I feel so happy now—like I'll never feel this happy again. Is that all right, do you think? she asked, and before I could answer, she took my hand and covered her mouth with it, to keep from screaming.

My father was sleeping on the couch again. I walked by him, went into the bathroom, took my pants off, and washed myself. Then I put my pants back on.

Get out, Jimmy, my father said.

I tried to be quiet. I didn't know you were still up.

Get out and keep going, he said. That's what you should do. You're a good boy. You never said nothing against me. They open the gate and then they close it.

Who?

Women.

Sure.

You know what my father taught me, son? So heavy is the chain of wedlock that it needs two to carry it . . . and sometimes three.

Sure, I said.

Do you get the joke? he asked.

I get it, I said. It's a good joke.

Listen, son—this is only temporary, my sleeping here. You know that, right? It's just until your mother gets off the rag.

Sure, Dad.

I went into my room. My kid brother Tommy was asleep, his baseball bat next to him on our bed, to keep us separated so that we didn't roll over onto one another. It was ten past three in the morning. On my desk was a new stack of letters waiting for me from all the Saint Colleges, but there was also one with a return address that said Department of Athletics, Brandeis University.

I opened it and read of their genuine interest in me as a student and an athlete.

It was March 17, 1955. I was 17 years old. I read the letter and I felt warm inside my chest, the way I did when Jane rested her head there. I thought of going into the living room, to wake my father and give him the good news, and I imagined how happy he'd be, how he'd want to celebrate my good fortune, how he'd pour drinks for us both and tell me I was going to have a swell life, not like his. He'd laugh and say we should wait until the morning to tell my mother, that she needed her beauty sleep. But if we woke my mother I knew she'd laugh more than both of us put together, that she'd kiss me and hug me and tell me that this was wonderful, having a dream come true—that this was always the best joke of all.

Connorsville, Virginia

SHERIFF JACKSON, he a good friend to the colored people. We got a small town without no mayor, so he acts for both, always comes to the funerals of colored folks and asks if he can help. I know it for a fact, if you ain't got enough to do it right, he gets it for you from the town money, you don't ask no questions.

Most folks here work out at the packing plant, black and white, and we ain't got no real troubles like you reading about in the newspapers. Maybe you heard of Connorsville Hams from Connorsville, Virginia. That's us. Me, I don't work out there on account of the smell. It's medical, the doctor says, from when I got hit in the war, makes me dizzy. The hole the doctors made back of my right ear, it never close all the way, so I got to be careful, always wear this fatigue cap they got with a steel plate to cover it. I take it off when I sleep.

People been good to me here, especially Sheriff Jackson. I got a standing order with him, come in every morning to his office, shine up his boots. He got the most beautiful boots you seen, goes to Norfolk to get 'em made, they this milk chocolate color, like the color my cousin Sally's skin. Me and Lucius, that's Sally's brother, we work together down by the square with guys like us, shining people's shoes, running things places, ready to do some lifting or picking for you, you need us. I ain't too strong, of course, but Lucius, he's a bull, bigger than any man in this town, which includes the Sheriff and Roy Barnes, head foreman at the plant, wrestles everybody at the fairs. Only things is, Lucius, he ain't got a hole in his head like me, with him they must of covered the hole up before he was born, but took out the sense first. He just don't remember much is all. He'll do lifting and pulling and shining for you, strong as five men, but you got to keep telling him how you want it done or he forgets. They try him out at the plant a few times, but it don't work out. He gets so angry with hisself when he does things the wrong way, people got scared he gonna hurt somebody. They been keeping him at home now.

Every once in a while some of the white folks live near the packing plant, they get to drinking or something, the Sheriff got hell on his hands. Sometimes they do something nasty to one of us, men and women both, and he don't stand for it. He finds out who did it, he makes 'em pay a fine and he always comes around sees if he can help out. Sometimes he just gives you the fine if you the one got beat up. The jail stays empty most of the time and he likes it that way.

The Sheriff ain't all good, of course. He gets mad at you, he beat you up pretty bad. He don't use nothing but his hands and his boots, though. Plenty black boys know how strong those boots are, but he says they help keep the jail empty and nobody disagrees with him. He lives out about seven miles, got a nice house by hisself, good soil, raises tomatoes and real nice sweet potatoes, he gets me to help him sometimes. Lucius tried once about six-seven years ago, I asked the Sheriff to give him a chance, but he messed things up, smashing the tomatoes and bringing potatoes to the bushels one at a time and the sheriff got so mad, he about ready to whip Lucius. He don't like it you don't follow his orders right. Once I seen him coming in from a hunt, this setter was acting ornery, the Sheriff started whacking him, didn't stop till that dog stopped. We never spoke about it after.

We don't speak much, you want to count words. Sometimes I helping him work on something big, painting the house, or putting up a new shed like we did last spring. I sleep over, but it don't create conversation. He pays me good money when I work out there, a dollar and a quarter an hour, says it's the wage you got to pay somebody if they do a man's work, "according to the U.S. government." I tell him cause of my head, I ain't all there he ain't got to pay me all a man gets, but he laughs and does anyway. He drinks a lot, don't offer me none, and when he goes up to sleep you can hear him walking and walking, I go up and say, "You all right, cap'n?" and he says, "Go on now, Homer," and by and by he sleeps like a dog. I go in and take his boots off and we eat together in the morning, he fixes the food, says in his home I'm his guest. He fries up scrapple real good, I put lots of syrup on it. Still, we don't talk much.

The other thing I got to tell you about is James, who's Lucius' younger brother, he ain't got too much more sense in his head than Lucius, only with him it's crazy sense. Ever since he a boy he been reading books it seems like and you can't always understand what he's talking to you about, so folks never paid him much attention, just listened and give him praise for knowing so much. He could always quote you long things, didn't matter what, plays or geography or how to build a airplane or love stories. Mister Turner come in to tell us about what happened to him in the morning when I finished doing the Sheriff's boots and we knew right away this real trouble. But maybe you expected it somehow. I was finished working his boots and he was letting me make some money cleaning his guns for him, polishing them up really, he likes to do the cleaning himself, but he trusts me to clean them on the outside. Lucius's family, it's hard to figure out, none of them got too much sense and their father, he was real respected among all of us, ran the medicine place you went to when you sick and need something. The mother, you look at her, you think she gonna break in two like a twig, dry and thin with yellow things been growing around her eyes long as I can remember, she can hardly see, but her children— they got three more after Lucius, James, and Sally—they all come out healthy and good-looking. There lots of white folks like to have Sally come visit them some dark night, you bet. If she not scared of what Lucius do, he find out, she prob'ly do it, she so simple. The others, two boys and a girl, they all married, working out at the packing plant, got kids of their own. James, though, he like his mother, got pigeon bones it looks like, seems he been wearing thick glasses since he was a boy—his father always feeding him pills to keep him alive. He always wiping his nose when I remember him, coughing too. But his father pretty proud on James's books and just before he gone to rest he send James off to this college somewhere, first one in the family, we figure maybe he get enough sense there to run the store when his old man passes on, but he comes back after the funeral, he ain't got drugstores on his mind. He come home again last summer, he talking about civil rights stuff, trying to organize us to vote and things. He got some good points, you listen careful, but after a while it get hard to follow him cause he throwing in things about animals or his mother or a movie he saw and I tell Sheriff Jackson he ain't got nothing to worry about, James so scared of you when he talks, people pretty satisfied the way things are, so long as he running things we don't got to worry. Anyway, I tell him, not for the fact folks don't want to hurt James's feelings they wouldn't listen to him much, you ask me. They just being polite. The college, they prob'ly do with him like the schools here, cause he don't hurt nobody and he ain't fit to work in the packing plant or places. His father, he a real good man, smart too, left lots of insurance so I guess they pay the college some to keep him there.

"Why anybody wanna kill James though?" That the first thing I say when Mister Turner brings the news.

The Sheriff turns on me real angry. "You shut up your mouth, hear?" Then he curses some and Mister Turner, he look real scared, twirling his hat in his hands like he courting some gal the first time. "C'mon, c'mon—the rest of it!"

"I swear to you," Mister Turner says, the Sheriff standing by the window now, next his guns, he don't like this none. Like I tell you, folks get nasty on us sometimes, but long as I can remember this the first one end in murder. "We tried to stop him, Jim. We did. But he was too likkered up. Got in some of that special stuff from over in West Virginia, and—well—I guess some of the other boys, we weren't too much more sober. But ain't none of us figger on what happened—I swear to you—"

"Okay, okay," the Sheriff says. He looks at me strange, but I go about my business like nothing happen, get my shine stuff together. "Where is he now?"

"Like I said, we figgered it don't do nobody any good, let the story out, so we kept him out at Hiram's place overnight. Nobody knows but you and us—and—" He looks over at me.

"Homer got a hole in his head, don't you know?" the Sheriff says. He seems calmer now. "Everything that goes in comes right out again. Right Homer?"

"Yes sir, cap'n," I say, smile some. How come I smiling though, I wonder, when I got a cousin just been shotgunned the other side this world? James, I guess nobody count him a real person somehow.

"I don't even think Ed meant to do it hisself," Mister Turner says. He sweating a river, the way the Sheriff looks on him, he can't stop talking. "We all just wanted to have a little fun with him. He was down by the square, see, handing out these papers about those kids got cut up in Miss'ssippi, Ed says let's take him along, tell us all about it. We just wanted to have a little fun with him is all—but then James keeps on about all this stuff—it was real hard to follow him, Jim—and before you know it he's getting Ed so riled up, we stop the car, Ed says there been enough talking. Still, James, he don't stop—starts in—lemme see—oh yeah, all about how kids right here in Virginia they don't go to school cause they helpin' with tobacco, their folks in debt to men like Ed, and Ed he takes a whack at him, the kid goes down and then he starts saying how he knows Ed gonna murder him, but he don't care cause freedom's coming." He wipes his mouth, we don't say nothing. "That was when he started in about how he knew Ed was gonna kill him, but he didn't care cause freedom's coming, he kept repeating, again and again—and then he started spinning on about changing this town—real loud—'I know I'm bound to die!' he kept yellin'—"

"Okay, okay," the Sheriff says, some starch wash out of him. He thinking hard.

"You know Ed," Mister Turner says. "He can't concentrate too much better than James once he gets stuff in him. But I—"

"You say you brought James home?"

"That's right," Mister Turner says. He swallows hard, remembering. "He's a real mess, Jim. We didn't leave no traces, though. Banged on the door and took our blanket from around him, left straightaway. I burned the blanket this morning, washed my car good. I pray to the Lord to forgive me, Jim—"

"Get out," the Sheriff says. "I'll be to Hiram's place later. You keep Robinson there, hear? And keep your mouth shut, too."

"Sure, Jim. That's why I come here first thing, before—" The Sheriff looks at him hard and Mister Turner shuts up, nods his head real nervous and goes on his way. He got trouble closing the door. The Sheriff don't do nothing for a while and it real still in the office, you can see the sun shine on the gun barrels. "Okay," he says after a while, I don't ask no questions, get in the station wagon with him, sit up front like always, we drive out to Lucius's house.

I tell the Sheriff I ain't feeling too good, could he take it easy over the bumps, he looks at me and smiles. "Relax," he says. Then, "I'm sorry, Homer." I tell him he didn't do nothing, whatever he do, we all know he just doing the best he can. "We know what you up against, cap'n," I say. He don't answer me.

We get out to Lucius's place, I remember that James, he belong to somebody. The Sheriff takes his hat off, leaves his gun in the car, locks up, we go inside. James's older brother, he thanks the Sheriff for coming, the Sheriff says he's real sorry, but everybody says the same thing to him I did. It's all right. We know he do the best he can. James's mother, she cries some she sees us, I try to say something, but I get so dizzy, they got to help me sit down. Doctor Kinnard, used to be a good friend to Lucius's father, he puts stuff under my nose, it wakes me up. Lots of cousins and aunts walking around the house, soft, we all look at each other, what there to say? Sally, she look real pretty in black, tells me the doctor got to give Lucius all kinds of needles to quiet him down. "He really love James," she say to me. "James used to read to him lots."

Going out, in the hall, you can see into the kitchen, they got something rolled up in the living room drape, tore off the window, you wouldn't hardly think a body could be so small. The Sheriff goes in with one of James's brothers, but I don't follow. Upstairs, old Aunt Emma, she singing like she does, it a song I like, makes my head settle down some.

> *"We all gonna be singing' then*
> *Nobody gonna be diggin' then*
> *We all gonna be singin' then*
> *Oh James . . . Oh James . . ."*

She sings it the same whenever somebody dead in the family, always filling in the name of the person. Lucius's mother calls the Sheriff back to the living room, asks him if it's okay to move the body yet, they didn't want to do nothing against the law. The Sheriff says he got to have somebody from the town come take it for a while, then they can go on with the funeral.

"I'm real sorry," he says. "But we got to have an autopsy. It's the law."

Lucius's mother shakes her head like she known it, then she looks straight at the Sheriff. "I hope there ain't gonna be no trial," she says to him. "That all I pray for, that there be no trial. Whoever done it, if you get him, he'll make fun on James's memory." She wipes her eyes, got her glasses in her lap. "That all I pray for, Sheriff, that nobody make fun on James's memory. That there ain't gonna be no trial. That the one thing I pray for—" The Sheriff, he don't say nothing, seems like he listening to Aunt Emma too. "Let him go peaceful," she says.

The Sheriff don't speak to what she says, but he says he'll be back tomorrow, they be sure to let him know if there's anything needs doing. He says that if they got any message and they can't reach him, to give it to me. I go out of the house without looking in the kitchen.

Lucius, he hiding on the other side the station wagon, we both step back we see him.

"I'm sorry about your brother, Lucius," the Sheriff says.

"Don't tell 'em I'm here," he says. "I snuck out."

"We won't tell," the Sheriff says. He tries to open the door to get in, but Lucius grabs his arm, I get scared a minute, you can see the veins in his neck spreading. "I got a big knife hid in the dirt," Lucius says. "I gonna get whoever kill James. Gonna get him the same way. I got a big knife hid in the dirt."

"You best calm down, Lucius," the Sheriff says. "You let me take care of it. That's my job."

"No, sir," Lucius says, he concentrating real hard to get his sense together. I take a look at the Sheriff's gun on the seat in the car, hope Lucius don't see it. "Momma says can't be no trial. No trial—"

The Sheriff pushes him to one side and gets in, puts his gun in his holster. I go round the other side, Lucius crouch down so nobody see him. "Please," he says to the Sheriff. "I be careful. Nobody ever know. I been thinking, Sheriff. I could do lots of things to him. Lots. Please—" I look at him, he trembling from his anger, but his eyes ain't crazy. They not moving ten ways, just open big. "Please—"

"You be careful," the Sheriff says, guns the engine. "Take care of your mother."

"Please—" Lucius says again, he almost crying. "I got to—"

The Sheriff pulls out to the road, Lucius hangs on to the window with his big hands, pleading like a schoolchild, till the Sheriff reaches over bangs him real hard on his knuckles with his fist. "Get off now," he says, angry, but Lucius stays on. "Dumb bastard," the Sheriff says and steps on the gas, Lucius's hands rip off, he bangs on the side of the car, falls down. I see him in the mirror, he run a few steps, then starts shaking both his fists, screaming after us.

We get out to where they got Ed Robinson hid, Mister Turner and the others they all in the barn. I know them. The Sheriff, he see Ed Robinson, first thing he does is haul off and slam him a shot to the jaw makes that little guy spin around, some blood starts at the corner of his mouth.

"You goddamn dumb bastard," the Sheriff says, stands over him, then says it again.

Ed Robinson, he shakes his head, he a kind of little guy, skinny and always moving his fingers 'gainst one another. He reaches inside his mouth, looks like the Sheriff loosed one of his teeth. The Sheriff breathing hard. "Let's go," he says, fixes handcuffs on Ed Robinson.

"I'm real sorry," Ed Robinson says, you can see how scared he is. The other men, they can't hardly look the Sheriff in the eye, just shuffle around. Ed Robinson stands up. He pretty old, got the skinniest jaw you ever seen, lots of sandy hair on his head still. He got a truck farm he runs by himself when he ain't working at the packing plant. "I didn't aim to make no trouble for you, Jim," he says.

The other men they try to say how they're sorry, but the Sheriff don't look like he hears them. "Let's go," he says, and pulls Ed Robinson along with him, we get to the station wagon, he cuffs Robinson and me together in the back seat, we head for town. Ed Robinson don't like being attached to me. He leans forward, right next to the Sheriff, we travel some and he don't seem all that scared no more. I guess he figures the worst is over.

"You still got power, Jim," he says, rubbing his jaw. The Sheriff don't answer. "Mind if I smoke?"

The Sheriff still don't answer. Ed Robinson, he jerks my hand toward him before I know it, lights up his cigarette. I don't say nothing. He gonna get his, I figure. But Ed Robinson, he figures different.

"I told you I'm sorry," he says. "I mean, I didn't mean to do it, Jim. That's the truth. But when he started screaming I was gonna kill him, it made something go wild in me. You know?" He laughs. "Crazy nigra—I'll tell you the truth, Jim—with all that stuff he was spoutin' about freedom and rights, he weren't ever gonna hurt nobody. I know that." He laughs some more. "Gonna miss havin' him around, if you know what I mean." The Sheriff don't answer. Ed Robinson, he start getting fidgety again, yanks me toward him so he can scratch his chest. This time I yank back, he looks at me hard like maybe he want to kill me too. "Ah, I wish it hadn't of happened, Jim," he says. "For your sake. It puts you on the spot, don't it?"

"You killed a man and you got to pay," the Sheriff says and I watch Ed Robinson's eyes move forward. He don't expect this. Me neither, you want the truth.

"Ah, c'mon," he says, his neck jerk out of his shirt like a turtle. "Stop kiddin' around. He was just a nigra—nutty one too."

"This is Connorsville, Virginia," the Sheriff says. "It ain't Miss'sippi and it ain't even Alabama."

Ed Robinson screws up his face like he don't quite get what the Sheriff trying to say. He chuckles some to hisself, though. "Hell, I'll just say it was self-defense, Jim—no jury round here gonna hang a white man for killin' a nigra."

"Maybe not," the Sheriff says.

Then Ed Robinson leans forward, touches the Sheriff on the back. "C'mon—you ain't serious, are you, Jim?"

"Get your hands off me. Pull him back, Homer. You got a job back there—do it."

"Yes sir, cap'n," I say, yank my wrist hard and Ed Robinson hit against the back of the seat, glare at me and I feeling pretty good, helping the Sheriff this way. Ed Robinson, he don't say much the rest of the trip, we get him to the office, though, you can tell he been cooking something under his skull.

"Thought you liked to keep this place empty," he says.

"That's right."

"C'mon, Jim—I know I put you on a spot and if I could take the whole thing back I would—but you only gonna be making more trouble for yourself, you lock me up."

"Maybe," the Sheriff says, sits down at his desk.

Ed Robinson breathes easy, seeing he ain't locked up yet. The Sheriff tosses me the keys, tells me to take the cuffs off. I get them off, move quick to the other side of the room.

"Look," Ed Robinson says. "You let me go and who's gonna know the difference? None of the boys with me ever gonna tell—nobody but us knows I did it—and the niggers around here, they respect you, they won't push. I mean, who's gonna know the difference?"

"Me," I say. "I'll know." Then I look around real quick cause I ain't sure where those words come from. The Sheriff and Ed Robinson, they booth look at me about as surprised as I am. The Sheriff he chew on his lip, just keep staring at me, wondering if he can understand me any better than I do. Ed Robinson, though, he starts laughing.

"Homer—" He waves his hand, brushes his hair back. "Everybody in this town knows he does what you tell him, Jim. Why the way I hear it, the N-double-A-C-P, they gettin' ready to prosecute you for slave-holding!" He laughs some more, a kind of crazy laugh, he got to sit down. "Look, Jim," he says, "I mean, you and me, we known each other a long time, right? And in this town we got things pretty good—nice and quiet, no trouble, you want to have a personal slave, you don't hear anybody holler, right?" He wags his finger at the Sheriff, I think to myself, you doing the wrong thing, Mister Robinson, don't be shaking your finger at the Sheriff. "But you put a white man on trial here for killin' a nigger, you gonna have that N-double-A-C-P down your neck for sure. They gonna come in here with their TV and their newspapers, make a hero out of that crazy James and before you know it, you gonna have the federal government buttin' in too." He closes his eyes narrow. "That James, like I say, we all know he ain't held together right in his head, but he was connected up with them groups up North and in Washington, and they gonna come down here, this town never be the same—ain't nobody gonna be thanking you for that. They gonna start messin' with our schools and they be wantin' niggers on the jury—oh yeah, you gonna have real trouble, Jim. And for what?" He stops talking. I look at the Sheriff, then back at Ed Robinson, then to the Sheriff. I feeling a little dizzy, count of what he say about me.

"You be committin' suicide, you run a trial here," Ed Robinson says. But he ain't getting any reaction from the Sheriff. He keeps trying, though. Scratches his chin and laughs. "Okay, okay—you know something? Not for the fact of all the trouble it make for everybody I'd kind of like the chance to testify in court. Never done that. You should of seen the way that James was carrying on—I'll tell you something—you can bet your best pair of boots I'd have that jury rolling in the aisle, imitatin' how he was going on—" He wags his finger again and I feel this nerve along my shoulder start heart-beating. "Long as things are peaceful here, long as you keep order, people stay pretty tolerant, Jim. They don't care too much how you go about doing it. But once they think this civil rights stuff gonna invade our town, you be surprised how quick they get together. Like I say, not for the trouble that'd come, I'd kind of like the chance to sit up there in the courthouse. Only I'd be the one they'd make a hero, Jim, and you better believe that." He stops. The Sheriff, I sure don't want to be him now, damned if he do and damned if he don't. Ed Robinson, he feeling good. He stands up and stretches, laughs nice and easy like him and the Sheriff good buddies again and he going to do his best to get the Sheriff off the hook. "Hell, Jim," he says. "You did the same thing yourself, you and me used to run around together." The Sheriff's eyes shift real quick, Ed Robinson see it too. "Things were different in those days, huh, Jim? I mean, I'm as sorry as I can be I put you in a fix—but I'm remembering the time, wouldn't of been no fix at all to take after a nigra. Remember in high school, we had nothin' to do on a Saturday night, we used to get those chains and ride around looking for a stray one?" He looks kind of wild in his eyes, remembering. "Jesus, I remember that time you got that big black boy out behind the old stone quarry. Some job you did on him—"

The Sheriff, he's done thinking. "Go on home, Ed," he says, real calm, but Ed Robinson, he a little surprised, hear the words so sudden. "You mean it?"

"Unless you want me to keep you here—for your own protection. I'll do that, if you want."

Ed Robinson, he only been putting up a front, you can see now, cause he starts laughing kind of hysterical, he so relieved. "Who's gonna touch me?" he asks. "That's a good one, Jim—for my own protection!"

"I thought maybe you were scared the nigras might find out—"

Ed Robinson howls now, slaps his knee. "That'll be the day, won't it though," he says. "When the niggers go after us. Why when that day comes, Jim, lemme tell you, I'll say okay, set 'em all free, let 'em eat where I eat, live where I live, drink where I drink. I'll say set 'em all free—even Homer here."

"Go on home, Ed," the Sheriff says again. I ain't looking up, the room turning kind of sideways, I not sure what I want to do to Ed Robinson, but it something awful.

"I'll see you tomorrow, Sheriff," I say when Ed Robinson gone. I head for the door.

"Stay put, goddamn you!" the Sheriff says.

"Yes sir, cap'n," I say.

He stands up, real angry—I didn't see how angry he is till now. "And stop saying that, hear? 'Yes sir, cap'n, yes sir, cap'n'—it's driving me crazy—!"

"Yes—" But that as far as I get, I get control of my mouth, stop the rest.

"Goddamn, just goddamn," the Sheriff says, walks around the room some. His jaw, it set so hard, he gonna break something. I scared of him now, afraid I gonna say the wrong thing. He come up close to me after a while, jab my chest with his finger. "You know where Ed Robinson lives?" he asks.

"Yes sir, cap'n," I say, and then he lets me have it—wham! I go flying, knock down a whole bunch of guns and things. The floor goes backwards and I slide some, the whole world racing around me and I got to catch hold onto something.

"Get up!" he says. "Goddamn you, get up!"

It a mystery to me, but his words they get me up. He don't look sorry at all. He just takes hold on my jacket and shakes me. "Do you?—And don't say it: just nod your head."

I nod my head. I know where Ed Robinson lives.

"Okay. Let's go." I fix my hat on the back of my head and go with him into the car, I see we heading back for Lucius's house, I try not to think on what's coming.

"Tell me something, Homer," he says, half-way there, just talking like nothing been happening. "You like it in the Army?"

"Oh yes—" I say, stop the rest of that sentence. "I like the Army. Would of stayed in it, not for what happened. It's good in the Army."

"What happened?" he asks. I slide toward the door, look out the window, it the first time he ask me this, and I know it ain't no use, so I tell him how this cook, I in the kitchen always making jokes to keep everybody laughing, but I go too far this one time—say something about his girl, a joke about a guy going in a camera store, gets asked what size camera he got. Only I so nervous now, I get all the funny parts about the Brownie and the box messed up, and the Sheriff don't get it. But I tell him that was how it happened, this guy got so mad he throw this chopper at me, right there in the kitchen, lay me out flat, I never even known what did it till they tell me at the hospital. I tell most people it happen while we killing Japs with tanks.

The Sheriff nods like he filing my story away, some of his anger gone, but we get to the house, he stride right up to the porch, I got to hustle to get inside with him.

"You can bury James when you want," he tells Lucius's mother. "We won't need an autopsy." She looks at him and the Sheriff lets out some breath, then speaks quick. "Okay, okay. There won't be any trial, either," and he turns direct and I hurry out after him. Aunt Emma, she still singing.

Outside the Sheriff looks at me and I look back at him. "It's the only way, Homer," he says. "You get Lucius, say I need him to do some packing down by the office—they'll be glad to get him off their hands. I'll drive you out a ways, you do the rest by yourself." He don't look right at me no more. "Can you do the job, Homer?"

I don't got to think. "Yes sir," I say. "Me and Lucius, we put our sense together this time, we do the job for you."

"You'll explain to Lucius—about not talking?"

"Don't you worry none, Sheriff," I say. "You done lots for us. You a good friend to the colored people."

"Sure," he says, but you can tell he don't believe it. "Sure." He shakes his head. There ain't no anger in him now. He just seem tired and old. I forget how old he is sometimes, he so big and quick. "God help us all," he says.

"Ed Robinson ain't no good," I say to him. "Lucius get him anyway somehow, Sheriff."

"Goddamn him," the Sheriff says, I ain't sure if he means Lucius or Ed Robinson. "Just goddamn him." Then he looks at me strange. "Am I doing the right thing, Homer?" he asks. My cap, it pressing on my head, his face sways some in front of me. He starts to grab my jacket but stops. "Am I? It's important. Do you think I'm doing the right thing?"

"Yes sir," I say. "Yes sir, cap'n."

He don't seem to mind me saying that again, it's something else don't satisfy him this time. "The truth—" he says, grabs me and looks like he gonna get mad all over again. "Goddamn you—give me a straight answer. It's important, damn it. Do you think I'm doing the right thing, Homer?"

"Yes sir," I say, answering the best I know how. "Yes sir, cap'n. You doing the best you can."

"Oh goddamn you," he says, shoves me away. "Just goddamn you." I wishing I could tell him other things now, but it only upset him, I figure. The Sheriff, he real good to me. My head still turning some, thinking on what gonna be, but I don't got to look, and like the Sheriff says, it's the only way. The Sheriff, he knows Ed Robinson ain't the guy to keep shut on a thing like this. That's for sure. Maybe he don't trust me neither. He let Ed Robinson get off free, we all gonna be in for worse troubles, how he ever gonna keep order? Like I say, I wishing I could tell him other things now. What I like to do is tell him how if he die before I do, I go out to his grave all the time, make sure they tend to it right, but I don't figure he wants to know about this none. I thinking about it, though. "Go on," he says to me. "Go on."

"Yes sir, cap'n," I say and go in the house, say what I have to and get Lucius. The Sheriff gonna drive us partway, wait to drive us back after. "Let's go, Lucius," I whisper upstairs, he must of got some needles from the doctor, he sitting on his bed pretty calm and big, humming to hisself the song Aunt Emma singing about his brother. "C'mon, Lucius," I say. "You got to dig up your knife."

The Year Between

WHEN THE IDEA first occurred to Mark Goldman—
that he and his wife should live apart for a year, and
that, afterward, they should never reveal to anyone, not even to each
other, what they did during that year—he was certain he was borrowing
it from an early short story by Henry James. The story he recalled
seemed to him a typical Jamesian ghost story in which, at the end, after
the husband and wife are reunited, the husband is slowly driven mad by
his desire to know, and not knowing, to create, in painful detail, each
hour and day, in his wife's life, of the missing year.

Mark mentioned the story to several colleagues in the English Department at Amherst College; he went through the complete New York
edition of James's stories and short novels, and then through the peri-
odicals in which the stories had originally appeared. He found nothing.

"Then you must have made it up yourself," Janet said to him one
evening, before dinner. He noticed that her cheeks, usually pale, were
flushed. "And I think it's wonderful that you did—haven't I always said
you had a marvelous imagination, if only you'd give it a chance?"

"I suppose so," he replied. "But listen. Give me your opinion. I've
been thinking that maybe—maybe I should write the story myself—"

"Or maybe—" she said then, her eyes shining "—maybe we should
live it."

He leaned toward her, his mouth half-open in astonishment—she
had, he knew, spoken for his own silent thoughts—and when she
laughed, he found that he was laughing with her. "Do you really think
so?" he asked.

"Yes." She seemed surprised by her own reply. "Yes. I suppose I do,"
she said, setting down her glass of sherry. She came to him and sat on
his lap. She unbuttoned the top two buttons of his shirt and slid her

hand inside. She rubbed his chest gently, and he could feel the warmth of her thighs through the thin cloth of her spring dress. "We're free," she said. "Don't you see? We can do whatever we want."

"I suppose so," he said. "But you're not really serious, are you? I mean, for a story it might be a terrific idea—a couple renewing themselves by inventing a ghost, by infusing their lives with the mystery it lacks, but to actually live out . . ."

She rested her head against his chest. "Oh Mark, why not?" she pleaded, softly. "Why not? It's just the thing we need, don't you see? It would be—" she laughed at the Jamesian phrase "—the great thing in our lives."

The next evening, after dinner, they sat in their living room and talked again. She had never seemed more beautiful to him. It was as if, he thought, his idea had somehow melted that cool New England reserve of hers that had, through the years, often infuriated him. He told her so and she smiled, allowing for the truth of what he said. Hadn't she always believed in his imagination? His mind, he admitted, did take flights at times, as it had been doing all day, and sometimes those flights brought with them painful questions. Would she mind if he asked her a simple question—would she answer him honestly? In all their years in Amherst, he wanted to know, had she ever been in love with anyone else?

"No."

He nodded, swallowed hard. "Even when we were first married," he confessed, "I used to fear that I wasn't enough for you, that I could never satisfy you. Did you know that?" He sighed. "I used to watch the way your eyes would flicker sideways sometimes when you were smiling at others—at faculty parties, or concerts. Sometimes when you were gone in the afternoon with your women friends, I'd sneak out and drive around town, afraid—wishing, I suppose you'd say—that I'd find you with another man."

She made circles on his chest with her fingertip. "You're sweet," she said. "You're very sweet, Mark. But no, despite the phantoms of your imagination, I've never been with another man. But tell me what you discovered today. Please? Don't let me—" she smiled "—hang fire forever—"

He told her that he had continued his researches in the Frost Library during the afternoon, but had discovered nothing. The story was, he concluded—like the missing year—a ghost. "I like ghosts," she said. Then she shuddered, and gestured to the darkened room. "What, really, do we have to lose?" she asked. "Sometimes I just get so scared for the emptiness of our life, Mark. Living here year after year, without children, without—please let's try it. Please?"

"But if we actually did it—I mean, be realistic, Janet—how could we face each other afterward?" he asked. "Acts have consequences—isn't that the point? If James had written the story, wouldn't that have *been* the point? That we're never *really* free, not even in our imaginations." He shrugged. "I know us too well. We're just too normal and moral—too possessive, too monogamous, too—"

"That's right," she said, and he heard a familiar coldness enter her voice. "That's exactly right."

He kissed her forehead, then recited the line he had often recited to her in their early years: "What do you think—can an intense Jewish boy from the streets of Brooklyn find contentment in the arms of the frail and beautiful daughter of a dying New England clergyman?"

"Can he?" she asked. Her body was very still now, against his own. "Tell me that, please. Can he, Mark? *Did* he?"

She took his face between her hands and kissed him. Her lips were warm. She flicked his tongue lightly with her own, and he felt himself harden at once. He closed his eyes and he saw her as she had been fifteen years before, in the sunlit bedroom of the parsonage, washing her father's gaunt face with a damp cloth. Such tenderness! He had, watching her from the doorway, held his breath. He had loved her most in that moment, he knew, when she had not been aware of his presence. He had longed to have her care for him with such single-minded and intense gentleness. And after the tenderness, he recalled, in her bedroom upstairs, such passion; and all the while their bodies were clasped together, her father was below them, dying and dreaming.

The next afternoon Mark cut his office hours short and surprised Janet by coming home at two o'clock. He took the papers he had prepared out of his briefcase, showed them to her, and told her that he had figured out the logistical details. All things were possible, he said. They would each choose one friend with whom, during the twelve months, they would be constantly in touch. Each friend would have the name of the other in a sealed envelope. If any emergency should arise, one friend would open the sealed envelope, notify the other friend, and that friend would notify one of them. He took out their bankbooks and checkbooks and explained to her how they would arrange their finances. They would each use a different travel agent. They would agree, from this point on, not to open or to read each other's mail, or to look upon each other's desks. In late May, when classes were out, he would go to New Haven for two weeks, to work at the Beinecke Library, and she could use that time to do whatever could not be done with him present. She would leave the house sometime before his return. He would then come home and would leave one week later. He would notify Amherst College about their plans to be abroad for his sabbatical; they lived in a college-owned house, and the college would take care of it in their absence. He spoke for more than an hour, working from notes, and when he was done speaking she burst into applause and declared him a genius, that rare man who could wed deep feeling and wild invention with practical realities.

Then, abruptly, she stopped smiling. "But Mark," she said, her brow furrowed. "There's something else. I've been thinking—are you sure you're up to this? Are you sure you don't just want to forget the whole thing?" She looked down. "I wouldn't mind. Really. I've been thinking too, and I can see now that it might be hard on you afterward in a way it might not be on me. I wouldn't mind. It's been wonderful to play with the idea, but—"

He took her in his arms and told her that he would be doing it as much for himself as for her. Hadn't the idea been his? Hadn't he worked out all the details? If he did not now put his character to the test he had imagined for it, he would live out the rest of his life, he knew, with the feeling of failure, with the knowledge that he had proven himself inadequate to the demands of his real self, his true dreams. He spoke to her with great intensity and while he spoke she sat across from him on their bed, cross-legged, listening; and when he was done speaking she was kind to him in ways that gave him the courage she kept assuring him he had.

2

NOW THE YEAR WAS over, and they were across the room from each other, at the first faculty party of the new academic year. While he talked with his colleagues and their wives, and parried their questions with noncommittal answers, he could not keep from grinning, he could not keep from searching out Janet's sparkling eyes, from thinking of their reunion the night before. She had seemed even younger to him than she had in the weeks preceding their separation. Her body was leaner, her skin smoother, and her hair—her lovely flaxen hair, which she had always worn just past her shoulders—now hung down almost to her waist. That had been her gift to him.

They had, during their last days together the year before, agreed that although they could not bring home souvenirs or purchases that might in any way reveal a place or an event, they would allow themselves to bring each other a gift, so long as the gift—a test of their ingenuity—was not in any way a clue. His gift to her was the story itself—"The Year Between," by Mark Goldman—and when she opened the manilla envelope and saw the title page, she had embraced him happily. Then she set the story on her night table and told him to close his eyes while she readied her gift for him. She undressed and removed the lavender scarf from her head; when he opened his eyes and saw her golden hair lying across her bare shoulders, he had gasped.

Their night together had been wonderful—not so much the sheer physical pleasures, he realized, but the obvious happiness they each felt simply in being with each other again, in touching each other, gently and tentatively, and in smiling at each other without the need for words; and all the while they were apart during the day—she on errands, he at the college—and now again, when they were surrounded by others who knew of their year apart, he was aware of the pleasure he took from the new way people looked at him. They were, he realized, in awe of him, almost as if he were a movie star or a well-known novelist. And he saw that the less he said, the more they felt this way.

"You look older somehow, Mark. More mature," the wife of one of his colleagues said to him. She reached out and touched his hair. "There's more gray in your hair, isn't there?" She smiled, her head tilted to one side, and then, speaking softly, she began to ask the inevitable—had they really gone and done it, and now that it seemed that they had, what was it like to return to ordinary life, to the humdrum reality of Amherst?

"Is this reality?" he replied, gesturing with his glass to the roomful of people. She touched his arm and told him how wonderful Janet looked. "Maybe—" he said, "—maybe this is all an illusion and the only real thing is—is—"

"—the year we'll never tell about?" Janet asked. She was at his side. She leaned against him, her fingers on his wrist. "Kiss and tell?" she asked. She kissed him on the cheek.

He shook his head. "I can't," he said. "I'm sworn to secrecy."

There were others around them now, watching and smiling. "Kiss and tell," Janet whispered again, and he noticed that as she pressed her chest against his, she raised one leg from the carpet, her shoe half-off, as if, he thought, she were a schoolgirl on prom night.

He put his arm around her and drew her close. He looked at the others. Their eyes pleaded with him to tell them something—anything. "Never," he said. He heard laughter. "Never."

Janet closed her eyes and he sensed that she was happy in a way she had never been before.

A week later they gave a party in their own house and, near the end of the evening, when he was walking a couple to the door, he caught a glimpse of Janet in the kitchen. She was leaning forward, and then, as he was about to turn away, he saw her leg go up from the floor, her ankle arch, her toe point. When he passed the kitchen again, a minute later, Janet was walking toward him, her arm in the arm of one of Mark's colleagues, a young poet the department had recently hired. She told Mark that the poet had just offered to write a sonnet sequence about their year—if only she would reveal a few of its details to him. Mark smiled. "What did you tell him?"

"I told him I'm holding out for an epic."

"Janet tells me that you've already written a short story about the year," the poet said.

"There's nothing about the year in the story," Mark stated. "It's the one thing that's left out. That's the point, of course, or else—"

"Of course," the poet said. "Or else Janet would have—"

"Precisely," Janet said, and she giggled. She walked the two men into the living room, leaning now against one and now against the other.

When the guests were gone, Mark asked her what she and the poet had been doing in the kitchen. In his mind's eye he saw again the slender curve of her calf, the delicacy of her ankle. "Kiss and tell?" she asked.

"Tell me what you were doing," he repeated. "I'm serious."

She breathed in deeply, as if to sober herself. "You're jealous," she exclaimed. "You're actually jealous—"

"I suppose so," he said. "Still, I want to know what—"

"Oh Mark," she said. "My sweet Mark!" She came to him and took him by the hand, drawing him back with her to the living room. "He *is* an attractive man and we were having fun with each other—at least *I* was having fun teasing him while he tried to find out what we'd really done and if we've kept to our vows—but that was all." She tugged on his fingers so that he sat beside her on the couch. "Do you realize that you haven't asked me even once about all those days and months I was on my own, and yet you see me for a brief moment in the kitchen with—"

"It is crazy," he said. "Isn't it?"

"Don't worry about me," she said. "Please promise me that? It would ruin everything if I thought you were being hurt in some way. I'm all right, and I wouldn't trade you for any man in the world, don't you know that? I chose *you,* Mark. I chose you, and I chose to stay with you."

"Yes," he said.

"Before—there were times before, I'll admit, when I often had an active fantasy life, but that's all behind us, don't you see? What we have now is so *real,* Mark. It's something nobody else has and I wouldn't give it up for anything."

"But I see the way other men have been staring at you ever since our return," he said, "and it—"

"And I've seen the way women look at *you* now," she said. "You are a very attractive man. You know that, don't you?"

He nodded. "That was always my ambition."

"Your ambition?"

"To grow up to be a very attractive man."

"I love you," she said, hugging him. "And I'll always be true to you and you won't ever have to worry again." She pulled away and looked at him. "You trusted me fully, and I don't ever need to test that trust again—for you or for me. Even in my imagination I'll be true to you now." She took his face between her hands. "I have what I want, Mark.

Can you understand that? Everything *is* different for me now and that's the great thing."

3

TIME PASSED, and Mark realized that the closer they drew to each other—now playfully, now passionately—and the more they talked and shared, without ever mentioning the year itself, the more tangibly it seemed to be there; so that he found himself beginning to wonder which was more real, the life they led now, or the year they would never talk about. He knew that she was right—that the year had changed them, and that the changes themselves were profound and good. She seemed to grow younger, and at the same time, more serious. She took up sculpture—an old passion—with great energy and intensity. When he arrived home from the college, and found her in the basement working in one of his old shirts, he was happy. He would bring a book and a drink, and sit and watch. For his birthday, she surprised him by presenting him with a sculpture of his head, in clay. The likeness was excellent, and though he thought it made him look more handsome and substantial than he actually was, nobody suggested that her love for him had made her blind to some weakness in himself that he feared she could not see. She had never had more energy, she had never been happier, and yet, most remarkable of all, when he was at home, she seemed, still, to have endless time to be with him—to cook for him, to sit and read with him, to talk with him about his work.

He wanted to take the story he had given to Janet, and to expand it into a novella, a novel. He wanted to write story after story—to give his imagination free rein—but he found that his teaching and committee duties required too much of his time. He was giving a new course, a senior seminar in the American novel that he had designed before his sabbatical, and it came as a surprise to him one day when one of his students pointed out that virtually all the books he had chosen, by his favorite authors—Melville, Hawthorne, James, Cather, Bellow—were set elsewhere than in America: *Benito Cereno, The Marble Faun, Wings of the Dove, Shadows on the Rock, Henderson the Rain King*. And even when the works themselves were far from great—Twain's *Joan of Arc*, Faulkner's *A Fable*, Malamud's *The Fixer*—it seemed significant that they were, usually, the favorite books of their authors.

If so many American writers had, for their major statements, to seek out some past from which they themselves, and their countrymen, had been cut off, where in his own life, he wondered, might there be an equivalent past from which he had been severed? Where, in his own past, did the origin of his idea lie? When and where had it been born?

In his memory he found that he returned frequently to a year during which he had lived, not with his parents, but with an aunt and uncle. Was this the missing year? His father had been overseas, in the Army. His mother, a fragile and hysterical woman, had been away in a sanitarium, suffering from one of her periodic breakdowns. He had been a year and a half old when his aunt and uncle had taken him in, and no matter how hard he tried he could recall nothing about the year, and—his parents and his aunt and uncle now gone—there was no way, he knew, that he would ever find out about it.

He returned also, in his memory, to the many times he would, as a child, accompany his mother for walks along Flatbush Avenue, in Brooklyn. She would push his baby carriage, and in the carriage there were treasures from home—scarves, silverware, pots, dishes, hats, toys—all of which she would try to sell to people along the street. Sometimes, he knew, his father followed, a block or so behind. His mother, he realized, had been truly happy during these walks, and he recalled, for the first time in many years, that he had, when he was in the third grade, written stories that he gave to his mother to put into the carriage and sell for him. He remembered how wonderful her smile had been, each time he brought her a new one. He remembered a neighbor who had bought one of his stories for three cents. Was the lost Henry James story somehow connected with these lost stories of his childhood? Had he sensed, as a child, from the reactions of others, just how strange his mother was? Or—Janet found this idea most probable—had he feared that, the possessions filling the space in the carriage where he had previously sat, that his mother had somehow wanted to sell *him?*

As Janet talked with him about his ideas and memories, she also urged him to work less hard. She noticed more gray hairs, new lines around his eyes, and when Mark looked in the mirror one morning, in the seventh month after their return, he realized, with some alarm, that he was beginning to look like his father. He stared at his image for a long time. His father had been a failure, in business and in life, and his mother, whether sane or insane, had mocked the man mercilessly. He asked Janet one night if she thought that all his efforts—his marriage, his New England home, his career—were, like the new life he had conjured up from some hidden recess of his imagination, nothing more than a thinly veiled attempt to avoid being the failure his father had been.

"No," she said. "Of course not."

"Then why—?"

"Because when you're tired, as you've been lately, from overwork, you do fear that you are somehow like your father." She touched his cheek. "But that's natural, Mark. You'll see—as soon as you get some rest, you won't feel this way."

"But there's something else," he said. He spoke rapidly. "Another idea I've been toying with. Tell me what you think, all right? I've begun to conceive of a book, half-fiction and half-memoir, part memory and part fantasy, in which I'd write about a man who'd imagined and done what I've imagined and done, and then had gone on to try, by looking backwards into his own life, as if through a series of glazes in a Renaissance portrait, to try to account for the origins of it all." He breathed out. "What do you think?"

She shrugged. "I'm not sure I quite understand what you mean by half-fiction and half-memoir," she said. "If it's really going to be about what you've imagined and done, then in what way will it be half-fiction?"

He felt weak suddenly. "I don't know," he said. "I mean, I haven't worked it all out yet—I haven't even begun the real writing—but it just came to me that way, as some new kind of prose form, as if, say, Twain had combined *Huckleberry Finn* and *Life on the Mississippi* in one book, or as if Bellow would rewrite *Henderson the Rain King* and mingle it with an account of his own psychoanalysis." He blinked. "That's all I meant."

She kissed him once on each eyelid. "I think you should go ahead and try it. I don't have to understand everything you do, after all." She laughed. "That's the beauty of it, isn't it, Mark?—that we're so close that we know each other so well, and yet what binds us together—our secret—runs so deep that we can never speak of it, that we ourselves hardly know what it is."

"I suppose," he said, and as he looked into her face, he felt a terrible weariness settle into his bones. "Maybe you're right. Maybe I need to rest more. All the reading I've had to do for this new course, and my freshman world literature survey—which I haven't taught for a half-dozen years—and then being adviser to some senior honors students, sitting on the Dean's curriculum review committee—it's been getting to me. I've felt tired all day, in fact, much more so than usual. Walking home through the snow this afternoon my legs felt especially heavy. I didn't want to worry you, and then—"

She felt his forehead with her lips. "But you have a fever!" she exclaimed. She darted from the couch, to the bathroom, and returned with a thermometer. "You're burning up."

He lay in bed for four days. She fed him, washed him, shaved him, and read to him, and she urged him not to be a critic of the writings of others, but to consider, when he was well, doing more writing of his own. She hoped, when his time was less pressured, that he would give himself the chance, yet again, to let his imagination take wing. But if he did or if he didn't, she would still love him, she would still be happy.

His eyes ached, his muscles were sore, his throat and chest were thick with phlegm. He thought of Milly Theale, in *Wings of the Dove,* dying in the room that overlooked the Grand Canal. He realized that he did believe that Janet was, truly, as happy as she claimed to be. Still, he sensed that it was his *idea,* and not himself, that had brought such happiness to her, and the difference disturbed him.

"Maybe—" he said, while she sat at his side, holding the glass from which he sipped his tea and honey, "—maybe I need a prolonged rest. I feel so damned exhausted sometimes, Janet. As if—"

"Don't be silly," she said. "It's just the flu. It's been hitting everybody. You'll get over it in another day or two."

"But—" He dropped back upon his pillow. "I can't ever remember feeling this bad, not even—"

"Shh," she said. "You shouldn't talk. You're tiring yourself more. You sleep for a while and then maybe—" she smiled. "—maybe I'll come join you and we'll attempt an old Biblical remedy—"

He tried to smile. "What they ordered for King David?"

"Mmm," she said. "Now close your eyes. Be a good boy."

When next he opened his eyes, the room was dark. He called for her and she came at once, wearing a white bathrobe. He remembered Susan Hayward, in a movie version of "The Aspern Papers," rustling through darkened rooms in a white evening gown. "Are you ready?" she asked.

"I'm in a sweat," he said. "I'm drenched."

"Good. The fever may be breaking." He watched her as, wraithlike, she turned her back to him and removed her robe. She let it fall about her feet, and then she stepped away. Her hair seemed longer and silkier to him. She laughed, lightly. "Did I tell you that this morning, when I went to the library to check out some books, they asked me for my student I.D.—?"

"I'm cold," he said. "I think I'm getting a chill."

"I'll be there in a minute." She stood in front of the vanity table mirror and brushed her hair. "I'll warm you. But—can you imagine?—that at my age they mistook me for an undergraduate?"

She turned to him, smiling with a kindness that numbed him. As he watched her move across the room, he found himself beginning to imagine for the first time how other men—in France, in Italy, in Spain, in Greece, in Morocco—might have looked upon her.

She lifted the covers and lay next to him. "Your skin is so hot," she said.

"Maybe we should take me to the doctor."

"Never," she said, gently, kissing him.

"I'm cold," he said. "And things seem to be getting dark suddenly . . ."

"The darkness before the light?" she laughed. "Don't talk—you'll tire yourself. Let me talk. Did you know the one time I doubted?" She stroked his forehead. "The one time I doubted was not when you asked me how we could, afterward, return to our ordinary lives, but when you said what you did about how James might have written the story—about how the point would have been something about acts and conse-quences, about our not ever being free, not even in our imaginations."

"You should have told me."

"But if I had, we might never—" She broke off. "And there's some-thing else I've wanted to tell you." She touched his face with great tenderness. "If I tell you that I haven't been able to read your story yet, will you forgive me? Oh Mark, I've tried—believe me—and I *was* so happy when you first gave it to me as a gift. It's just that . . ."

He closed his eyes. "It's all right," he said. "It doesn't matter."

She kissed him. "I know," she said. "Because now that I've told you, I feel better. I'll be able to read it." She rested her cheek against his. "Until now I haven't felt free to. I've been frightened of it somehow, and not because of anything I might find in it, but by the idea that you finished it. Can you understand that? Whenever I've looked at it I've been frightened by the idea that it has an *ending*—and yet our life itself goes on and on—"

"You should have told me before," he said. "There's really nothing . . ."

"Shh," she said. "You've been sweet never to have asked me if I'd read it. But you don't have to say anything now. We don't have to explain to each other anymore—not ever again." She pressed against him. "And promise me too that you'll try not to worry about how you look—your age; I've always liked older men, haven't I? Wasn't that what first attracted me to you?"

He closed his eyes and let her do what she wanted with him, and while she did—and all the while she talked to him, comforted him, and loved him—he realized that if he would now dare to ask her about her year, and if she would tell, he would not be jealous, either of real acts or of those he might imagine. He believed her. He understood that what she'd said was true—that, now that she had had her chance, now that they had done the great thing—she would be faithful to him forever. And yet being free of the thing he had feared most hardly comforted him, for even as he realized that this fear was gone, and even as Janet ministered to his needs with a kindness and passion he could hardly endure, he sensed that a new and more terrible fear was settling within him and taking hold. He looked away, toward the night table, toward the envelope that contained his story, and he saw, finally, that he had been wrong: his great fear was not that she might reveal her acts to him or that he might be jealous, but that, having revealed herself fully to him—all that she had and had not done—she might look at him with her bright and eager eyes and plead with him to do the same, and that he would have to think then, for the first time, of all that, having at last given himself the chance, he had, nonetheless, failed to do.

Your Child
Has Been Towed

WHEN I WAS A BOY growing up in Brooklyn during the years after the Second World War, my favorite place was our local library. On Saturday mornings while my parents slept late, I'd sneak out the door, then run the three blocks from our apartment house until I came to the squat white stone building. The children's room was on the right side, a large rectangle with enormous windows that ran along its three outside walls. The windows were high up above the shelves of books, and when I sat inside the room, I used to look up and imagine there were machine gun nests perched just outside the glass, machine gunners in camouflaged helmets firing down on me and the other children—spraying us with pellets of brilliant sunlight.

I loved going to the library on Saturday mornings because that was when Mrs. Kachulis, my fourth-grade teacher, was there. Each Saturday morning she came with her daughter Demeter. Mrs. Kachulis always called her daughter, who was in the third grade, by her full name of Demeter. At school, Demeter's girlfriends called her Demmy and sometimes, if no teachers were around, boys would circle around her and call her Dummy. The first time I met Mrs. Kachulis at the library was by chance. I'd gone to synagogue with my father, a block from the library, because he had to say Kaddish for his father. Otherwise, since my father was proud to be what he called a godless Jew, he never went. On the way home we stopped at the library so I could get some books to read over the weekend. He had taken me with him to synagogue because I was, he said, his *kaddishel*, the person who would say Kaddish for him all the years after he died.

My favorite writer during those years was John R. Tunis. I knew the names of the ballplayers on his imaginary teams as well as I knew the names of the players on the Brooklyn Dodgers. I'd read all his books several times each and I was looking through *The Kid from Tomkinsville* again when Mrs. Kachulis found me. She grabbed me by the arms, helped me up from the floor, smiled at me as if I were the one human being in the world she had most hoped to meet. This is what she said:

How wonderful to see you here, Jason! I come here every Saturday morning with Demeter. We'll meet again. You know Demeter, of course. Demeter, come here, please, and meet Jason Klein. Demeter, this is Jason Klein, the most brilliant and generous student I've ever had.

A blast of air entered my mouth and shot down my throat. It breathed heat into a bundle of dry twigs that lay waiting just below my chest. The twigs burst into flame.

Hello, Mrs. Kachulis. I'm pleased to meet you, Demeter.

Mrs. Kachulis asked to see what I was reading. I offered the book to her and I wondered if she would know what I loved most about holding the book: that the straw-colored binding made me imagine what the sun felt like on the Kid from Tomkinsville's back when he was out on the ballfield somewhere in Florida, far from home, on his first day of spring training.

My father came to get me. You must be proud to have a son like Jason, Mrs. Kachulis said. I'll tell you a secret—he makes my days worthwhile.

Jason's a good boy mostly, my father said. Especially when he sleeps.

Look at the books he's reading, a boy his age.

Sports books. Always sports books, my father said. Athletes and horses and grown men chasing little balls. When I was his age, I read books by Ralph Henry Barbour, but I read other things too. On Saturday afternoons I studied Talmud with my father. Jason should be interested in the world, in history, and in how things work. He should read about President Roosevelt and the Depression and the internal combustion engine and why we won the war.

Ah, but he does—he reads everything. He devours books, Mrs. Kachulis said. I've never met a boy more curious.

He's a strange one, my father said. That's true enough. You never know what goes on in that beautiful head of his, behind those golden curls. He certainly doesn't think like you and me.

For our history project, he did a report on lend-lease, Mrs. Kachulis continued. He made marvelous drawings of battleships and destroyers and fighter-bombers. He made a meticulous chart showing how U.S. industry mobilized miraculously for the war effort. I put his work on display for the entire school to see.

He's no slouch, my father said. His hand moved toward my head as if to ruffle the curls. Then, without touching me, his hand retreated to the back of his own head, to the spot where all the hair began, and he scratched himself there. We have to get home, he said. Your mother will be waiting for lunch.

Demeter was the goddess of agriculture and fruitfulness, the protectress of marriage, the mother of Bacchus. I liked the name Bacchus because it had two c's in it. I liked the name Demeter because it was the name of a rookie outfielder for the Brooklyn Dodgers—Don Demeter— I'd been following since he came up from Fort Worth in the Minor Leagues. Despite his frail gifts, I hoped Demeter might someday become the heir to Duke Snider's centerfield kingdom. In his first at bat in the Majors, pinch hitting against Don Liddle, and the very first time he swung a bat, Demeter blasted a home run.

Each week when we met in the children's room of the library, Mrs. Kachulis asked me what I was reading. Each time she found me there, sitting at one of the low blond wood tables, or on the wine-colored carpeting near the far wall, she seemed as surprised and delighted as she was the first time. On the third Saturday we met, she told me to come with her to where the grown-up books were.

And after that first time, she took me with her to the stacks every week. The stacks were positioned directly behind the squared-off area where you checked your books in and out, there for you as you entered or left the library. The stacks were dark—you could switch lights on yourself for whichever aisle you were using, and Mrs. Kachulis would walk along, singing to herself in Italian—she loved opera, would sometimes stop class, clap her hands, and proceed to tell us the story of one—taking down books and handing them to me even while she kept walking and singing. Try this one and tell me what you think of it, she'd say, and pass the book backwards to me as she moved forward.

I had often become attached to ballplayers simply because of the way their names sounded or were spelled: Ramazotti, Lavagetto, Medwick, Jorgenson, Loes, Mikses, Cimoli, Roebuck. Now it was the same with names of authors: Shellabarger, Undset, Fuchs, Yerby, Zugsmith, Slaughter, Ullman, Wouk, Buck, Brace, Cather, Saroyan, Baasch, Jewett, Bemelmans, Lagerkvist . . .

In class, when I'd finished my work before others had, I'd tell her about the books—not *about* them really, for what I did was simply to retell the stories. When I was done, or when we had to stop so the class could continue, she'd smile at me and say, Oh you're such a careful reader, Jason. I love having you tell me stories.

I never thought Mrs. Kachulis was a beautiful woman, but I loved her smile more than any smile in the world, since when she offered it to me I felt that no least part of it was meant for anyone else. Some of the students called her Mrs. Horseface because of how large her teeth were and the way her long jaw quivered slightly when she laughed. I loved her more because they mocked her. Had I been strong enough to defend her with my fists, I would have, but knowing that I could not defeat *all* the boys who made fun of her, and that, therefore, when the fight was over they would only mock us both, I did nothing. Except to imagine a time when my mother might die, when my father might, in his grief, despair, and when I would be put up for adoption. Then Mrs. Kachulis would put out her arms and embrace me. Of course I'll take you as mine, she said.

Mrs. Kachulis never told me what she herself thought of books or which ones she liked more than others and I never asked. This was so partly because I was afraid I might discover we disagreed, and partly because what she preferred to do was to tell me about the lives of authors, of what they did when they were not writing. Most writers, even if they were doctors or statesmen, explorers, gamblers, or scientists, had had ordinary and lonely childhoods, she said. What made them different was how much time they had spent living inside their imaginations. That was why she thought I might be a writer someday, for despite all the words and energy I summoned up to retell the stories of others, she seemed to know what I dimly perceived—that I had worlds of my own inside me I'd never told anyone about, and that they were as terrifying as they were beautiful.

So I said I would write a book for her. At night, after my parents and sisters were asleep, I sat up in my bed and, writing by flashlight, I began. When I wrote, I felt as exhilarated as I did when I read my favorite books, except that when I was done writing I felt both happier and more exhausted. My story was about a young baseball player who contracts an incurable disease, leaves the Major Leagues after one glorious season in which he's both Rookie of the Year and Most Valuable Player—and journeys around the world on a boat he builds himself, having dangerous and splendid adventures at various islands, and in exotic ports in Africa, Asia, South America, Australia, and Greenland. Pursued by envious enemies, his great desire is to meet as many worthy people as he can and to tell them the story of his life—of all he's learning in the time left to him before he must die.

Each Monday morning I brought in a new chapter and each Monday morning, after the Pledge of Allegiance, Mrs. Kachulis said: And now it's time to hear Jason read to us from his book. Then I'd rise from my seat and walk to the front of the room and read. When I was done my classmates applauded—some even whistled—and afterward, when we had conversation time, or at lunch, or recess, or after school, they'd come up to me, always wanting to know the same thing: what happens next?

Some promised to be my best friend if I told them—*Tell me, tell me,* they'd implore—but the truth was that until I sat up in bed by myself, picked up my pencil, watched the scenes begin to take place in my mind and began to translate what I saw into words, I myself never really knew the answer.

Now I am a grown man. I still live in Brooklyn, within walking distance of my childhood home and library. I am forty-eight years old, divorced twice, a full-time single parent. My one child, Carolyn, is nine years old. I am presently involved with a woman, Lynne Douglas. She is thirty-seven years old, also divorced twice, the full-time single parent of a seven-year-old boy named Timothy.

We met in the children's room of the library. Things happened quickly, with great heat. On Saturday mornings we came, regularly, to leave Carolyn and Timothy in the library and to adjourn to her apartment or mine, for this was the only time all week when our apartments were available to us—the only time when our children were not at home while we were not at work.

The first time we went to her apartment and she mounted me, this is what she said: We can do anything we want, Jason—anything we can imagine—anything at all.

Lynne is a lawyer specializing in property law. She teaches at Brooklyn Law School, is a consultant to a public television series about citizens' legal rights. I am a science writer, executive editor of the textbook division of a large publishing house. In addition to the writing I myself do, I oversee a staff of nine writers. We write of recent discoveries about why and how things are: about plate tectonics, neurobiology, black holes, the origin of the universe, punctuated equilibrium, frozen stars, the structure of matter, neural plasticity, the chemistry of the brain. My own special interest, about which I have written a short and well-received book, is grand unification theory, a theory that gathers into its ken all the phenomena of physics, excepting gravity: from the squealing of tires to the shining of the stars, from radioactivity to the blazing of the sun, the fuel-injected engine, the compass needle, the magnetic cartridge, the microchip, and nuclear fission.

After the first time we made love, when Lynne said to me that she had but ten percent of her brain left, I found myself talking to her of the major prediction of grand unification theory—that the proton, a subatomic particle out of which all matter is created, will decay, and its consequence: that all substance dissolves into light.

I'll say, Lynne said. She glowed. The brain, I told her, contrary to popular belief, was not at all like a computer. It was anything but binary. A given neuron may have several thousand synaptic connections with other neurons. And if, as we believe, it has 10^{11} neurons, then it has at least 10^{14} synapses. The number of possible synaptic connections among nerve cells in any human brain, therefore, is virtually without end. The number of possible interconnections between the cells in a single human brain is greater than the number of atoms in the universe.

Are you done? she asked, and when I said that I was, we went at each other again, on the carpeting beside her bed, until she whispered that what was left of her brain had melted to pure heat and light, to the beginning of time.

While she slept I lay awake, my fingertips caressing her forehead, circling the bones around her eyes. I thought, with pleasure, of quarks, which make up the proton, of how they combine into a new particle, survive briefly, and decay, either into original elements or into something else: an anti-electron. And here the strange and wonderful thing occurs, and that it does had never occurred to me in precisely this way before.

The process of decay allows the proton to transform itself into two elements—a pi meson and an anti-electron—that race away from each other, and decay into light itself. It is the remarkable prediction of grand unification theory, then, that since all things are made of protons, and all things decay, then all things glisten.

When Lynne woke I spoke the words that had come to me, words that named both what I felt and what I thought: We are composed, I said, of incipient radiance.

You're a wonderful man, she said.

We met at the library for eleven consecutive weeks. We did not see each other at any other time. We did not go out for dinner or to the movies together, or to the park or to museums with our children. We did not call each other, at home or at work. I did not send her flowers or playful notes, and she did not send me frivolous gifts and clever cards. Did we miss each other, during the six days we were apart? I couldn't tell. Neither of us ever addressed the subject.

When we talked, we talked about our work and about our children. We shared the problems of single parenting—the frustrations and joys, the emotional burdens and logistical complexities of doing it all ourselves: chauffeuring, car pools, music lessons, athletic teams, medical and dental appointments, emotional burnout, housekeeping chores— and we shared, too, a firm belief that, to our surprise—since we had previously been so invested in family life—we thought it better for children to be brought up by a single parent than by a couple. Because our children were aware that while they were left in the library we were elsewhere, and because they asked about the future—would they become brother and sister?—Lynne bought us T-shirts to wear in our apartments that she'd had imprinted with two words: *Separate Households.*

Three Saturdays ago, when we returned to the library shortly before noon, our children were gone. Notes were tacked to the corkboard next to the checkout desk in the children's room, each with our name on it, along with the simple declarative sentence: Your child has been towed.

We laughed. We asked the librarian if she had seen our children. She had—during morning story hour—but not since then. We looked around. We walked through the library and searched all rooms, stacks, bathrooms, closets. We went outside and walked, in opposite directions, around the block, returning to the library entrance. We went back inside and searched again. We spoke to the head librarian. She telephoned the police station and told us that the officer on duty advised us to come down.

We hurried. The officer at the desk, a handsome young man named Galen Kelly, took the information from us and asked if we could supply him with photos. Lynne took a photo from her purse and I took one from my wallet: head and shoulder shots against blue pastel backgrounds, taken by school photographers. Officer Kelly advised us to check our apartments, to notify friends, relatives, and neighbors, to inform the schools. He made several phone calls, but came up with no information about children resembling Timothy or Carolyn. He suggested we go to our homes and check there, and then check the library again. He asked if he could keep the notes and run them through the police laboratory.

Although he would, of course, send all data about our children to the National Center for Missing and Exploited Children, he added that, in his experience, the Missing Children problem was overblown by the media. Most missing children were not missing at all: they merely crossed state or city lines, after separations and divorces, to return to one or another parent. The greater problem, about which nobody was talking, he said, was missing parents.

We thanked him and left. I went to my apartment but Carolyn was not there. I checked in her closet, under her bed, on the fire escape. I checked the refrigerator, the freezer, the hallway incinerator, our storage area in the building's cellar. I telephoned the library. I telephoned Lynne.

Maybe we're being punished, she said.

Oh Lynne, I said. Come on. What did we do except to have a good time—?

You don't understand anything, do you? she said. I'm not talking about right and wrong. What scares me is precisely that this seems to have happened so arbitrarily—*without* any discernible reference to who we are or what we've been doing. I just don't get it, Jason. That's all I mean.

I thought of Schrodinger's Cat. I said so to Lynne—that perhaps our children were actually in their rooms while we were talking on the phone, but that each time we looked in their rooms, they disappeared.

She found no humor in my remark. I had thought Lynne a woman who knew what she wanted from life and went after it, who was not subject to panic when she didn't immediately get what she was after. When she spoke now, however, her voice reeked of desperation. What if they never return? she said. I've already fantasized the abuse Timothy might suffer, the feelings I'll have when I see his picture on milk cartons, cereal boxes, movie screens. I've imagined his death and mutilation nine ways till Sunday. I can deal with facts, Jason. But what if we simply never know what happens? What if this waiting for the news never ends?

I recalled a joke my father loved to tell, about the Jew who sits at the train station, tearing his hair and wailing. What's the matter, his friend asks. I missed my train, the Jew replies, and recommences his wailing. When did it leave? Three minutes ago, the Jew says. Ach, his friend replies, waving away the Jew's suffering. From the way you were carrying on I thought you'd missed it by an hour!

Given Lynne's mood, I kept the joke to myself, and asked instead if she wanted me to come to her apartment. I left a message on my door for Carolyn, spoke to the doorman, to neighbors, and to the parents of some of Carolyn's friends. I informed them of what had happened. Everybody looked at me with a terrible mixture of sympathy and admiration—I was, after all, an anomaly: a single hard-working man who was parenting a single child full-time—and assured me that Carolyn was a good and sensible girl, that she had probably wandered off for a while along Flatbush Avenue, or to Prospect Park, or to a friend's house, and that she would soon come home.

Carolyn did not return that day, or the next. Lynne and I took turns staying in each other's apartments. We drank heavily, watched movies on our VCRs, and slept. We neither talked nor touched.

On Monday we returned to our jobs. On Monday evening Officer Kelly visited me at home. He took fingerprints, hair samples, the pajamas from under Carolyn's pillow. He sat with me in the kitchen and wrote down a family history. I told him about Carolyn's birth, about Carolyn's mother, about Carolyn's early years, about my first divorce, and about my divorce from Carolyn's mother. I gave him the names, addresses, and phone numbers of my two ex-wives. I spoke of Carolyn's schooling, her habits, her hobbies, her idiosyncracies, her favorite books and television shows. I talked about how wonderful it felt, in the simplest way, when, in traffic or in a crowded store, she took my hand, or when she looked up at me in an elevator, say, and asked me a question to which I knew the answer. I told Officer Kelly about how hurt I'd been when Carolyn's mother left us, about my drinking problem, about the arrangement Lynne and I had been developing. I left nothing out, yet I sensed that he found my account cold, that he did not believe I truly loved my daughter.

When he left, to visit Lynne and secure data from her, I telephoned and told her he was on his way. She asked if I would stay with her after he left. I arrived at her apartment near midnight. She took some tranquilizers and a glass of bourbon. We sat in her living room and had nothing to say to each other. I felt depleted. I didn't ask her about her day at work and she didn't ask me about mine. I didn't ask her about her interview with Officer Kelly and she didn't ask me about mine. I had no desire to touch her and I wondered about all those hours when, for eleven mornings, I'd been transported physically into a rapture beyond any I'd previously known. Where was it now? Where were the feelings that had, for a time, seemed to comprise the universe?

It was as if my memory were detached from my body, or, more exactly, as if, like a patient operated on for removal of the hippocampus, I was now destined to live forever in the present: to have permanently lost the ability to learn new things or to remember my own experiences. Like the patient who, distracted, has no memory of the person he has been talking to a moment before, I looked at Lynne now and wondered who she was. And if I had known her, what exactly was it I had known if I could conjure up no true memory of what it was I had felt when we'd been together?

On Saturday morning we went to the library. Carolyn and Timothy were not there. The librarian asked me about my father, whom she remembered from the years when I was a young boy. He died four years ago, I said. Had I heard that Mrs. Kachulis had passed away only two months before? Cancer of the spine. She was sixty-eight years old. What of her daughter Demeter, I asked. The librarian said that the less I knew of Demeter the better. Demeter had not turned out well. The last anyone had heard, Demeter was wandering in the West somewhere. Demeter had not come to the funeral.

Lynne sat at one of the low tables on the far side of the room, her hands clasped in front of her. Was she afraid she would forget Timothy—all they had done together, all he was? Old memories, I wanted to explain to her, are rarely lost, are impervious to anything short of brain damage. New memories, in comparison, are fragile, though about memory itself, its structure and architecture, we still knew virtually nothing. Why is it that almost all children have virtually perfect photographic memories, yet lose these at about the time they learn to read and write? Persisting photographic memory—iconic memory—is much more common in adults of preliterate cultures. Was learning to read and write, then, even as it worked to help us retain what was most beautiful, good, and true about our lives, joined in an eternal bond with the very loss of memory and feelings about those things we wished, by the act of reading and writing, to hold to?

Officer Kelly visited me each night that week. He was the only person who seemed concerned. Friends, neighbors, relatives, and school officials stopped inquiring. Officer Kelly sat in my kitchen and asked me about my day at work, about Carolyn, about my relationship with Lynne. I spoke to him of what I was working on at the office, of theories and mysteries concerning memory, evolutionary change, the origin of time, the riddle of space, the psychoneurological basis of feeling.

We watched ballgames and movies together. He talked to me of his life as a policeman, its banality and violence. I continued to tell him everything I remembered about Carolyn and our life together, but the more I told, the less I felt I knew. It was as if by remembering and naming what had been, I was losing the very things I was hoping to find. On Friday night of the second week after Carolyn's disappearance, Officer Kelly said that it would make no difference to him—to his regard for me—if I never spoke about Carolyn again. He would not think my love for her, or my feeling of loss, any less authentic.

The following morning, when Lynne and I were sitting in the children's room at the library, a young man dressed in jeans and a red and blue checkered sport shirt, came up to us and asked if our children had returned yet. How did you know—? I asked, and then realized that the young man was Officer Kelly, dressed in civilian clothes. He told us that he had resigned from his job as a policeman. He assured us that our cases would be followed up on a regular basis, through regular channels. He sat at our table and began to talk about himself. He had no parents, no brothers and sisters, no wife or ex-wives, no children. Until the age of twenty-one, he said, he'd had only one desire: to be a policeman. He'd fulfilled that desire, and didn't see why, at the age of twenty-five, he should still be bound by a dream he'd had when he was five, or ten, or twenty. He needed some time to reconsider his life. I asked him if he wanted to stay with me. He thanked me and offered, in exchange, to take care of the apartment while I was at work—to do the shopping, the housekeeping, the preparation of meals. When Carolyn returned, he would, of course, leave.

Lynne had supper with us that night. We ate by candlelight and I repeated a saying of my father's, that when you lost the most precious jewel, you searched for it with a candle that cost but a penny. Neither Lynne nor Galen reacted. Our children might be lost, I added, but our childhoods were not. We could talk to one another of all we remembered and when we were done remembering, I said, we could make up stories and give them to one another. Again, neither Lynne nor Galen showed any reaction. They ate in silence, and while they did, I tried to imagine what they were thinking or imagining or feeling. I could not. So I suggested that Lynne consider moving in with us. She could sleep in Carolyn's room and Galen could sleep in the living room. There was no reason, until we knew what would happen next, for any of us to be alone.

What Is the Good Life?

So, I asked. Are we in love then?

Probably, she said.

Probably?

She laughed. The surface of the Mediterranean was smooth, and I imagined peeling off a thin layer of it, offering it to Aldy—I imagined her furling it around her neck, smiling lovingly at me. I imagined that I could, by such an act, please her in a way no one else had ever pleased her.

She took my hand. But here, she said. Here, Carl. Come. This is the place I wanted to show you—where the car plunged through. It landed down there.

She pointed to a spot about forty feet below, told me that Doctor Duplay, head of neurosurgery at Nice Hospital, was convinced Stephanie had tried to pull up the hand brake. There were other stories—that Stephanie, and not her mother, had been the one driving; that Prince Rainier covered this up since Stephanie was under age; that the Prince's marriage, twenty years before, had been part of a deal whereby the United States—with the French about to withdraw militarily from NATO—would secure a strategic base in this part of the world; and that the death itself was not accidental—that it was, instead, merely the last bit of a long and lousy piece of foreign intrigue. Aldy believed none of these stories—she believed that Stephanie had, in fact, tried to pull up the brake and save her mother's life.

Will you say so?

Yes. God, but the press went after her—not because she survived and her mother died, but more, I think, because she didn't attend the funeral.

I kissed the back of Aldy's neck, watched the frail gold hairs there uncurl. I thought of how peaceful I'd felt the night before, driving home from Nice airport, along the coast—of how happy I'd been, knowing Aldy would be waiting for me.

I've never felt this way before, I said. I never imagined I could love anybody the way I love you. I'm still surprised.

That you love me?

That someone like you finds me interesting. Sometimes I just want to tell you *everything*—all I feel, all I've done.

The height must be getting to you, she said. It's eight hundred feet above sea level here.

Don't, I said. Please. Don't make light of what I say. Tell me instead. Tell me what *you* feel.

You're the dearest man I've ever known. She kissed me gently, on the mouth. I'm surprised, Carl. Astonished really, by what you make me feel.

She turned away from me again, so that she too was looking down at the sea. We stood close to the wall of the Moyenne Corniche, and she leaned back into me, then reached behind, slipping her hand under my shirt, letting it rest against my stomach.

This is the way it was, she said. The gear shift was in drive. The parking brake was up three notches. Grace lay unconscious in the back seat. They pulled her through the rear window of the car. Stephanie suffered a hairline fracture of one of the vertebrae on her neck, but that wasn't what kept her from the funeral.

Shock?

Yes. She'd taken it in the neck before—no pun intended—for absenting herself from obligation: she stayed away from the grand ball the night before her sister Caroline's wedding. Why? Because her mother had denied her request to wear slacks.

So then, I asked, *are* the rich different from you and me?

I wouldn't know, she said. I'm very rich.

And very beautiful. Sometimes, even when we're together, I don't believe it—that a woman as beautiful as you cares for me the way you do.

Stop. She pulled away. I've told you not to tell me that anymore. Why should I value what I didn't cause and can't help?

I didn't apologize for what I'd said. I lifted her chin, kissed her.

Aldy spoke: Here's what Stephanie said—"I don't understand why people are interested in me. I want to be an ordinary girl. I can't stand for my friends to call me princess."

But you're not her friend. You're a writer—a reporter.

I have an appointment with her tomorrow. And I'll interview Caroline next week, while you're away. Which reminds me—my father wants to meet you. He'll be here this weekend.

Then he approves?

Princeton *uber alles,* Carl. She moved her hand down, below my belt buckle. I grew hard at once. You like it when I do this—here—don't you?

Yes.

I'm doing this at the very spot where Grace Kelly's favorite car, her brown Rover 3500, an eight-cylinder automatic, plunged through the crash barrier. Are you thinking of Grace Kelly?

No.

Do you still love me?

Is this a trick question?

In third grade, at the International School in Geneva, I was madly in love with a Danish boy named Peter. I sat behind him and slipped notes to him, under my desk and through the opening to his seat. "Do you love me? Please answer yes or no." When he wrote "yes" and passed the note back I'd write a new note: "Do you *still* love me?"

Her white blouse shone in the sun as if, I thought, it were made of fiberglass. I moved a hand to her breast, but she pushed it away.

I asked you a question and I expect an answer: Do you still love me?

Yes.

I touched her, at the hip, leaned on her there, for when she began to make love to me like this, I became dizzy. She lifted my hand. Don't move, she said. Don't touch me. I used to dream of doing you this way. Even at Princeton. Her mouth was at my ear. Some dreams do come true, you see.

I could hear my heart pumping, could feel blood swirling through me. I closed my eyes, saw blood pouring down the mountain, rushing past cypress and wild olive trees, circling the highway from Roc Agel to La Turbie, from La Turbie to where we were, and then down again, down into the green sea.

Do you recall what she looked like? Aldy asked. Do you remember her in *Rear Window?*

No.

She was flawless. Pure Irish cream. Would you like it if I looked like her? Or like Stephanie? I could talk with Stephanie about us getting together—getting it on together, to be exact. Stephanie trusts me, you see. Why? Because she fears I may find her uninteresting. Aldy stopped. *Rear Window*—it just occurred to me—they pulled her through the rear window. Character is fate, yes? So tell me. Tell me what you want, Carl. I want to give you everything you want.

I want *you*. I want—

She placed her free hand over my mouth. No, she said. Tell me something else: Will you talk with my father about how I lusted after you when we were at Princeton? My father saw you play against Yale and Colgate. He said you had a superb spin move—that you could stop and turn on a dime. He said you were amazing in the open court, that you had a marvelous sense of where you were. Like Bill Bradley. She leaned her cheek against my chest. I love to hear your heart, she said. I love to know how much I excite you. I'll do anything for you.

Just love me.

Shh. Princess Grace dated the Shah of Iran when she was in acting school, Aldy said. She dated Onassis. She was a guest on his yacht, where the bar stools were made from the scrotums of whales. Frank Sinatra was her close personal friend. Frank Sinatra's close personal friends sell crack and heroine to children on street corners.

Why are you telling me this now?

She pushed me against the wall until I felt the warm stone cut into the small of my back. She dated and fucked the scum of the world, Aldy said. She was President of the local Le Leche League. She had two miscarriages. She said that a woman's natural role is to be a pillar of the family. It's their *physiological* job. The emancipation of women, she stated, had made them lose their mystery. Am I still a mystery to you, Carl? In what ways do you *not* still know me?

I said nothing. I watched her eyes, the strange glazed surface, the fire below. Aldy kept talking, whispering in my ear: When Marilyn died, people in mental hospitals went berserk. When Grace died, nothing. Flowers and diplomats. Grace would never have done to you what I'm doing now.

I dug my nails into her back. Grace didn't drink and she didn't smoke and she didn't take pills and she worried about her weight. Women only work, she claimed, to avoid their true responsibilities. She was as dull as coal dust in a dark Pennsylvania mine.

You know why I love you? I asked.

Tell me.

Because you do your homework so well.

Aldy smiled. I'm considering a series: Marilyn, Liz, Jackie, Madonna, Jane. You've heard of "Lifestyles of the Rich and Famous"? My series will be called "Leftovers of the Rich and Famous." We photograph the insides of their refrigerators. We run elaborate layouts of their bathrooms and bedrooms. The back seats of their cars. When they're gone. When they're dead.

Her touch was gentler than her voice. Are you happy, Carl? she asked. I like hearing you breathe against my neck. Will you come in my hand? I want you to. Now, Carl. It was a safe life for you here until I showed up. That's what you said to me, our first night together—afterward. Remember? You said you'd had a safe life here until I entered it. Now you don't.

The villa Aldy's father was staying in for the weekend was in Cap d'Antibes, less than a quarter mile from the villa that had once belonged to Somerset Maugham. I sat on the patio, gazing at the green sea, Aldy beside me, while her father poured wine for us, talked to Aldy about the Riviera, about who—Picasso, Modigliani, Chagall, Francoise Sagan, Graham Greene, Brigitte Bardot, Jean Marais, Jimmy Baldwin, the Countess Tolstoy—had lived in which villas and which villages, about who she would write about when she was done with the royal family. Aldy said she was going to write about me, of course. She was going to interview me to find out what a gifted and graceful athlete imagined life would be like when his playing days were over. What would he think and feel during those hours and years when his body could no longer do what it was born to do so well? After me she would interview Baryshnikov and Michael Jordan, Nureyev and Magic Johnson and Martina and Gretzky and Flo Jo. She already had a title for the series—"Life after Grace."

Aldy's father asked me questions and I answered him, explained how the system worked in Europe—what American players like myself were paid, how each team was allowed to have two of us on its squad, what the differences in the rules were: a lane that opened out, zone defenses to keep the scores down, a thirty-second time clock. The World Championship would be held in Spain during the second and third weeks in June. My team, representing Nice, was the best in France, but the French teams were invariably weak internationally, inferior to the Italians, Russians, Spanish, and Yugoslavians—even to the Greeks and Israelis.

Aldy leaned over me, kissed me, upside down. Her tongue tasted like wine. Carl came here in search of the good life, she said. Carl majored in philosophy. He can tell you about the difference between an object and the name of an object. He can explain Wittgenstein's theories of epistemology.

Aldy left. I've never seen my daughter happier, her father said. She's always been amusing, if in a mordant way—life after grace is right—but she seems to be truly enjoying herself, even her cleverness—in a new way. You're a good influence on her, Carl. I'm pleased. He paused. Only she shouldn't have followed you here. I warned her. She's in danger, you know. They'll use her to get to me.

They knew that an American airliner was going to be blown out of the sky, and they knew who was going to do the job. Americans and Jews would be killed. They were trying to make a deal, but things were getting tricky, and if they were unable to come to terms, they would, afterward—were their foreknowledge exposed—need deniability. I could help. And if I helped, not only would I be aiding my country and my people, but I would also be saving the woman I loved.

I would not have to know anything. In fact, the less I knew, the better; not knowing reduced my liability and vulnerability. My presence was, as Aldy said, merely a convenience. As a regular part of my vocation—my team's schedule—I frequently crossed borders. I met with Russians, Israelis, Greeks. I would be given messages I would not understand, to deliver to people I did not know. It would not be unusual for a basketball star to talk to a fan, to give an autograph, to buy American magazines at kiosks, to order room service, to celebrate after a victory or, after a loss, to keep to himself—or to brood during long solitary walks. The championships in Madrid—my two weeks there—were an ideal cover, their timing excellent. Now that Aldy was here they would use her—to pressure her father for concessions. Now that Aldy was with me—was being threatened—how could I not be involved?

I thought we believed in never submitting to terrorists, I said.

Everyone submits to terrorists, he said. Even the Israelis. How else did they get into Entebbe? It's all deals. Like point spreads, yes? The best team usually wins, but there can be refinements, profits for shrewd and knowledgeable bettors along the way.

Then you fix games too.

If we also saw to that, where would the sport of it be?

Nobody gives us a chance, but I want to win, I said. And I was angry with myself at once, for saying so.

Then forget all the people on the plane you and I have never met, he said. Forget what Israel will do to civilians in retaliation. Forget the Israeli children who may be kidnapped, tortured, killed. Just think of Aldy.

You like this, I said. You get off on it, don't you?

Please. I *like* knowing that my career endangers my daughter—that it may result in her death? Don't be absurd.

No. You like the danger—the sport of it.

Aldy came toward us, carrying our Sunday lunch on a tray. I took the tray and set it on the table. So, she asked. What *is* the good life—have you decided?

We drove along the Costa del Sol, Stephanie singing to us from the tape deck: *Ouragan.*

She has no voice, I said.

But she has an island—Mauritius—and she's offered it to us.

If we have to escape?

If we want to. I won't write my article if you won't play in your game. We go to the airport, get on a plane, leave this world behind. Your choice.

You're not scared, then, are you.

No. Daddy's still Daddy. I don't expect to change him. I've lived with it—the threats, the games, the *stuff*—my whole life. Alas, he's not as mature as I am, yes? He still wants to change me, and he'll use anything—even you, sweetheart—to have his way.

Which is?

To get me to return home. He can't understand why a young woman with my gifts would want to spend her time writing about people less interesting than I am. He probably still thinks I should make a suitable marriage, breed grandchildren—the rest of that Wasp jazz. Strange. He has such conventional hopes for me, yet I often suspect he's secretly happy about my unconventional life—happy I'm like him in this.

In what?

My love of a free-lance existence, of danger. Nobody's ever owned Daddy. I was there once, eavesdropping, when they told him that if he didn't perform a certain act, his name would go to the top of a shopping list.

A shopping list?

He would be terminated with extreme prejudice. Eliminated. "You do what you have to do. I do what I have to do." That was all he said.

Maybe he staged the scene for your benefit.

I considered that.

Maybe your coming here—your pursuing me—is merely defiance of him.

Let's not be tedious, all right? If Daddy wants to reduce the fate of nations to the personal—Will the man save the girl?—that doesn't mean we have to do the same.

Perhaps you and your father have staged the whole thing these past few weeks, not because you're in danger, but to set me up, to use me.

She drew away slightly, said nothing for a while. I waited.

She turned off Stephanie's voice. I love you, Carl, she said. I love being with you. There isn't anything in life—no man or woman—I've ever loved or desired the way I love and desire you. And you're not forcing the words from me. It would be harder to hold them back than to let them flow. She smiled. Perhaps I lack the energy to hold back feelings that strong. It's a wonderful weakness you bring out in me. She touched my cheek. I can't wait to arrive in Madrid, to get to our room, to lounge there, to make love to you, to watch you dress, to see you play. This is the first time it's ever happened to me.

Love?

Being dazzled more in my life than in my fantasies. Caring about somebody else this way—wondering what that person thinks, and feels, and desires. She looked away. You've never let me down.

So far.

Don't, she said, and now she leaned on me, held tightly to my arm. Please.

I loved her most when she was like this—when I heard urgency in her voice, felt it in her touch. The softness of her lips, when they touched my cheek, chilled me. The road curved to the left and a wide arc of sky and beach stretched before us, as far as we could see. I imagined our car moving straight ahead, gliding soundlessly through air, landing far out to sea.

What Aldy desired most of all, she said, was to find something in her own life she could love as much as I loved playing ball. Now that she was falling in love with me, she said, she felt optimistic. She was only twenty-seven years old. Most things were still possible. She would never play in the NBA or be a chess master or a concert pianist. Certain kinds of genius flowered—and died—young, she said. Mozart, Keats.

Bias, I said.

Biased against what? I'm *for* you, Carl. Don't you understand? I may have joked, with Daddy present—irony always gives comfort—about aging athletes, but it does hurt, to think of what you may feel one day when your body won't do for you what it does so wonderfully now.

Not biased, I said. Bias. Len Bias. He was an All-American basketball player who overdosed on cocaine and died at the age of twenty-two—shortly after he was drafted by the Celtics.

Did you know him?

No.

Are you nervous? she asked.

About what will happen in the hotel room?

What else would I be referring to?

I'm nervous.

Has anyone contacted you?

Yes.

And—?

They gave me the date on which the plane will be blown up. It's the day you fly back to the States. You're safe, they assured me, but if I inform anyone of their plans, they'll transfer the bomb to your flight. If you cancel, they'll simply get to you some other way. If I cooperate and do what they ask, there's nothing to worry about. If your father is reasonable, nobody will be hurt.

Are you surprised?

No. I don't even know which side the person who called me was on. Maybe he didn't either.

She.

Aldy laughed. Affirmative action—on the job in international es-
pionage, she said. Sometimes I think the major part of their work, my
father and his counterparts, is simply keeping one another from the
unemployment lines. You threaten our operative, we'll threaten yours.
You bust our code, we'll bust yours. You get somebody to kill my kid, I'll
get somebody to butcher yours.

Why didn't you tell me you were planning to go back to the States
next week?

Because I didn't want to worry you before the championships. Because I thought this might happen. Because I wanted to be able to
escape, by myself or with you, if necessary. I spend a large portion of my
life devising contingency plans. It's one thing I'm good at.

True.

And because I promised the magazine I'd finish the article this
month—that I'd retrace the family's journey: from the peat bogs of
County Mayo to the pink palace in Monaco. From Rutland, Vermont,
where the clan first settled, to upstate New York, where they moved
next, to Schuylkill, Pennsylvania, where they settled at last.

And worked in coal mines?

Textile mills. She stopped. Damn! she said. I hate having to give
anybody reasons for what I do.

But you just did—and with great exactitude. You were ready for my
question.

For my important interviews, I always prepare especially well. Didn't
you say you loved me because of how well I did my homework? So
here's another question for you: What did you tell them when they
called?

To go fuck themselves.

She rested her head on my shoulder. My hero, she said.

Not quite.

Because saying yes would have implicated you and thereby involved
me? Or because you're like me—willful, competitive—even while you
fight *for* me—because above all what you want is *not* to give my father
what he wants?

Why answer? You seem to know what I think before I do—to have me
all figured out.

Not at all. Shit. She touched my hand. I'm sorry, she said. I watched
her eyes and saw something flicker there that I'd never seen before. I

thought: If a woman was beautiful, intelligent, wealthy, and gifted—if she was born and raised taking for granted that whatever she desired in life, she could have—how would she ever come to experience or feel anything that resembled doubt?

I meant to ask—are you pleased with how the article on Stephanie's coming? I asked.

She shrugged. Monaco's half the size of Central Park, she stated. Did you know that?

No.

Grace Kelly didn't get into the colleges of her choice—did you know that?

No.

Thanks, Carl. Thanks for asking about the article. Know what else?

What?

I'm glad I'm not Stephanie.

Me too.

Know what I'd love most of all?

No.

To have lots of *ordinary* conversations with you.

Yes.

She caressed my wrist. Do you remember your first day of grade school, Carl—who you held hands with, on line? she asked. Do you remember tying your shoelaces for the first time by yourself—or each of your teachers from each grade and what you imagined their lives were like when they weren't teaching?

Yes.

I used to dream about falling in love and when I did, I imagined that that's what people who were in love did—that that was how they knew it was true love: That, quite simply, they spent their time together telling each other the stories of their lives.

God created the world because He loved stories.

He did?

I laughed. Maybe. It's a saying I found in a novel—I hadn't remember it for years.

I haven't had much practice at this—at answering questions, at being in love. I'm fine at getting others to tell me their stories—it's my job—but I've never given anyone my own. I'm nervous.

I'm dangerous.

Yes.

Your father said that to me—that your being with me endangers you.

She touched my mouth with her fingers. Then let's just go. Please? Let's just go now. Let's go to that island you dream of, where nobody knows us, where we can tell each other the stories of our lives, and if ever we're done doing that, we'll just make things up. We can *lie*. We can imagine new lives and then live inside them.

You'd really do that, wouldn't you? If I said yes—if I drove to the airport instead of the hotel—you'd get on the plane with me and leave everything behind.

Yes.

You think we could make each other that happy.

Yes.

Beyond the pleasure principle is the reality principle.

Too bad.

Not at all. The reality principle protects our ability to experience pleasure.

Who cares? I don't want theories, Carl. I want you. I want us both to *live*. I've thought about it a good deal—I've thought it through, this far: If I can't have me, then nobody else can either.

I want you.

But you're choosing not to have me forever.

You're serious, aren't you—about leaving everything behind?

I suppose I am.

I thought of saying something about how unpleasant she became when she didn't get her way—how petulant—but I didn't. We drove on, not touching each other. A few miles past Castellon de la Plana, I turned inland. When the sea had disappeared behind us, Aldy spoke again: I once asked Daddy about what he actually did—about torture. I was eighteen years old, visiting him in Salzburg during winter break— the first time we were together, over here, after Mother's death. He told me not to worry. In my profession, he said, sadism is a liability.

A good line to give to a beloved and beautiful daughter. Eichmann loved children and dogs.

Be fair, Carl. Daddy's a kind man.

In his profession, kindness is an asset. If he enjoyed his work, he'd be less good at it. He murders people, Aldy.

Only out of choice.

Only out of *what?*

I laughed. Aldy turned away, and I pictured the green of the sea in her eyes. I said nothing to bring her back to me. In the distance I could see towns I would never enter, where people who spoke a language I didn't know would never know me.

They telephoned me too, Carl.

And—?

Daddy had already booked my flight back to the States. Under a different name. I have several passports—black wigs, thick glasses, various and cruel identities. Once I'm gone, you're free again. You'll have what you want, after all.

I'm free now, I said. I've never not been free.

She put her hand on top of mine, drew it to her, placed it on her lap, then lifted it so that it rested against her bare stomach. Her skin was warm. She unzipped her slacks.

You always do what you want, she said. It's why I love you. I can't ever make you do anything. I can't even make you love me.

It's why it's called love, I said. Because it's given freely.

And this? she said, pressing my hand with hers, moving it where she wanted it. Is this free too, or will you want something in return?

I said nothing. She pushed me deeper inside her.

I tried to withdraw my hand, but she held to me, told me not to stop.

You want to hurt me, don't you, she said. You despise me when I get like this. I know it. You're angry with me. You're furious. Tell me it's so. Tell me.

Yes. I want to hurt you.

Ah, she said. Self-knowledge is a wonderful thing.

She gasped. Deeper, she said. I want you deeper. Tell me what you want me to do for you later. Tell me. You can do anything you want to me. Anything you imagine. Please. And consider this too—it's all tax deductible—our travel, our room—your game, my article. So let's transact business, yes? Tell me: What *will* you feel ten years from now when some twenty-one-year-old boy, without thinking, skies over you on the court—does to you what you now do to others? What will you do when your glory days are done? Run summer camps for boys? Open bowling alleys or restaurants? Coach preppies at Princeton? Enter into partnership with your father-in-law?

She shuddered once, then again, then lay against my shoulder and whispered that she was sorry, that she wished she could have stopped herself from being the way she was.

You're trembling, I said.

You don't hate me then?

No.

Ask me a question—any question. Please? Ask me to do something for you.

Can you make a sentence using the words Euripides and Eumenides?

Euripides pants, Eumenides pants.

She laughed and when I laughed with her, the rage I'd been feeling slipped away. Her head was back, her eyes rolling up in their sockets, her golden hair streaming behind. She was gone with pleasure again. I thought of Grace Kelly, by Jimmy Stewart's side, his crutch near the couch on which they made love. I had lied to Aldy about *Rear Window,* and I knew it would please her if I said so. I said nothing. Aldy couldn't stop laughing. She told me how wonderful it was that I was such a great ballplayer—that I could go either way, that I was so good with either hand, that I had such a soft touch. Her mouth was wide open and I wanted to drift down, to drop inside. I wanted to taste her hair, to sleep inside her as if in warm water. I thought of sea anemones and they were high up in an ice-blue sky—thousands of them—and then, like silk parachutes, they all came floating slowly down.

I gave away more than six inches to Shea, point guard for Il Mesaggero Roma, but he was thin, with little upper-body strength, and I was doing what I wanted, wearing him down. They were ahead by one, in over-time, and I ran the base line, stopped, pivoted, and spun—not to get free, but so I could, reversing direction, ram my shoulder into his chest. I heard the air go out of him, then moved to the top of the key and the ball was there for me. I started to go up for the shot and Shea, hustling back on defense, was in the air to slap it away, but I was under him, a full step ahead, flying toward the basket. Their big man moved toward me, to cover for Shea—what I expected—and I fed off to his man, Boisvert, for an easy layup.

Now I was tight on Shea and I could see, in his eyes, that he could not understand where my stamina came from. I was not the player he

was—I didn't have his pure athletic gifts, but I was as strong now—
stronger—than I was at the game's start. It was always this way with me:
the longer I played, the stronger I got. Shea dribbled between his legs,
faked left, started right, and I was there, nice and low, my eyes on one
thing only—the ball—and I stripped it clean, headed for open court, felt
the cheering of the crowd inside my head as if the ocean were there. I
rose at the foul line, drifted up, all alone—suspended in air—and let the
ball slip from my fingertips, into the net. We were ahead by three with
twelve seconds left.

To everyone's surprise, Il Mesaggero Roma had given Shea a million-
dollar contract after his rookie year with the Celtics, but Shea's money,
like the words that came to me on the phone—from Aldy's father, from
others—was nothing to me. The only thing that mattered was what I
was actually doing. If Aldy was right in what she often said, that I had a
hard time trusting others—it was why, she laughed, imitating Garbo, I
wanted to be alone so much—it was not true that I didn't trust. I trusted
the ball. I trusted the net. I trusted my hands. The ball came to Shea
and I was on him—harassing, hawking, making him work to bring it up
court. I asked him what his accountant would do about taxes on his
windfall, if his Italian was improving. The sweat poured from him as if a
machine were pumping it through his pores. He was lean and sleek, but
if he was a greyhound, I thought, then I was a groundhog, and I could
rise up and snap his toes and heels off because my jaws were strong and
hungry, because my timing was fine, because I knew how to wait.

We trapped him as he came across the half-court line—six seconds
left—and, in desperation, he heaved the ball toward the far corner. Too
far. Out of bounds and I was already streaking across the court, taking
the ball out, handing it to Merle, our shooting guard, then taking it
back, going behind my back—first one way, then the other—and we
were home free and Shea knew it. I looked to the stands, saw Aldy
standing and cheering, looking the way she might have looked before I
knew her: a happy and beautiful young college girl at an Ivy League
game. The buzzer sounded, my teammates surrounded me, lifting me
from the floor, screaming at me in French that they loved me. Shea
made his way through the bodies, shook my hand. I wanted to tell him
that even though what they were offering me—Aldy's life, a challenging
government job when my playing days were over, the opportunity to

travel the world alone on a generous expense account—was less lucrative than what he received, I had nonetheless turned it down.

You were wonderful, Aldy said. She took my hand. I saw tears come into her eyes. I'm surprised, she said.

That I was wonderful?

At what I feel.

We were eating dinner in a small restaurant just off the Rue d'Alcala, a block south of the Place de Cybèle. I don't think I ever saw you play with such ferocity. You were wild, Carl. Pure energy, sheer grace.

It's weird, I said. When I'm out there playing, it's like you said—I can't remember ever thinking of what to do next. I move before I think.

Moveo ergo sum?

Something like that. Only listen—before the game—they called again. They asked me to lose. Why? How would our losing—we were supposed to lose anyway—but how would that transmit a message? I don't get it.

They just wanted to see if they could control you. Or perhaps not. They're like you, yes? Sometimes they don't have the vaguest idea as to why they do something—they just want to keep things in motion. Maybe they figured if they asked you to lose, you'd be sure to be fired up, to defy them. Maybe they bet a wad of money on your team as a way of transferring funds.

If you're so rich, how come you're smart?

Yeah. She shrugged, seemed embarrassed. She started to say something, but couldn't speak. I watched her swallow, lick her lips to moisten them. I know all about my supposed sense of entitlement, how assured I seem, she said, and it occurred to me that had she not previously rehearsed what she was now saying, she could not have gotten the words out. My intelligence is the only thing I've ever felt truly confident about, she said. I believe in it, in its chemistry. I was doing an article last year—new discoveries about how the brain works— and I became fascinated by the study of faces, by how and why the brain is so impressed—actually, literally—with faces. Infants know faces much earlier than we ever thought. When they can barely make out anything else they can pick out their own mothers from hundreds of others. Mere millimeters of difference in configuration, affect, coloring, and babies live and die by it. Maybe love *is* chemistry, Carl. The way you look and move and sound and smell excites a few neurons in a small fold of some obscure lobe.

A lobe of brain, a jug of wine, and thou?

She smiled. The more we know about how the brain works—how mysterious it all is—the more it seems the poets and philosophers were right all along. Love enters through the eyes and travels to the heart, except it first detours to . . . She stopped. Why am I mouthing off like this? she asked. Why do I love to talk to you so much? And yet it's not what either of us *says* that matters. It's something more purely physical. I perceive you—your goodness, yourself—the way I feel the sun on my back, or a stone in my mouth.

I took her hand, spoke: Carl the philosopher says, "All philosophers are liars." I waited, spoke again: I love you, Aldy.

Epimenides' paradox, right?

Right.

We feel before we think.

Yes.

Alzheimer patients will recognize famous people—tests show they react to them, that their bioelectric fields—the conductivity in their skin—indicate recognition, even though they can't name them. We see somebody and we know we know the person, though we may have to go through an internal multiple choice test as to when and where and who to get to the name. I say to you, "Look—there's Grace Kelly," and you turn and say, "Oh yes—there she is." With somebody famous—Grace or Marilyn or Liz—we don't, unless we're brain damaged, respond, "Grace Kelly—who's she?"

Grace Kelly is dead.

Probably.

Probably?

We laughed. She pressed her lips to my wrist. I know I love you, Carl. I can't ever get you out of my mind, even when you're beside me, even when I'm touching you. Chemical basis or Platonic myth—who cares?—but it seems true, after all, what lovers have always said to one another: I feel as if I've known you forever.

We always know more than we can say.

If you're making fun of me, don't. Please.

I'm not making fun of you.

The old Platonic stuff about knowledge being memory brought to light—that knowledge is always within us, and that what we think is knowledge is merely remembering what we didn't know we'd forgotten—I fell for that big once upon a time.

You know what I'm wishing now?

Tell me.

That I'd said yes when you made your offer. I wish we hadn't come here. I'd love to be somewhere else now, with you—somewhere so peaceful we wouldn't ever have to speak or to know the difference between a thought and a feeling—to be so far from anyone and anything we knew that all we'd need to do, to tell each other our desires, would be to touch.

What stopped you?

Your voice. There was something desperate in it that put me off. Desperate, and angry.

You felt that?

Yes.

Then it was there, she said. Aldy's cave—not unlike Plato's. Which reminds me. Did you know that Rainier has a thing about animals—a private menagerie? Tigers and monkeys and wolves. He gave me a tour. He's an interesting man. He knows my father.

Your father wasn't at the game. He telephoned me this afternoon from a hotel in Madrid. Do you think he's all right?

I'm sorry, she said.

For what?

For changing the subject. You were very happy, talking like that just before—talking *with* me.

Yes.

She stood. I'll be right back.

She started to move away, but I reached out, held her wrist. She looked at my fingers, pressed against her tanned skin, said something about Cary Grant on the rooftops of Monaco—they had filmed *To Catch a Thief* there—holding on to Grace.

Your skin is ice cold, I said.

Let me call Daddy and then I'll come back. I promise.

You're frightened.

I love you. I'm glad I saw you win. It must be a wonderful feeling, to be able to do something you love so well. Her eyes shone, so that the green seemed flecked with blue. I thought of warm rain on a calm sea. It's strange, to desire you so, Carl—to feel so wild with you, yet the part you stir most deeply in me is tenderness. That's what I've been wanting to tell you, what I never expected—what I never knew I knew, yes? I feel an enormous urge to take care of you, sweetheart. I've never wanted to take care of anybody before in my life.

Then, before I could respond, she had kissed me—I let go of her wrist, to touch her face—and was gone.

Aldy's father sat across from me, where Aldy had been. A few minutes after Aldy left, to telephone him, he had appeared, had told me that we were to stay and talk for a while, until someone came for us. If all went well, Aldy would be waiting for me in our room. I wondered about the switch they had made—father for daughter—and if and when they had arranged it. But I asked no questions. The point of our conversation was for me to learn and know as little as possible. Think of our talk, Aldy's father said, as philosophic minimalism. After all, didn't Aristotle say that philosophy began in wonder—didn't Socrates believe that the wisest man was he who knew that he knew nothing?

Then to know you is to know nothing, I said.

Precisely.

In the hotel I moved from the sitting room to the bedroom. Aldy was there, under the covers, a small bullet hole in her forehead. Her expression was calm, as if she had not been surprised.

Her father covered her, said that they would never kill him, because he knew too much. If he died, his knowledge, which others coveted, went to the grave with him. Aldy had known nothing and was, therefore, expendable.

Then you lied to me, I said.

Of course. You knew that, didn't you? Didn't Carl the philosopher say that all philosophers are liars?

I thought of lifting him and throwing him against a wall, or through a window, but the thought—the picture—of what would happen if I did—of what would ensue—was there before the feeling: he would be prepared for my anger. He was expecting it, I knew, and would be armed, and though he might not kill me, he could wound me in severe ways, so that I might never play again.

He had lost somebody he had known for her entire life, I thought, whereas I had lost somebody I had hoped to know for my entire life. Neither of us seemed surprised at Aldy's death. Neither of us showed any outward signs of grief, and I did not sense this was because our feelings lay too deep for tears.

Will you mourn? I heard Aldy ask.

Probably, I said.

Probably?

Aldy's father talked to me about the arrangements—how her death would be reported, how her body would be taken away and cared for, what he and I would do next. Our best hope lay in trusting each other. He touched my arm, said that he had tried to get to the restaurant before Aldy left—to intercept her, to propose a plan that would save us all—but that she had lied to him on the phone, saying that she would wait for him with me, that the three of us could have dessert and coffee together. He said that if she had not deceived him and returned to the hotel by herself, without me, she would now be alive and I—so she had believed—would be dead. They only wanted one body and they preferred, given a choice, to use the less newsworthy one of those available.

He left the room, and I heard him speaking on the phone, attending to details. I did not look at Aldy again. I wanted to think of the small hole in her forehead, the smudge of powder, as a blemish that, bringing imperfection, would have pleased her. She could at last be valued for qualities other than the physical beauty that had been hers and that she had not chosen. She would not be able to interview me in order to tell the story of my life, and I thought of saying to her that with nobody to tell my story, my life would remain unexamined and unverified. It would not, however, she replied, remain unlived. I could now have, she said, what I had desired before I knew her. It was why, she suspected, I was feeling so little after she, to her surprise, had been feeling so much. I could now be more alone than I had ever, in my philosophy, dreamt possible.

In Memory of Jane Fogarty

N THE GLOOM and fog of Dublin, who'll ever notice my difference?

Your difference, she replied.

My difference, damn it! You know what I mean—my *craziness!* She showed nothing. Simon looked down at his hands. In the gloom and fog of Dublin, for that matter, who'll notice me?

In the deserts of the heart, let the healing fountain start.

Surely Simon had had that verse in mind when he spoke to her of Dublin—and surely, too, he'd had it in mind when he attached to his flight insurance policy a sheet of paper on which, in block letters, he printed five words: IN MEMORY OF JANE FOGARTY.

She reached to the night table, lifted her glass of white wine, drank. She chose not to answer the telephone. Tom's glass was empty. He had left two hours before, at 6 A.M. She listened to her own voice, recorded, asking callers to leave messages at the sound of the tone. She listened to Simon's father telling her that if she didn't agree to meet with him, he would instruct his lawyer to take action against her.

She walked to the bathroom, downed two aspirins, squatted on the toilet, removed her diaphragm, listened to Mr. Pearlstein's voice—like bright morning sun, she thought, like an ocean of holy light!—pour into her apartment. How pleased Simon would be, she thought, could he hear the sound of his father's helplessness and rage.

"We'll give you one more chance. Please call us by noon so we can try to settle this like reasonable human beings. My wife and I have decided that we're prepared to compromise—to give you something. At a time like this we certainly don't intend to drag our son's memory through unpleasantness."

But you will, Jane said. If you get angry and greedy enough, you will. For a half million dollars, there are lots of things we'll do we never suspected we were capable of.

Simon was dead and she was a wealthy woman. Amazing. Simon Pearlstein, twenty-six years old, her patient of nineteen months—thirteen months at the state hospital, six months as an outpatient—had perished along with 221 other passengers when their Boeing 737 charter crashed three days before as it passed over Gander, Newfoundland. Simon Pearlstein—dear, sweet Simon, who brought her a gift each time he came to her office—had outdone himself this time. Before boarding his plane, Simon had taken out a $525,000 accidental death and dismemberment policy, and on it he had named Jane Fogarty, M.D., his psychiatrist, as sole beneficiary.

While his plane sent a small explosion of light into the sky above Newfoundland—a supernova to a passing dove, she thought—she had been in bed with Tom, on top, banging away at him, waves of orgasm passing from her thighs to her brain and back again, blinding her, making her wish she would never have to look at anything in this world again. Still, even in memory, even while that warm ocean had come roaring through her body, the thought of having to talk with Tom afterward—of having to act as if she cared for him more than she did—wearied her.

So now that you can do anything you want, what is it you want to do?

She laughed. I'm not sure, Simon. Let's wait and see.

Sure, he said. I'm good at waiting. Where I am now, I can be patient in a way I wasn't able to be before. It's the best kind of patient to be.

Simon had asked her often about her childhood. It wasn't fair, he would protest, that she knew all about him and he knew nothing about her! Why was she hiding from him? If you tell me all about yourself, he said, I promise I won't criticize you or make fun of you the way you do to me.

I grew up poor, Simon. I was an only child. My father was a handsome man who loved to drink and who would, in my presence, sometimes beat my mother. Mostly, though, he'd fall down drunk and beg her forgiveness. My mother worked as a cleaning woman at St. Anthony's Hospital in Newark. My father died of a heart attack when I was eleven and he was thirty-seven. It happened on a trolley car, though for years I told friends—boyfriends especially—that he'd died in the saddle. I made up stories about him. In high school, he was in love with a beautiful girl who later became a movie star. Stopping over in Newark on her way to New York—the weekend of their twentieth high school reunion—she called him. In her luggage, in addition to her lavish wardrobe, she carried with her, always, her own powder-blue satin sheets.

So now that you know that, what do you know?

Simon looked away, as if ashamed to have drawn such information from her—as if frightened, Jane sensed, that she would abandon him because she had told him about herself.

The difference, she thought, answering her own question. The difference between what I was and what I am. Between outside and inside. Between then and now. Well. If Simon could not know her—know her life—he could do the next best thing: he could, from the grave, alter it.

The aspirins were taking effect. Jane watched her headache lift, the fumes curling from her hair, rising to the ceiling. She remembered, as a child, buying tubes of magic smoke, rubbing the sticky substance between her fingertips, watching the feathered plumes lift off. In the mist below the ceiling, Simon coalesced, drifted down. He sat next to her.

Money was the one thing my mother talked to me about freely, Simon. Money was the matter of her lullabies. My mother taught me how to budget, explained on a daily basis how she managed the bills, the shopping, the rent. When she wrote a check, I sealed the envelope. When she held up two cans of beans in the grocery, I chose the less expensive one. If I had not existed, she would surely have moved to the shore—to Asbury Park, where her sister Regina had found a husband, an accountant, who bought her a house of her own and who treated her like a lady. But her sister would not let her move in while my mother had a child with her.

The phone rang and Tom's voice came through the answering machine. He had been in touch with his lawyer, Emlyn Schiff, who was expecting her call. Tom had two questions for her: If Simon wanted her to have all the money, why did he send a copy of the policy to his parents? And if she was so rich, why wasn't she smart enough to fall madly in love with him?

Jane smiled. She had known Tom for nearly a year, had seen him or spoken with him almost every day for the previous four months. He was handsome, intelligent, generous. He was marketing director for a large New York publishing house, had been a senior editor before that. He had a wonderful sense of humor. He loved her. She doubted neither his constancy nor his wit. So what kept her from returning his love, from feeling free to say, All right—you're it. She was splendid, as with Simon, at taking care of others—at helping them learn to take care of themselves, to know themselves. But when somebody else—Tom—wanted to care for her . . .

She closed her eyes and, with Simon, silently recited the opening lines of Auden's poem in memory of Yeats:

> *He disappeared in the dead of winter*
> *The brooks were frozen, the airports almost deserted . . .*

Simon had brought copies of his own poems to her office, had sometimes inserted into their conversations snatches from the poems of others and then, afterward, asked if she noticed the difference: which words were his, which belonged to Yeats or Auden, to Thomas, Jeffers, cummings, Dickinson, Hopkins, Donne, or Blake. Most of the time—though she did not let on—she could have answered, could have passed Simon's tests.

Yet, as with his parents, Simon had his small victory with her too. For she could neither return his last gift nor talk with him about it. She knew all about accepting and not accepting gifts from patients. Well. If she was entitled to the money, he'd been entitled to the pleasure—had it been his—of giving it to her, of letting his parents know he had.

She wondered, though: now that she could have virtually anything she wanted whenever she wanted it, would she be less horny? She felt almost giddy, finding the question there. Would being free financially enable her to be more patient with herself sexually? What Tom didn't know about her adventures during the past year—brief, delightful flings, usually at out-of-town professional meetings—surely didn't hurt him, and surely, too, she had been clear about her own sense of their relationship, about the freedom she desired for herself and allowed for him. She understood her own needs and patterns well enough. When the sex came first—and early—what need was there for trust? The sex *represented* intimacy. Genuine trust was something that, by definition, came only with time—something that, as she knew better than most, was built and sustained slowly.

Trust was not infatuation and infatuation was not love and love was not sex and sex was not love and love was not infatuation and infatuation was not trust.

Yes? Tell me more.

To know something in the mind is not to feel it in the heart, and to feel it in the heart is not necessarily to know it in the life.

You're confused, aren't you?

Yes, Simon. I'm confused, if mildly.

I can tell from how general you're being about yourself—the words you're using—about trust and money and love. Simon paused, leaned forward. When he spoke again, his voice was hers: would you like to talk about it?

She laughed. You're wonderful, Simon. You really are.

I always thought it was so.

That you were wonderful?

No. That money was at least as wonderful and confusing as sex. So what do *you* think?

Jane sighed. What I think is that I want to be loved—most of all, endlessly—by a handsome, strong, attractive man, and yet . . .

Yes?

I feel ashamed of my desire at the same time that I fear it will never be fulfilled. Such an ordinary sentiment, alas.

I disagree.

She dressed for work. She thought of her day: an hour's drive to the hospital on Long Island for a staff meeting, then back to the city for four hours of individual therapy at her Manhattan office. Jane wanted to get to the poems before Simon's parents did. She worried that if his parents found the poems he had written expressly for her, they might, in their rage, destroy them. Some of the poems, she thought, were publishable—Simon had been too terrified of rejection to send them out—and so she would ask Tom to look at them, to give her his opinion. If the poems were neither publishable nor good, she wanted, still, to be able to use them in her own work, for a paper she was preparing on dissociative mechanisms in posttraumatic stress disorders.

Through the static of her answering machine, Simon's father returned. He had checked at the hospital, at her office. If she insisted on avoiding him, he would be forced to take actions they might both regret.

Simon had once talked of composing a poem made up solely of messages from people's answering machines. His own "Hic and Ille," he said, about a convention at the World Trade Center, where answering machines gathered in the darkness of an auditorium to exchange greetings and messages.

Simon's father, unable to provoke a reaction from Jane, was now railing against her—about how she had taken advantage of Simon's good nature, of his vulnerability. "He may have been out of his mind—which is why your case won't hold up in court for a minute—but he's still our son," Mr. Pearlstein declared. "There's a difference."

Jane raised her glass to Mr. Pearlstein's voice. Together, she and Simon watched the bile travel upward to Mr. Pearlstein's mouth, out and into the receiver, through the wires, down into the walls of his apartment building. It rolled below the city's streets, gathering speed, tumbling toward her apartment. The underground cable was slick and sticky. Like what? Jane smiled, made an incision in the sidewalk, lifted the cable—a gleaming, slippery large intestine—unfurled it, stretched it to its full length so that the liquid rage within could flow more easily, so that she could see where, at each end, to slice the tube.

Simon passed the scalpel to her, complimented her on how deft she was. He said he would trust her to remove his brain, to cut out the sections of it that made him ill. He bent over the white sheet, sniffed it so he could determine which sections were rotting. He had read about Phineas Gage, he said. Phineas Gage was a railroad crew chief through whose brain, in 1845, a three-foot-seven-inch-long, 1.25-inch-diameter iron rod, weighing 13.5 pounds—dynamited into his skull—had passed. Phineas and others who suffered penetrating bifrontal brain injuries often regained full physical independence. Their characters and personalities, however, suffered major disorders.

Their brains survived, Simon said, but their minds didn't. How come?

Jane cupped Simon's brain in her hands, set it on top of the water, watched it bob, dip, drop downward. She imagined it becoming part of the coral reef, the reef turning to flesh, throbbing, Simon waking from sleep, rising from the bottom of the sea, grinning.

The question remained: what would she do with all the money?

She could pay back her medical school debts, look for a larger apartment in a safer neighborhood, redecorate her office, get her mother into a better nursing home, buy books, clothing, records, antique jewelry, eat elegantly in expensive restaurants, take long, luxurious vacations . . .

But where would she go, and with whom?

With me.

Why you?

Because I'm paying for the trip.

You're dead, Simon.

Says who?

She spoke with the building's superintendent on West 74th Street, told him she wanted to see Simon's apartment, to gather some items for a memorial service. The superintendent—a young Puerto Rican with the jaundiced, creased face of a man twice his age—stared at her ankles, her breasts. He lifted his T-shirt, scratched a scar that ran in a jagged diagonal across his stomach, said that he couldn't do it. He had orders.

I'm Simon's sister, she said.

He shrugged.

She handed him a fifty dollar bill. This is for all you did to make Simon comfortable. He liked living here.

It's your choice, lady. Only I never gave you nothing. If you want a key, I might arrange it.

She gave him a second fifty dollar bill. He gave her the key. Money is a wonderful thing, she said to him.

Better than sex, he said, articulating, to her surprise, the very words that were in her mind.

She unlocked the door, closed her eyes, imagined that she was entering a commercial for California wine. A handsome executive, in midnight-blue tuxedo, stood at the window, gazing out at the city. The slow movement of Bach's Second Violin Concerto floated toward her in crystalline waves. The carpeting was linen-white, the furniture and draperies shades of ivory, mauve, lavender, ruby. Jane blinked. A plush leather couch, armrests of gleaming chrome, curved under billowing drapes at the far end of the long room.

She moved forward, across a handsome oriental rug. Simon had left his small apartment in order. There was an oak buffet, a glass coffee table with three geodes on it, a couch upholstered in navy blue corduroy. On the walls were prints: Chagall, Klee, O'Keeffe. A framed poem, inscribed to Simon from Seamus Heaney, hung on the wall beside the couch. Jane looked into the narrow kitchen, saw the chef's wrought-iron pot rack above the butcher block island, noted the microwave oven, the blender, the espresso machine. The white countertops glistened.

Beyond the sink and refrigerator, next to a window that led to the fire escape, there was an old mahogany telephone bench, where, as in a love seat, you sat to make and receive calls. She imagined Simon's parents telephoning the *New York Times Sunday Magazine* to come and photograph the apartment, the *Times* running a sidebar featuring one of Simon's poems. In death, as never in life, he might, with enough luck and hype, join some of those poets whose reputations, he argued, had been inflated by suicide: Plath, Berryman, Sexton, Jarrell.

She moved to the bedroom, imagined that she was walking across the sleeping bodies of hundreds of Angora cats. Simon's desk, a wide rectangle of golden oak, was at the far end of the room. The bed itself, between her and the desk, was, to her surprise, queen-sized, covered with a quilt, the quilt stained in deep parallel bands of purple, vermillion, cobalt blue. She moved to the desk.

A velvet-encased box—IN MEMORY OF JANE FOGARTY inscribed upon its cover—waited dead center, an electronic typewriter to its left, two volumes to its right: *The Collected Poems of W. B. Yeats, The Collected Poems of W. H. Auden.* She sat in Simon's chair, untied the lacing of the case, looked at the title page. Once, during her junior year abroad, she recalled, she had pretended to be wealthy, had sat for two luxurious hours in a fancy London art gallery, opening such boxes, going through Flemish engravings.

She looked beyond the desk, to the fire escapes on the backs of facing buildings. She closed her eyes, thought of Dutch landscapes, of low horizons and wide vistas, saw the land slip downward so that there was nothing in the frame but sky. She could enter that sky with Simon, were he to trust her enough. If he could have closed his eyes and let himself fall into the white space, believing that she would never let him fall all the way—if he could have learned fully to depend on her until he could depend upon himself . . .

"We knew you'd be here."

She turned.

"That's her, officer. Jane Fogarty—the lady we told you about."

"She told me she was his sister and that he gave her the key. I don't know nothing else."

Simon's father held up a camera, took her photograph.

The police officer moved forward, spoke to her about her rights, about trespassing, about pressing charges. Jane saw other people standing in the doorway, to either side of Mr. and Mrs. Pearlstein, assumed they were Simon's older brothers and sisters. She saw children. Simon's nieces and nephews?

"And I'm Samuel Axelrod, Dr. Fogarty—Mr. and Mrs. Pearlstein's attorney."

"I'm sorry, darling," Mrs. Pearlstein said. Mrs. Pearlstein touched the hem of her skirt, turned in a half circle, like a young girl. She touched the quilt. There were tears in her eyes. "Where did he get the money?"

"You've never been here before, have you?" Jane said.

"Don't answer her," Simon's father said.

"It's like magic, being here," Mrs. Pearlstein said. "That I should live to see the day my son had an apartment like this. When he was a boy he always helped me clean. He scrubbed the kitchen floor. One time he scrubbed the oriental rug and I yelled at him because it was so hard to get the Ajax out. He asked for the rug when he moved out of the hospital."

The police officer had his pad in hand. Jane stared at the black leather holster that held his revolver, at the handcuffs that dangled from his belt. The children were laughing at her. She counted: there were nine of them. She wanted to tell them about the note Simon sent, with the policy—how he had mistyped a word, writing that he had *attacked* the policy to the note when he meant *attached*.

"I'm sorry," she said. "I'm very sorry. I liked Simon."

"I'll bet you did," Mr. Pearlstein said. "I've read articles about what you people do with your patients—"

"Shush," Mrs. Pearlstein said. "She's a nice young woman. She helped Simon. Look around to see the proof. He needed help and she was there."

"With her hand out."

"Max is too upset to notice anything except revenge," Mrs. Pearlstein said to Jane. "The first time Simon got into bad trouble—when he had spiders crawling over him and tried to kill his brother—Max was the one who calmed him down, got him to go to the hospital before he hurt anybody. Sometimes I think Max loved him more than I did."

"I won't argue with you, Norma," Mr. Pearlstein said. "It's not the time."

"How?" Simon's mother asked. "How did he do all this?"

"I gave him money on the side."

Mrs. Pearlstein kissed her husband. "I'm sorry I yelled at you when we were short on cash. I love you."

Jane smiled.

"I don't need your condescending looks, young lady. You know when my son changed? When he stopped taking the pills you gave him. Because they were poison. If it was up to you people, you would have stuck a funnel in his mouth like for a goose and poured pills down him forever." Mr. Pearlstein nodded to the officer. "Officer, do your duty."

Jane almost laughed, even as the officer moved forward.

"Hi!"

Everybody turned toward the living room.

"I'm Tom Hoffman, a friend of Dr. Fogarty. And this is our lawyer, Emlyn Schiff." Tom moved through the room as if he were a politician working a crowd.

Emlyn Schiff and Samuel Axelrod shook hands. Jane kissed Tom on the cheek. "My hero," Jane whispered.

"She's sick," Mr. Pearlstein said. "Didn't I tell you? Our son—her patient—is dead, and in his bedroom she makes jokes."

Jane started forward. The police officer put up his hand, as if at a school crossing. Emlyn Schiff whispered to Samuel Axelrod. Samuel Axelrod whispered to Mr. Pearlstein.

"Okay. Let her go for now," Mr. Pearlstein said. "But we haven't finished, believe me—not by a long shot."

Jane tied the case, showed the officer that it had her name on it.

Tom was asleep. Jane slipped into his T-shirt, sat at her desk, sipped wine, began reading through Simon's poems. Tom had saved the day and had done so, it seemed, simply because he was worried about what she might be getting into. He wished, he said, she would act as impulsively and instinctively toward him as she did toward her patients. Though she had laughed with Tom about the scene—how crazy, pathetic, and comic it was—she felt now as if it were all a dream. She smiled. Of course. It *was* a dream—Simon's dream come true—and she was living in it.

"What are you reading?"

"His poems."

"May I?"

He kissed her neck, and she reached up, stroked his cheek, his hair. He lifted a page.

> *In the prison of his days*
> *Teach the free man how to praise.*

"That's good," Tom said. "He had a gift, didn't he?"

"That's Auden," she said. "Not Simon. Here's Simon: *In the prism of his daze / Teach the free man how to craze.* Simon did that sometimes, to see if—"

She broke off, saw again the dazed expression on Mrs. Pearlstein's face.

"I like you, Tom. I like you a lot." She turned and rubbed her forehead against his stomach, wanting to burrow into him as far as she could. "I'm trying. Really."

"I know. You're very trying."

She stood, pushed him out of the way. "Don't make jokes," she snapped.

Jane looked around the table: five doctors, three aides, two social workers, three nurses. Only one of the doctors—Feinstein, fast asleep to her left—could speak English with any fluency. Two of the aides routinely beat up their patients. One of the nurses, she knew, was on morphine. Another drank heavily . . .

She had called her travel agent in the morning, had inquired about flights, cruises, tour packages.

What does an Irishman do on his vacation?

He sits on somebody else's stoop.

She saw her mother's mouth, heard her mother howling with laughter. Her mother's head was way back, her mouth so enormous Jane imagined it could catch whole fish, the fish pouring down from barrels, the barrels at the edge of the tenement's roof. She and Simon were children, on the roof, tipping the barrels over, raining the pickled water down on the grown-ups. Her mother laughed harder, repeating her old jokes—about the stoop, about the priest and the chorus girl—and when her mother stopped, to get her breath, Jane heard Schiff's voice, advising her to settle out of court, fifty-fifty. Yes, they probably could prove that Simon was in his right mind when he made out the will. But that didn't matter: one did not have to be mentally stable to purchase life insurance. Yes, he would take her case, and yes, he was confident they would, in the end, prevail. But the end might be a long way off. Axelrod was very smart and very persistent. He would delay, appeal, drag the case through the courts interminably. He would claim undue influence, would try to prove that Simon had been particularly susceptible to Jane's charms. The Pearlsteins would sue the hospital, would use the newspapers, would move for a change of venue due to the publicity, would get the insurance money put into escrow on suspicion of fraud. Jane would be attacked publicly, professionally, personally. The hospital might think itself within its rights to suspend her temporarily . . .

Mental Patient Leaves Fortune to Female Shrink. Bereaved Family Claims Alienation of Affections. She thought of Simon's Crazy Jane poems, considered supplying him with new titles: Crazy Jane at a Staff Meeting, Crazy Jane and the Pearlsteins. Men come, men go, she recited to herself: all things remain in God. And what, Schiff assured her Axelrod would ask, had she *really* been doing in Simon's apartment? Had she been there before? How much would it cost, after all, to get the janitor to testify that she often spent the night there?

I had wild Simon for a lover, she mused, though, like a road that men pass over, my body makes no moan but sings on: all things remain in escrow.

Who paid for the apartment? Who encouraged him to fly to Ireland? Why did he write love poems to his psychiatrist?

Across from her, Dr. Kandrak was whispering to Dr. Ramanujian. She didn't know if the language they used was Pakistani, Indian, or a regional dialect.

How, Simon had asked, could doctors help crazy people get well when they couldn't even talk with them in the same language? Wouldn't Dr. Fogarty agree that communication was a moderately important part of a true healing process?

With great gentleness, she had asked why he asked her about the doctors of other patients.

Because I'm afraid to talk to you, to tell you what I feel.

Yes. But try, Simon. Try if you can.

I am trying, he said. Can't you tell? Why don't you trust me when I tell you I'm afraid? Why do you always want to criticize me?

Do you really think that?

Yes. No. But I think you like me. You're very beautiful when you smile. Sometimes.

Sometimes.

Sometimes I think you like me. You're always beautiful.

I like you, Simon. I like you very much. But try not to be afraid of telling me what you feel.

You're not out to get me then?

What do you think?

No. But—

But what?

But I feel you are. I'm sorry.

She had seen the tears come to his eyes then, noticed the way he turned his wrists, as if he were shaking down a batch of silver bracelets. She thought of his bones, on a beach, bleached and hollow like the bones of gulls. Had Simon reached for her hand—she suspected he wanted to, though she was not sure he knew it—she would have given it. Instead, he made a fist, chose that moment to tell her he was going to take out the insurance policy before his trip.

I know it's a nutty idea, he said, but you said not to hide anything so I'm telling you what I was thinking of doing if I ever get well enough to be on my own. I want to go to England and Ireland, to visit their homes. I want to be one upon whom nothing is lost. I want to meet them at close of day. But I don't know if I can.

Can what?

Can go to Ireland and take out an insurance policy in your name. So what do you think?

About what?

About how you'll feel if I die, damn it! Let's say I get well enough to really go—let us go then, you and I, right?—and I'm not etherized on anything other than those dolphin-torn seas and far from dives on 52nd Street and you think: if I hadn't helped him get well, then he wouldn't ever have made the trip and he would still be alive.

Yes?

I want both. I want both lives. I want all the lives I can have! I want *everything!*

Good.

Good?

The others were standing, gathering papers. Dr. Feinstein lit a cigar, whispered to her that he was the Red Auerbach of the state mental health system. "I think we're going to win," he said, his Viennese accent thick. Feinstein had known Freud, Rank, Abraham, Jones, Ferenczi. He claimed to have been analyzed by Eitengon. Eitengon had not, of course, worked for the KGB, as was now claimed, though who knew, despite his small stature and plain looks, what might have passed between him and the actress Plevitskaya . . .

"Win?"

"When he believes the basketball game is, as you say, in the bag, he lights up a cigar."

"Mimesis then," Jane said. "Now I understand: you and Auerbach."

Feinstein touched her hand, lovingly. "Ah, Jane, why are you here?"

"And you?"

"A different life. I've already been everywhere else, yes?"

She walked across the hospital lawn, thought of lying down, of blowing on the young spring grass as if it were hair along Tom's forearm.

Don't!

Don't what?

Don't betray me so soon when I'm scarce in the grave. Doesn't anyone believe in grief anymore? I saw you last night, the things you did with him. You never touched my arm with your breath—never made the soft hairs sway, never let me lie emptied of my poetry.

Have a good trip, Simon.

That's *all?* Have a good trip? I pour my heart out to you and you won't even tell me how you feel about it? I mean, what if something goes wrong? What if the IRA bombs the pub I'm in?

You yourself told me they always telephone the pubs first, as warning.

But the phones never work in Irish pubs! That's why—

Jane laughed. Oh Simon—you're wonderful!

I am?

She did not reply.

But listen to me. What if it happens? What if they kidnap me? What if the plane blows up before the pub does? What if the trip is a mistake? What if my *life* is a mistake?

We'll talk about it when you return.

We'll-talk-about-it-when-you-return, he mimicked. Maybe you're the one who's making the mistake. Maybe it's too soon. Maybe I should be back in the hospital. Maybe I shouldn't have trusted you with my life. Goddamn it—stop smiling and say something—your smile's driving me crazy! You're just so damned beautiful and I'm just so damned scared, can't you understand? Maybe if you were plain, this would be easier.

Have a wonderful trip.

Sure.

I'll miss you, Simon.

He went to the door, opened it, turned.

Oh, he said quietly.

It was the last time she would ever see him. For her, she thought, it was his last afternoon as himself. He started to apologize for having become angry with her, but stopped himself. God! he said. I'm really doing it.

On the Long Island Expressway, traffic hardly moved. Jane passed three separate accidents, thought of getting off the Expressway in order to telephone that she would be late. But whom would she telephone? She had no secretary. In Manhattan, her patients would arrive at a locked door. Damn! She prided herself on always being on time. She agreed with Auden that tardiness—not lust—should be one of the seven deadly sins. Her patients had to be able to trust her fully, to know that she was, for them, no matter the world's vagaries, dependable—that her commitment was unconditional.

Her engine coughed, died. She turned the key in the ignition; it ground noisily, metal on metal. The gas gauge showed empty. She got out of her car, slid sideways along the door, took a deep breath. It had occurred to her on the way to work several hours earlier to stop for gas, but she had forgotten to do so. She relaxed, made the association: she had forgotten because at that moment—knowing she might run dry—she had, instead, begun thinking of herself as the heroine in a ghost story, and she had begun doing that because the possibility of running dry had led her to think of Simon's statement about being one upon whom nothing was lost. She had full recall of such trains of association, prided herself—the great dividend from her analysis—on being able to relax enough to trace any series of thoughts or feelings to their source.

Lying in Tom's arms the night before, she had talked with him about how surprised she was not to be happier about her windfall. With some hesitancy she told him of her imaginary dialogues with Simon, of how uneasy they made her. Survivor guilt? Surely it was more complicated than that, yet she couldn't get a handle on it—on why she felt so unsettled. Tom lifted her hair, ran his tongue along her neck, told her he was encouraged to learn that she did, in fact, have an active fantasy life. "I think it's great that you and Simon are still having sessions. Even if there are no third-party payments," he said. "It's what saves us. The lack of imagination, as you've said before, *is* directly connected to the instinct for cruelty." She said nothing. "If we didn't imagine lives other than the one we have," he went on, "we'd die." He touched her gently. "Can't you see that yet?"

She turned toward him then, unable to speak, but feeling an overwhelming tenderness for him. She kissed his collarbone, licked his chest, bit at his nipples, then suckled there. When he sighed with pleasure, she felt happy. "What I love about you, since you asked," he said then, "why I feel each time we meet that I'm meeting you for the first time, all over again, as it were, is that, of all people, you seem the last to know the obvious about yourself: about your dreams, about how they work to keep *you* alive. Sometimes you seem hardly to know you have an imagination."

Simon, she sensed from the beginning, like others she treated, had the capacity to get well—to heal himself with her help—precisely because he had the ability and willingness to imagine lives he never had, to have lives he never imagined. People who loved stories, she believed—who could think of their lives *as* stories—could learn to trust, no matter their childhoods, no matter the psychic and emotional devastation visited upon them.

She had been happy, then, in the morning, thinking of Simon. She had been happy thinking of the small miracle of his life, of what he had, finally, by his act—no matter his death—done. He had done something that was truly him. What followed because of it—the drama she and his family were now embroiled in—was nothing more or less than a story that he had begun and that they would finish.

Driving to work along the Expressway she had let herself imagine, word by word, how she might, for Simon, have summarized that story: A young woman who has never married or fallen deeply in love inherits a large sum of money due to the death of a young male patient of hers. The patient, on the point of setting out for the Continent, there to visit the homes of the poets he loves, has been dependent upon the woman and, cured by her of his profound malaise, has rewarded himself with the gift of this adventure. He has decided, after all, to live. Yet he dies, and the woman, suddenly wealthy, is now visited not only by the ghost of this young man, but, to her surprise, by ghosts from her own past that, for all her knowledge and dreams, she has never before acknowledged. Realizing that she has been giving to others what she herself was never given—trust, love, and the will to risk all for life itself, with whatever pain and loss this risk may carry—what does she now do? Perhaps she sets forth for the Continent, to take up the very journey her young man has not taken. If so, what does she discover?

That she is out of gas.

Simon laughed.

Jane laughed with him and pulled herself up onto the hood of her car. She sat there, enjoying the warmth of the metal against her thighs. Well, this *is* a gas, isn't it, Simon?

It's lovely seeing you smile this way. I never saw you look so happy before. I never saw you let yourself lose control.

Jane's car was stalled in the middle of three lanes. The heat rising from the engine was hotter than she had at first realized, and she wondered if it would, through her thin cotton skirt, burn her. The sun shone brightly on her even as she felt the rain hit her face.

It's only a sun-shower, she said to Simon. It'll be gone soon.

And then what?

Then I'll call Tom and tell him I love him. I'd like to try that on for a while—see if it takes.

And then?

Then I'll call Emlyn and tell him not to settle—that I'll never settle. I want it all, Simon. The whole half-million.

The rain washed her hair onto her face. Her blouse and skirt stuck to her skin, and she imagined peeling the cloth away, wrapping herself in warm towels. The water ran crazily, in narrow rivers, over her ears, eyes, nose, mouth, down her neck, along her back, into her shoes. She heard horns, saw blurred faces staring at her from behind windshields. She thought she could hear the pleasant click and swish of wipers, and she had no desire to do anything but sit on her car's hood and let the rain pour down upon her while she wondered if Simon could actually see her, while she wondered if she would ever be able to give herself what she had given so well to him.

What was that?

Her mouth was open now, as wide as it could go, so that her jaw ached with pleasure, and the sound that rose from deep inside her—as if fueled by the engine's brutal fire, through cylinders, valves, cast iron, and tempered steel; through thighs, stomach, chest, and throat was, she knew, nothing else but her mother's drunken howling. With the years, her mother had come to drink at least as much as her father had. As her mother had comforted her father, so she had come to comfort and care for her mother. But knowing that, what did she know? Their drinking was not them, after all; addiction did not explain their lives—it merely explained them away. To discover what it was that kept her from loving a man such as Tom, that kept her from fully enjoying her legacy from Simon—to accomplish such things she would have to do more than relive the ordinary pain that had come with loving her mother and father. She would have to do more than she felt capable of.

She tipped her head back so that it rested against the windshield. The rain, like sorrow itself, would wash over her and pass, and she would still be there. It might wear her and use her, but she could wear it and use it in return; for it was blind, whereas she after a manner saw. She smiled. Do you know who said that?

Sounds like one of the James boys, Simon said. Very Irish.

She was surprised that he knew, but then, as he noted, he was now everlastingly what he had previously been only for a time: one upon whom nothing would ever be lost. She wanted to talk with him at length—at leisure—but before she could do that, she had to let the sound inside her out, and she was afraid she could not. She was afraid that, no matter how much she let go, more would be there—that it would keep boiling up inside her forever. Still, she knew that she had to begin, and so she let it ride through her and out—let it all loose—and she watched it rise through the falling rain until it reached into the heavens and tore through, like dynamite blasting open enormous slabs of concrete.

Then, as suddenly as the rain had begun, it stopped.

Tolstoy in Maine

SMOKE, LIKE early morning mists, rose from her cupped palms. The woman was lighting a cigarette, shielding it from the breeze. Martin watched the smoke thin, spread, dissolve—veils of frayed linen disintegrating, drifting into the fog beyond. Was she aware of him? She stood on the pier behind the fish market, talking to the men who worked the boats. She seemed at home, and he liked watching her without being able to hear her words. He liked the easy way she had with the fishermen. She glanced toward him, but without either invitation or curiosity; he looked away at once, embarrassed.

He closed the door to his car, walked toward the docks, let the reels inside his head spin, play back images from the previous few days. Long Shot: the woman laughing easily, soundlessly. Medium Shot: the woman leaning against a railing, flipping the stub of cigarette into the harbor. Close Up: the woman staring directly at him, a lopsided stack of lobster traps behind her, out-of-focus. Two Shot: the woman inclining her head toward one of the lobstermen, smiling with casual affection, touching the man's forearm. This was, then, the fifth morning in a row that, by the time he arrived, she was already there.

He was a stranger in the Maine fishing village, there for a few months—to get his bearings, to prepare for his next project, to recover from what had been the most difficult year of his life, a year that had included divorce, a brutal custody battle, loss of his two children to his ex-wife, heavy drinking. He reached into his side pocket for a coin, then remembered that he didn't need a coin, that the reason he drove in each morning to use the phone next to the fish market was because it was the only public touch-tone telephone in the town.

The phone rang twice, clicked, his message came on, and he listened impatiently for a few seconds to the sound of his own voice, then cut it off by tapping in his personal code. The modern world, he thought. Fishing nets and microchips. Divorce and silicone. He looked up, toward the pier. She was gone.

He listened to the swish of blank tape, to his answering machine, some five hundred miles away, preparing to play back messages. He wiped the screen inside his head clean, forced it to go black, and in that blackness he imagined giant squid moving steadily forward. The water was a dark block of blue-black stone, the bodies of the squid, caught suddenly by the camera's fan of bright arc-lights, seemingly transparent. The tape stopped. Silence again. His children had not called. His lawyer had not called. His agent had not called. His ex-wife had not called.

He wanted to be alone, to be left alone—it was why he had left job and home and city and moved here, taken the small house in Tenants Harbor. Yet he was disappointed. He missed his children. He missed cooking for them, shopping with them, helping them with their homework. He missed touching them and being touched. He smiled. He even missed breaking up their fights. He put the receiver back on its hook. Sure, he thought. Don't call us, we'll call you.

He turned, saw the woman standing no more than ten feet away, at the entrance to the fish market, her hand on the screen door. She looked past him, to the telephone, her eyes mildly inquisitive. He wished he could keep her there by coming up with something clever, but there were no words in his head. What he saw instead were stones—millions of them, like enormous pearls—and they were tumbling through water, piling one upon the other, becoming a wall beneath the sea. He tried to smile at the woman, but in her presence he felt like a young boy. She hesitated, as if to give him time to regain his confidence. Her eyes were pale gray, flecked with white, nearly translucent, and as he stared into them it became very important to him that she not think him foolish. She smiled slightly, the corner of her mouth lifting as if to receive a cigarette, then said good morning and walked off, her hands deep in the pockets of her suede jacket.

The boat came with the house: a sixteen-foot-long fiberglass training shell with a sliding seat and nine-foot oars. The topsides were green, the deck blue with white trim, the craft so wonderfully new that when he looked at it each morning he felt as if he were looking into an enormous jewel that had been split open, the crown lifted off so that he could explore the facets below. But he couldn't recall what the cut of the jewel—oval, pointed at the ends—was called.

He pulled the boat from the shed, hoisted it onto his shoulders, carried it to the water some fifty yards away, wondered why it was that the name of the stone kept slipping from his mind. Two years before he had made a documentary film in which he traced the journey across the world of a single diamond, from its mine four hundred feet below ground in Kimberley, South Africa, through stops in Johannesburg, Tel Aviv, Antwerp, and New York City, until it arrived in Rahway, New Jersey, and was placed on the ring finger of 22-year-old Katherine Bak's left hand. He had interviewed each of the people whose lives were in some way touched by the diamond—the black miners and those for whom they worked; the diamond dealers in Johannesburg; the Israeli merchants; the diamond cutters in Antwerp; the jewelers on 47th Street in Manhattan; the jewelry store owner in Rahway, New Jersey; the engaged couple and their families. He had alternated the interviews—the story of the stone's journey—with sequences in which, via time-lapse microphotography, he journeyed deeper and deeper into the diamond itself, light and color exploding from the screen as the stone was divided, cut, ground, rubbed, polished, set. The film had earned him an Academy Award for Best Feature Documentary. It had brought to him the recognition and audience he had, during a quarter century of work and hope, been longing for.

He returned to the shed, picked up the oars, the Wetproof bag in which he kept his charts. He thought of the final sequence in the film, a triptych: the diamond in the center, the engaged couple to the left, the black miner to the right. The miner, 19-year-old Joseph Kenaba, was shown on an ordinary day of work: rising from sleep, washing, dressing, eating breakfast, tending his rabbits and goats, boarding a bus, arriving at the mine, descending into blackness.

Was Joseph still alive? He would write again—perhaps later in the afternoon, in the hour before dinner that he set aside for correspondence, for working at his journal—and he would hope, yet again, to receive a reply. In his mind the fire in Joseph's eyes—the pride, the rage—more than equaled the fire at the diamond's heart. This fire had drawn Martin to Joseph and surely, given events in South Africa in the three years since Martin had been there, now marked him as a man in danger.

Marked him easily, Martin thought. Sure. Mark-ease. Marquise. There it was: the diamond that resembled his rowing shell was called a marquise-cut diamond. The light given off by a diamond reflected through its side facets and the marquise cut, he recalled, somewhat shallow due to its elongated shape, did not break up the light into as brilliant a display of prismatic fire as did the round or rose-cut stones. Martin nodded. When he let his mind wander lately—when he didn't force things—he could sometimes retrieve words, pictures, and feelings he feared were lost.

River, a pure white touched lightly with blue, was the name given to the color of the highest quality diamonds. Martin set the boat in the water, climbed in, pushed off with an oar. The water was steel gray, darker than the granite shore. Mists hung along the banks like smoke from dying campfires. He thought of dew riding the filaments of spider webs, recalled a fifteen-minute film he had made a dozen years before, a film still used in schools, about the spider and the fly, Burl Ives singing the ballad on the sound track.

He loved the tidal coves at this time of day, when the wind had not yet come up and the air was still, the water calm. The shell drew only an inch and a half of water, so that even later in the day, when the tide would run out and large sections of the cove would turn to mud flat, he could, if he wished, find enough water to keep going. But he would be home by then, at his desk. He would be writing to Joseph. Perhaps, too, if he felt easy and confident enough, he would write letters to each of his children. Perhaps he would find something clever—a phrase, a joke, a self-mocking description of his solitary life—that would make one of them smile, would make one of them think of him with affection.

He leaned forward, pulled on the oars. The seat whirred gently along its stainless steel runners. The cove stretched before him, some twenty-five to thirty yards across, widening gradually until, at the headlands a quarter of a mile away, it bent and angled west, away from the sea. Later, when he returned to his house, and after he had split wood, showered, and eaten lunch, he would let his mind play back the things it had seen and experienced. Then, like a schoolboy doing his homework, he would spend the early afternoon studying in guide books, encyclopedias, and dictionaries, learning about all those things he had not until now known much about: trees and shrubs and flowers and fish and rocks, boats and clouds and weather and tides and the movements of the stars.

In his films, he often believed, he had cheated: he would learn just enough about a subject so that he could make the film, could render for others the *illusion* that he knew things. Were a merchant to show him a dozen diamonds, though, could he type them, grade them? If he looked through a jeweler's glass, what would he really *see*, other than the same fractured geometry, the same gorgeous slashes of light the camera had seen?

His film had earned him both the admiration of his peers, and honor in the world. It brought him offers—from producers, studios, foundations, corporations—of a kind he had yearned for through most of his life. He was happy in a way he had never expected to be happy, and to his surprise the happiness had been soiled neither by bitterness nor by cynicism. But what had the film done for Joseph's life? And what had it and all the films before it done to keep his own life from blowing sky-high? What had it done to enable him to keep his wife from betraying him, to keep his children from turning against him? He had loved his family more than anything in the world. He had worked hard at being the man his own father had never been. And then, at the moment when he thought he had it all—the life *and* the work, the family *and* the career—everything came crashing down.

If your mother tells you one thing and I tell you the opposite, what are you to believe? Christ! He was the one who had cheated on their mother, they said. He was the one who had refused to get back together. He was the one who had destroyed their family. The litany of accusations became painful, crazy, familiar. *He loved his work more than he had ever loved them.* Well, he thought. Short of telling them that their mother had lied to them as maliciously as she had to everyone else, what else could he have said or done? And once used to destroy his happiness at home, his success in the world came to seem hollow, repugnant, deadly.

He pulled hard on the right oar so that the boat curved to the left, turned into a narrow channel lined on either side by high banks. He noted pin oak, mountain laurel, birch. He recalled the first time his children had come to his new apartment, after the court decision, how awkward it had been, how happy he had been before their visit, when he was alone in their rooms, making up their new beds for them, touching clean linens that they would soon touch.

A flight of black duck shot out from the steep bluff to his right, crossed the cove like an arrow, disappeared. The bluff was covered with swamp maples, their leaves a wild explosion of vermilion against a wall of green. He rowed on. There were no houses along this arm of the cove, no signs that, less than a mile away, most of the world was waking, was going about its daily business.

There were black workers in South Africa who traveled eight hours a day in old school buses, back and forth on small hard seats, from their settlements to their jobs, their jobs to their settlements. They worked ten to twelve hour days, averaged less than three hours sleep a night. What, other than death, could ever burst from them the way colors now burst from the trees he passed? If his children could understand why it was he had tried for so many years to get the images that were in his mind—that exploded *there* endlessly—onto strips of celluloid, would that allow them to understand that he was not the kind of man who would have done the awful things their mother claimed he did?

He saw the woman's face again, and she seemed to be asking him questions, encouraging him to talk. What she wanted to know was this: *If he was not a film maker, who and what was he?*

He pushed off with his legs, pulled harder, felt sweat slide down his back. The faster the shell moved through the water, the more stable it became. When he was rowing well he could do nearly five miles in an hour, the shell racing along as if it were riding *on* the water, not in it.

He saw the woman reach toward him, to touch his mouth, and then the boat was rising crazily from the water. He gasped, held his breath, saw the water churn inches from his face, felt his heart crash against his chest. He screamed, raised the oars high, shifted his body to the right. The shell rocked violently, took on water, righted itself. He sucked in air, imagined his heart falling from his chest, sinking through the surface of the icy water. He saw a young boy in a row boat, the boy letting his dropline down, hooking the heart, hauling it in, gazing at it with curiosity.

The boy was his son, Dan, he saw at once, and Dan looked the way he himself had looked when he was Dan's age—twelve—visiting his Uncle George in Orleans, on the Cape. Martin started rowing again. He had caught a crab, he realized, playing the scene back—he had hooked the water with his left oar while pushing the oar forward, while the woman reached toward him. The boat had veered, tilted. In his mind the woman was smiling at him still, as if she had noticed neither his error nor his panic. Blood rushed to his heart, then flowed from it: to his arms, his hands, his legs. In the bottom of the shell, water sloshed back and forth, drenching his sneakers, his socks, his jeans. He had long ago stopped trying to explain who he was by the craziness of his childhood, by what had gone on hour after hour in the three small rooms of his Somerville home. Everybody had parents. Everybody had a childhood. He rowed harder, let images refract inside his mind, let light play on the planes of the woman's face. She was about his own age, he guessed. But why were her eyes suddenly sad, and why, when she began to speak, did her upper lip tremble slightly? It occurred to him that he could reach toward her if he wanted. He could reach toward her and reassure her with the touch of *his* hand. The movement came to him as a sequence of matching shots: she looking into a silver mirror, he looking down at the plum-colored water. He saw crow-black hair threaded with gray, high foreheads, sad pearl-gray eyes, wide mouths that were slightly open, as if about to speak. Her face was his face.

She explained to him that the single-engine planes he often saw circling about the harbor were there to spot sets of herring and to radio their locations to the fishing boats. The boats used large nets called purse-seines. When the fishermen surrounded the herring with the net and pulled a cord, the cord would cinch the bottom and trap the fish. Then the fishermen would haul the net up and suck the fish out of it with enormous hoses. The hoses measured two to two-and-a-half feet across. The fishermen salted the herring, layer by layer, until the boat was down to its gunnels, then transported their cargo straight to the factories in Rockland. A single set of herring might fill three or four twenty-four-foot trawlers. As a girl she had begged to go out with her father in the boats so she could see the herring come hurtling from the hose in a silver stream, as if spangled in sequins. Wouldn't he want to film that?

To film her as a young girl watching the men fish? he asked. Of course he would love to film that. But how? She talked about growing up in Tenants Harbor, about how things had changed. October was her favorite month, she said. It was a time when the tourists and summer people were gone, when the harshness of a long, dark Maine winter had not yet moved in, when life, suspended between autumn and winter, made her feel that time itself moved more slowly, that her home and town were closer to what they had been thirty and forty years ago. He listened, with interest, but what he really wanted to do, he knew, was to take her face gently between his hands, to kiss her, to press her body to his, to have her mouth open to him, to have her hands move through his hair, across his face, down his sides, along his back.

Her name was Nancy Medeiros. She was forty-two years old, divorced once—ten years before—and she had no children. Her house had been built in 1922 by her father and her grandfather. She had gone to Wellesley College, and now lived and worked outside of Boston. It had taken several mornings for him to work up his courage, and when he had done so, and had begun a conversation, she had responded pleasantly, easily. This was the third evening in a row they were together—they had driven north to Rockland for dinner the night before; and the evening before that they had gone for a walk along the beach in front of his house.

Her face moved in and out of focus. Soft focus. Deep focus. He had had too much to drink, he knew, and he wondered if she noticed. He imagined a camera dollying in, centering on her eyes, the film a grainy black and white. He remembered what a director had said about Garbo: about how during a take the scene would seem ordinary, but that when he played it back on the screen you could see something behind the eyes that you never saw until you had photographed them. You could see thought, the director said.

He went to the window, trying to walk a straight line, trying not to sway. He felt light-headed. Go slowly, he told himself. The fog was moving out again, so that, in the dusk, the islands began to appear as if from nowhere, as if rising from the sea itself, like ghosts. He saw himself on the beach, Nancy materializing suddenly in front of him, out of the fog. Her cheeks were moist, her black hair glistening. Had she been crying? He imagined a Close Up of a single raindrop on her cheek. He could make the drop of rain appear to be a tear, he knew. He could turn a tear into a river, a river into a waterfall, a waterfall into a flood, a flood into a lake, a lake back again to the calm gray of her eye. On film there was nothing he could not do.

She was talking about the tidal coves, about how it still amazed her to know that the water could rise and fall a full ten or twelve feet in a day. Voice Over, he thought: Nancy talking about her childhood while the tide moved out, while a blue heron poked aimlessly in the mud. Her voice, like the film, had a mottled, grainy quality to it. Still Shots: Nancy at 10, Nancy at 15, Nancy at 20. Had he known her through those years he imagined that they would have been good friends, in the way cousins could become friends. He did not imagine that they would have let themselves be drawn to one another sexually. For if they had, it would have destroyed the safety of a friendship in which they could confide anything and everything.

That, he decided, was what frightened him now: if he kissed her—if they made love—would he still be able to talk with her as if she were a friend? He didn't know which scared him more: the possibility that she would reject him, or the possibility that she might not.

She offered him another drink and he declined, said something about having to get up early the next morning, about wanting to stop in town on the way home to telephone his daughter, Carol. It was her fifteenth birthday. Nancy said he could use her phone, that she would leave him alone and go to the kitchen, make some supper for them— would he stay?—and he found himself feeling flustered and dizzy, talking about his answering machine. He told her that when he called in, he would sometimes imagine a Close Up of a telephone, and then a deep voice booming through static: *Hi! You've reached Yasnaya Polyana. This is Leo Tolstoy speaking to you on a recording. I'm sorry I'm not here right now, but if you'll leave your name and a brief message . . .*

She laughed and refilled his glass. He sat in a rocking chair, his back to the living room window. She set the telephone down on the table beside him, then sat across from him, a Hudson Bay blanket across her lap.

"How are you, Martin?"

The urgency in her voice startled him.

"What?"

"How *are* you?"

He shrugged. Her voice was warm, close. He pressed his eyes tight, saw white lights swirling as if being drawn into an amber whirlpool. Bourbon. He had not drunk this much since he had left Manhattan. He opened his eyes and she was still there. He started to tell her that he felt fine, that he was in the best physical shape of his life—from the rowing, the wood splitting, the walks, from being on the wagon the past two months—but she interrupted him and asked him why he was here *really*. She could understand his not wanting to make a film for a while, his wanting to be in a place where nobody knew him and he knew nobody. But why not go to Paris to *not* make a film? Why not go to Florence, to Vienna, to Bangkok?

He said that an old friend from college, Phil Yarnell, aware of his troubles, had offered him the house. She nodded, said that she knew Phil.

"You've had a hard time, haven't you?"

"Yes."

"Phil told me about it—not the details—just that you'd been through hell, that he didn't quite know how you had made it to the other side."

"Me neither."

"What I wanted to say—to put on the table between us, as it were—is that he told me about how difficult things had been, how discouraged you'd become. I probably should have said something that first morning. It hasn't seemed quite fair these past few evenings, me knowing and you not knowing that I know."

"It's all right. Who cares?"

"I do."

She was beside him then, lifting the glass of bourbon from his hand. Her hand touched his. He felt chilled, wished that he could ask her to wrap him in a blanket, to set him on the porch and rock him back and forth. He imagined the porch coming detached, moving out to sea. He wanted her slender fingers to be ribs cradling him, her fingertips touching, her hands a small boat riding the waves in the harbor. Fade. Dissolve . . .

She asked him if he would like to talk about it—about what had happened—and he said that he preferred not to, that it was the same boring horror story most men had to tell these days, filled with the same standard items: infidelity, jealousy, rage, divorce, depression, humiliation, insolvency, lies, pain, fear.

"That's *all*?"

He shrugged.

"What's the hardest thing, Martin?"

The directness of her question surprised him. "The hardest thing is not having my children around," he said. He was relieved to hear his answer, yet afraid to look at her. "I miss being *near* them. I brought boxes of photos, some old home movies, and when I first got here I thought I might make a film, using family material and mixing it with whatever I might discover here—something about daily life in the town." He stopped. "I don't know what I'm saying," he stated. "I mean, I'm not sure I'm being clear—if *I* knew what I really wanted to do. I just had an idea that maybe I could alternate scenes of my life here with scenes of the life we used to have, then put it all together and send it to them for a Christmas present or something."

He looked up. Nancy was smiling, her gray eyes fixed on him, asking him to tell her more. "But I haven't begun yet. I haven't had the heart to begin, if you want the truth."

Martin shrugged. The ice cubes swirled in his glass, creating arabesques of pale amber. He felt dizzy, vaguely nauseated. He wanted to lie down, to sleep. He thought he could hear Dan's voice, asking him if he would buy him a Ferrari. Dan pleaded with him, promising to pay him back out of his allowance, week by week, saying that he knew he could pay the whole thing back some day . . . at least by the time Martin was dead. Astonished, Martin looked at his son, and then, an instant later, saw the light in Dan's eyes, the pleasure Dan took in teasing him this way.

"I had the epigraph chosen," Martin offered.

"Yes?"

"All intact families are alike," he recited, "but each divorced family is crazy in its own way."

"Listen, the stories *are* familiar enough, Martin, even routine these days," Nancy said, "except that when there are children involved, when the kids are endlessly torn, endlessly in fear of losing one or the other, of being abandoned—" She stopped. "All right. So listen. Do you know what *my* idea is, about what grown men and women should do to avoid all the crap they put themselves and their children through?"

"Tell me."

"I think that once the parents decide to get divorced, and if they both want the kids, then they should flip a coin and the loser should put a bullet through his or her head."

Martin applauded. She clinked her glass against his and then her voice came to him from a distance. She was in the kitchen, telling him that he could have privacy while he telephoned his daughter. He walked outside, inhaled enormous quantities of salt air, tried to sober himself up. He wanted to feel better. The islands in the harbor were dark brown mounds on a disc of black glass. He imagined a cold room, a tub full of warm water, the steam billowing up. He imagined the camera rising to reveal a layer of clear air just above the tub, between the water and the steam. The camera dipped slightly and he saw himself in the tub, his eyes closed. Was he asleep? He imagined intercutting, from one scene to the other, from the mists in the room to the mists on the bay. He saw his head sinking below the water, the water turning red, the red bleeding to pink, to white.

He came back inside, went to the bathroom, splashed cold water on his face, looked in the mirror and imagined a Sony camcorder on a shelf in the medicine chest, behind the mirror. He saw himself in a black scuba-diver's suit, underwater, filming the fishermen as they dragged the bottom of the harbor with their balloon nets, raking in cod, hake, halibut, haddock, and thousands of tiny plastic capsules. The capsules came spraying out through a hose and the hose became his mouth and he leaned forward, wanting, he knew, to smash his head against the mirror. Would he ever, *ever* stop seeing the world as if through a camera lens? Maybe he really *didn't* love anything in life more than the images that roamed through his mind. Maybe his wife and children had known something he still didn't know.

In the kitchen, while they ate, she asked him questions and he found that he wanted to answer, that he wanted to tell her everything. He went through the story, sometimes summarizing, sometimes going into detail. Nancy didn't say much while he talked, except to ask a question now and then, and her questions seemed eminently sane: Why did he still seem to feel the need to justify himself against accusations that were so patently ridiculous? Why had he chosen, so rigidly, to hold back the truth about their mother from his children? There was something about his actions that didn't make sense—some part of the story he was leaving out.

They finished their coffee, returned to the living room. He didn't understand why he had felt so free suddenly to mouth off to her the way he had, why he was able to listen to her questions without feeling much need to argue against them. Was *that* crazy? he asked. She replied by saying what he had been hoping to hear—that she thought he was a very attractive man, more attractive now when he seemed less sure of himself, now that he had given her his story. She said that what he'd been through *was* horrifying, but that she figured he had spent enough time during the past year or two feeling sorry for himself. The last thing he needed was for her to feel sorry for him, too. Still, she wondered about something he had said on their first evening together, about his feeling that he might not make films for a while because he didn't *know* anything. She couldn't understand that. He knew how to make films, didn't he? She had seen a few of them, on public television, and they were excellent. Why, then, should he feel that knowing about fishing nets or sea breezes was more valuable or real than knowing about how to make a film?

He stood, said that he had to go. Could they get together again the next day? She stood next to him. She smiled and touched his arm, told him that she hoped he wouldn't regret having told her so much that was so private. The next time they were together, she promised, she would tell him the story of *her* life. Fair enough?

Fair enough, he said, and then, to his surprise, he took her face in his hands, very gently, and kissed her. It was the first time in nearly twenty years that he had tasted the lips of a woman he was not married to. Nancy's lips seemed amazingly warm and soft, and when he heard a slight whimpering sound come from her throat, he saw no pictures, imagined no camera angles. Her mouth opened to him, her hands went to his hair, then moved along his neck, his face, his sides, his back.

In the morning, at breakfast, he felt very happy, very shy. She talked about the errands she had to run, and he talked about the call home he had never made. They talked about the weather, about lobster traps, about his racing shell, about answering machines, about his children. He wanted to ask her how she felt, if it had been as wonderful for her as it had been for him, but when he alluded to their love-making she stopped him by remarking, sharply, that such comparisons were always invidious.

After breakfast they lay down on her bed again, and later, when they woke, she sighed, nestled close, rubbed the muscles of his back, marveled at his shoulders, asked him how old he was. Forty-three, he replied. Keep rowing, she said. She moved away from him, sat up and then, her cheeks radiant, said that she had one other question for him: Was he absolutely certain this was his first time out?

Toward dusk, walking from his house to hers—a mile and a half along the rocky beach—he kept seeing her face, the light in her eyes as he had begun to answer her question, to tell her that of course he had been telling the truth. The smile that burst from her then—playful, teasing, affectionate—gave his heart the ease it had been yearning for.

He had spent the afternoon going over notes for films, sketching ideas, blocking out sequences, making lists of people to call. He decided that the idea of making a film for his children in which they appeared was as sweet as it was wrong-headed. Instead, he thought that the next film he would make, the one that might *begin* to show his children what the love of parent and child was about, would be the film about Yoshiko Fukuda and her daughter. Yoshiko was a concert violinist, born and raised in Japan—a single parent—who, when she was forty years old, adopted a six-year-old black girl from Savannah named Jean. Jean was now twelve, and she toured the country with her mother, as her mother's accompanist.

Martin was eager to tell Nancy about the film—about the excitement he had felt when it occurred to him that he could do it, that he could make it—but when he arrived at her house, her car was gone and a blue Ford pick-up was parked in the driveway. An elderly man in khaki workclothes was on the porch, repairing the screen door. Martin said hello. The man turned, nodded, went back to his work. Martin asked if Nancy Medeiros was home and the man said that she had left early in the afternoon. Martin's heart lurched. Did he know if she would be returning later?

Without expression the man told Martin that Nancy was gone for the season, that she would not be coming back for another year. Martin walked up onto the porch, tried to remain calm, hoped that the man would not sense his confusion, his panic. He felt betrayed, abandoned. The man worked methodically, steadily, and seemed unaffected by Martin's presence. Martin began talking. He told the man where he was living and how long he had been there. He told the man that he and Nancy had spent a few evenings together, had had dinner together the night before.

The man responded with the standard Maine "ayuh" to most of what Martin said, but after a while he did offer some information about himself. His name was Frank Cahill and he took care of Nancy's house for her when she was away. He had worked for the Medeiros family since he himself was a boy—before Nancy was born. The house needed a lot of work—a new roof, a paint job, some rewiring, new flooring for the porch—but he was gaining on it, he said. Martin liked the figure of speech, one he had heard others in the town use occasionally.

Martin took his time, told himself that time was the one thing he had plenty of. With or without a camera, he had always been a good interviewer. He had always been able to get people to talk to him. People liked him, trusted him. He had always, with others, had a talent for mixing patience and curiosity in the right proportions.

When the sun set, Frank put away his tools and sat with Martin on the porch. They watched the lights come on in the harbor. Martin talked about the rowing he had done that morning, about how the fog never seemed to come into the coves. Frank nodded, said that it was so. He said that most of the local fishermen knew the coastline so well that they could tell where they were in the harbor from the sound of the water against the shore. Frank went to his truck, came back with a six-pack of beer, offered one to Martin. They sat and drank beers, looked out to sea, talked, and after a while Frank allowed as to how he remembered Nancy saying something about a friend named Martin—he was the film-maker, wasn't he?—and as to how he might be stopping by.

Martin said that he didn't know Nancy well, but that he had enjoyed her company, that he had rarely met a woman who had seemed so calm, so sensible, so forthright. Oh yes, Frank said. Nancy was a fine woman. Quite a story there, though, he added, and gradually Martin's patient ways won for him what they had often won before. Frank told him the tale: Nancy Medeiros had always been the smartest girl around, the kind of young woman you knew would leave Tenants Harbor one day to make something of herself. Her mother had been a schoolteacher who died when Nancy was eight and her younger brother, Nick, was five. Nancy had been the apple of her father's eye. But when she was sixteen, out with her father on his fishing boat one afternoon, the weather went sour suddenly. The wind—a fall northwester—came tearing through in a bad blow. While they were trying to batten things down, Nancy's brother had tripped, skidded, fallen overboard. Without hesitating

Nancy's father had leapt into the sea after him, rubber boots and all. Nancy watched them go under, then had gone below deck, waited out the storm, brought the boat in by herself. The father and son were found two days later, washed up in the mouth of a cove about three miles north of Nancy's house.

Nancy came back every year at this time—the anniversary of their drowning—and stayed for about two weeks. Nobody knew much more about her than that. She had gone to college, and then to medical school for a while, but she hadn't finished. She had married briefly and badly, and nobody had ever met the man. She had had a series of breakdowns, had spent a good portion of her adult life in and out of hospitals and rest homes. Her father had provided for her pretty well, so that when she felt the world going out from under her, at least she was able to be taken in by places whose surroundings were reasonably pleasant.

Frank said that he thought Nancy seemed in better shape on this visit than she had in many years. Maybe what she had seen and felt a quarter of a century ago was finally wearing off a bit. She was a smart and good woman. He figured she deserved better in this life than she had received, so far. But she was gaining, Frank said, as he stood to go. She was definitely gaining.